CRASH & BURN

SAVANNAH KADE

CHAPTER ONE

M aggie Willis bolted upright in her bed, the sounds of the old springs squeaking obscured whatever might have woken her.

Her heart raced from a bad dream ... or that's what she told herself as she pressed her palm flat to her chest and strained to hear over the pounding of her own blood.

It's just the old house. Old houses creaked.

She was in a new place—new town, new job, new life—and that's all it was. All the new combined with the old—old bed, old house, old fears—was making her jumpy.

She strained again to listen for more strange noises but now, of course, everything was quiet except the wind. And no one could blame the wind for blowing.

I should have gotten a cat, Maggie told herself as she punched at the pillow again. Then any odd sounds could have easily been written off. Because, *seriously?* Who would even bother with this old place? It had cabbage rose wallpaper and hand cut wood floors that would have been beautiful had they not been gouged and scratched by her great aunt Abbie's tenants over the years. The place needed enough repair that, if anyone did break in,

1

Maggie should threaten them with a hammer and put them to work.

Aunt Abbie's house had often felt sinister to Maggie. As a kid, when she'd first come to visit, the creaks had sounded like the house was attempting to talk. Though the house seemed large and borderline-haunted, Aunt Abbie herself had always been warm, giving, and loving. And Maggie, the oldest of her sister's grandchildren, had been Abbie's favorite. Thus, the old place was hers now.

The reading of Aunt Abbie's will, had made hope bloom in her chest. This old house and Abbie's legacy had seemed like the perfect escape from all the sides closing in on her in Los Angeles. Now, not so much.

Laying her head back down, exhausted and knowing that she would wake up again at the slightest sound, Maggie tried to ignore the noises. But once her ear hit the pillow, everything was magnified.

She heard a door creaking open downstairs, and she sat up again, stunned.

Was someone really in the house?

Aunt Abbie had always told her that her pillow would magnify small sounds into something they weren't. But ...

Her chest heaved with cold fear as she debated heading down to search—what weapon did she even have?—Maggie listened again.

Nothing.

But as her ear hit the pillow she couldn't tell if what she heard was footsteps or just the amplified rush of her own pulse.

CHAPTER TWO

P ushing the stroller, Maggie wheeled Hannah into the fire
station and hoped the guys weren't out on a call.
Everything was going wrong today so it would just figure if she
walked all the way down here and they weren't even in. If there
was a fire, they could be gone for hours.

At least she and Hannah had a good walk, and she consoled
herself that she'd be done babysitting soon. Still, hanging out
her shingle and trying to start up a solo legal practice in a small
town was turning out to be no easy feat. She didn't have time to
wait around.

As she peered in through the bay doors, she didn't see
anyone. That wasn't a good sign. Still she rolled the stroller past
the shiny red engine.

As she reached for the door that led into the station offices,
it swung wide and Hannah squealed.

"HannahBean!" Sebastian grinned at Rex's toddler daughter
as he leaned down to pick her up, his blond surfer hair trying to
flop into his eyes. "How's my favorite redhead?"

The little girl's arms went up and the tall, broad-shouldered
firefighter handily unclicked her from the seat and scooped her

up, eliciting another squeal. Maggie sighed. Though he seemed to stiffen just a little as she settled in his arm, Maggie thought Sebastian was much better with Hannah than her own father was. Then again, she cut Rex a break, Sebastian didn't have the toddler full time and out of the blue.

Without thinking, Maggie flipped her own auburn hair over her shoulder with a cheeky grin. "She's your favorite redhead, huh?"

He grinned, and shrugged, hard to do with the toddler in his arms. "I'm open to suggestions."

Her heart skipped a thump. She shouldn't have fished, but she couldn't deny the zing that shot through her.

Just before a truly awkward silence could settle in, he gave her a wide smile but asked a little more formally, "What can we do for you?"

"I have something to show Rex." Her chest clenched just thinking about it. The box she'd found gave her very bad vibes —enough that she wanted to get some other eyes on it and … Well, there was nothing she could put her finger on, but what Maggie really wanted was someone to tell her that she was right or that she was being ridiculous.

"Rex is in a training class … we all are."

Random afternoon trainings were normal, Maggie knew. She was both a firefighter's girlfriend and a volunteer. She worked at the station eight hours a week, usually with A-team. But since she'd started watching Hannah while Rex was at work, she'd had to move to another shift. "So why aren't you in training?"

"I'm already Search and Rescue trained." He shrugged as though it was no big deal and she wondered how many other certifications he casually held. "It's probably another twenty minutes before they finish. Do you want to wait?"

That was always the question with a firefighter. She could wait and he'd be done in twenty minutes. Or she could wait and he'd come out and the bell would ring just as she started to ask her question. Off he would run, and she couldn't even be mad about it.

She thought for a moment. "Do you have to go back in?"

Sebastian shook his head, the motion calling out that his hair was just a little long for the firehouse rules. Apparently, no one had called him on it yet. "What do you need?"

Maggie wheeled the stroller toward the open family room where the firefighters hung out if they weren't sleeping, training, or at a fire. Right now, it was empty though she could hear the soft murmur of class just beyond the wall. Sebastian followed, setting Hannah down to let her play.

"It's this." Maggie pulled the gift bag from the back pocket of the stroller and set it on the table.

"An early Christmas present?"

"Ha. No. This was the only bag I had." Sighing, she reached in and pulled out the carved wooden box. It looked Haitian or Caribbean to her, but what did she know?

Sebastian looked at it but didn't seem put off by it. Maybe he would tell her she was being an idiot and shouldn't worry about it. So she plowed ahead.

"See the scratches? That's because I pulled it up from where it was wedged under a floorboard. The board squeaked, I went to fix it, I found this." She motioned harshly with her hand.

"Okay? That's weird, but it's yours now. You own the house, right?"

Maggie nodded. Practically everyone in town knew by now that she'd inherited Abbie's home. "I don't think this belonged to my aunt."

"I thought she was your grandmother," Sebastian sidetracked then shrugged. "If it was in the house, then it's yours."

She sighed. "It's not the box itself that concerns me. Look what's in it." Then she watched as he lifted the lid and saw the tangled mess of jewelry.

"I'm confused."

"Who does this?" she asked, trying to pinpoint why the mass of gold and silver made her so uneasy. "Look at it ... the one bracelet is turning green, so it's probably ten carat gold." He was still frowning at her, and she kept chattering, hoping to make some kind of sense. "That necklace? I think that's a real diamond ... probably half to three quarters of a carat, so it's worth some money."

He reached for it, but she gently shoved his hand away, still not sure why she didn't want to touch it, but she didn't.

"What's this long bracelet here?" Sebastian had caught on and only pushed the other jewelry aside with his pinky ... as though he was preserving evidence.

"That's an ankle bracelet." She watched as he turned just a little pink. It was cute that he seemed embarrassed about the error. "And it looks like real sapphires to me ... also valuable."

"You can sell it if you don't want it." He clearly still didn't understand.

"That—" she pointed to another piece, hearing the sounds of the training meeting behind them breaking up, "—looks like a gumball machine prize."

The necklace was half of a 'best friends' heart, the gold tone rubbing off.

"So, you think it's not all one person's jewelry?" he asked as, behind him, the other firefighters poured out of the training room. They turned on the TV, swung Hannah around, or came over to the table to see what she had.

"Hey babe!" Rex offered her a workplace-appropriate peck on the cheek. "Did you bring your jewelry in?"

Maggie had tried to tell him about the box for two days ... but he simply hadn't had time to listen. He was up to his eyeballs with his job and his daughter. A month ago, Hannah's mother had announced that she needed rehab and dropped the girl off. Rex hadn't heard from her since and it was appearing the change in custody was permanent.

Though it wasn't Rex's fault, Maggie was frustrated. Hannah needed her dad, but Maggie found herself doing a lot of the parenting and she barely had a boyfriend. She forced a smile and an explanation.

"I found it under a floorboard in one of the old tenant rooms." She still hadn't told him she thought she'd heard something in the house the other night.

Now a good number of the firefighters were crowded around. Though several reached out, Sebastian motioned for them to not touch.

"It is weird," Kalan commented from over her shoulder, and Maggie turned to smile at the tall, black man. She was glad someone else thought so.

She repeated her words from earlier. "This jewelry probably doesn't all belong to one person." Finally, she managed to state what bothered her. "Who collects and hides jewelry that doesn't belong to them?"

Though he was laughing, thinking he made a joke, Kalan's words froze her blood.

"Serial killers. That's who."

CHAPTER THREE

Maggie wheeled Hannah's stroller into the open bay of the fire station for the second time in twenty-four hours. This time the place buzzed with a shift change. Men were already cleaning the engines while others were throwing their bags over their shoulder and heading out the door.

She looked for Rex in the crowd as A-shift left and B-shift came on.

"Hey, Maggie!" Sebastian headed toward her.

She smiled back at him until he asked, "Are you okay? You look tired."

"Jesus, man!" Rex butted in. "Never tell a woman she looks tired!"

Maggie wanted to laugh, but she couldn't. Rex offered a quick kiss and a quicker thanks. "Thank you for taking Hannah, babe."

"Of course," she told him, resenting the words even as they rolled off her lips. He'd told her he was going to find a sitter, but it was a small town, and he hadn't found anyone yet—not for the twenty-four hour shifts he worked.

She'd been up several times during the night with Hannah

and she now had eight hours of volunteer work at the station. She was exhausted but she'd readily signed up for the position before Hannah had come into the picture.

Rex took the stroller from her and commented, "I don't know how I'm going to keep up with her after working a shift."

Maggie's irritation flared. "I just had her for a full day and I have a shift to work now, too."

"But you only have eight hours." He smiled as though he wasn't devaluing her extremely generous donation to his family. That's what it was: she was watching his daughter for free.

Tamping down her feelings, Maggie handed over the diaper bag, and told him what Hannah had eaten and when she'd slept. Then she watched as he wheeled his happy daughter out the door. When she turned back to head into the station house, Sebastian was still standing there waiting. She could tell he was a bit upset.

"I'm sorry I said you looked tired."

This time she did laugh. She shouldn't have, he looked sheepish and fully regretful, but she'd seen the mirror this morning. "I'm not offended by the truth, and I'm exhausted. Hannah didn't sleep last night and now I've got an eight-hour shift to work."

He looked like he wanted to say something else, but Sebastian motioned over his shoulder toward the house and B-team. "I hope they go easy on you … I miss having you on A." Then he turned away as though the conversation were over and he was starting to leave.

She missed A-team, too. Maggie didn't like the resentment that kept creeping up about Rex and Hannah, but Sebastian's shy smile softened some of her irritation.

With his bag slung over his shoulder, he looked like the quintessential bad boy. What Maggie had discovered in the past few months, was that his bold looks and on-site confidence were deceiving and he was actually quite shy.

She was about to wish him a good day when he turned back and popped an unexpected question into the space between them. "You don't want kids?"

Her heart sank. There was no good way to answer this. So she fumbled it. "I do want kids. Just not like this. Not yet."

Sebastian nodded. "Rex got dealt a tough hand."

That was understating it, and probably why Maggie didn't resist more than she did. Though he'd known about his daughter and paid regular child support, he didn't have much contact with Hannah. Then, when he'd moved here, training as a firefighter after he left the Los Angeles Police Department, Hannah's mother had done her best to cut Rex out of his daughter's life completely.

But suddenly, Maggie's carefree boyfriend had become a full time dad. And she'd somehow become his full-time babysitter. So now she looked at Sebastian, wondering if she had dated the wrong guy in the first place. *Not that Sebastian had asked her ...*

She had what she had. "He did get dealt a rough hand, and I adore Hannah. I would do anything for her, but ..." She shrugged, letting the words fall away.

Sebastian might not be loud, but he was relentless. He still stood there, bag over his shoulder, clearly ready to go home after his own shift, but he wasn't budging until she told him what was up. "But what?"

"I'm supposed to be renovating the house, which, of course, is going slower than it was supposed to."

He tilted his head. "You've got your offices all set up in the front room. You've been seeing clients."

She smiled, glad that he knew that. Then again, Sebastian just seemed to know things. Maybe it wasn't clear to everyone that she was fully set up despite the shingle she'd hung out front. The crowds weren't rolling in yet. Advertising needed some of her time, too.

Maggie almost sighed, it was just one more thing on her list.

"The rest of the house needs work—more work than I estimated. I'm supposed to have more rooms to use ... And now I have a toddler every third day."

And then some. But she didn't add the last part. More than once, Rex had asked her to babysit so he could sleep or go to the grocery store or run some errand. She was going to have to start saying no.

Sebastian nodded, the move looking a little tight, as though there was something else he wanted to say. When he did speak, it seemed he was biting his tongue. "Well, I'll see you around then."

Once again, Maggie wondered what would have happened if Rex hadn't asked her out first. Was she brave enough to find out?

CHAPTER FOUR

Maggie pulled her front door open at the knock, hoping it was a client.

"Come in!" she offered cheerfully, still looking down at the document she'd just printed. That was bad form, and she swiveled her head to glance at him, her gaze traveling up the tight-fitting jeans and navy blue t shirt. She hadn't needed to get past the biceps to recognize that it was Sebastian Kane standing on her doorstep.

Surprise, she thought, *he knows where I live.* Then again, he had commented she was seeing clients, so clearly he knew how to find her. *Small Town,* she reminded herself.

Maggie really hadn't considered that factor when she decided to live and work in the same place. She'd simply wanted to get away from the city, away from running into her ex-fiancé or anyone who wanted to talk about her canceled-at-the-last minute wedding. And she needed to get away from a job that she hated. Had she gone too far coming to a town as small as Redemption?

"You look nice," Sebastian told her as he stepped across the threshold. The floorboards squeaked underneath his feet as he epdins. Yet another thing she really needed to fix. She could just add it to the very long list.

Maggie closed the door behind them, suddenly feeling intimately close in the small, poorly lit space. She wanted to blurt out, *why are you here?* But she didn't. Maybe he was here as a new client. So she left her voice professional. "How can I help you?"

"Oh," he replied, his smile almost shy. "I just wanted to check in. Make sure you got some sleep ..." he let his voice trail off.

Maggie waited him out. Was he being sweet, checking up after she was clearly upset about the box of jewelry and Kalan's offhand serial killer comment? Or was there really nothing else to do in town except check on the neighbors?

"I'm sorry, I didn't mean to overstep. It's just that you seemed a little upset when I was leaving the station the other day and I wanted to be sure everything was all right."

For a moment Maggie paused. Everything was not all right. In fact, she'd tried twice to sit down and talk to Rex, but he'd brushed her off, not even able to find a few minutes to listen to her.

She needed him to find a real babysitter for Hannah and she wanted him to check into the jewelry. He was, after all, a former cop. As far as she knew, Sebastian had no such background. Yet, Sebastian was here and Rex had been a relatively crappy boyfriend of late, though that wasn't his fault.

"Maggie?" Sebastian pressed, leaning a little forward and trying to catch her eye as, clearly, she'd hesitated too long.

So, she gave in with a sigh and everything tumbled out. "I'm not as good at DIY repairs as I thought I would be. I have these creaky floorboards ..." she started to point toward the back room, but that was ridiculous, they almost all creaked! "Actually, I have a lot of them."

"I can help," Sebastian offered, maybe a little too quickly and she must have looked at him oddly because he explained. "My dad's a carpenter. I can build a mean bookcase, install a new doorframe, and repair squeaky floorboards like nobody's business."

Maggie found herself smiling when she hadn't expected to. His grin was infectious. *Thank God for Sebastian,* she thought. Heading toward the back room, she heard him follow. "This was the squeaky board I tried to fix where I found the box."

His curiosity was obviously piqued and as she led him into the room, she asked, "What do you know about the house?"

He took a deep breath as though this were a pop quiz. "Well, it was a boarding house for a long time, up until a handful of months ago when Sabbie passed away."

"Why does everyone call her Sabbie?" Her aunt's name was Abbie, and Maggie thought she'd been mishearing everyone until now.

"She was always Miss Abbie ... and my dad always knew her when he was little and couldn't say it right. He said a lot of the kids called her Sabbie." He paused a moment. "It's sweet that she left you the house."

"She had no kids and I was her favorite of her sister's grandkids. She left me the house and everything in it. The money—not very much—went between the other three grandkids." Maggie replied. "I thought I could do an estate sale for the furniture and things in the house to cover the cost of repairs, but there's not enough of it for me to have any furniture if I do that."

"They're not antiques?" he asked.

"Honestly," Maggie stopped and turned toward him there in the hallway. "I don't know enough to tell what's valuable and what's not. So I'm still at the stage where I need to find someone to tell me what to keep and what to sell." She didn't add *someone I can trust.*

And she also didn't add that it should have happened well before now, but the house was rapidly becoming a money pit and time suck. The to-do list had been long when she arrived. Then, each thing she attempted revealed three more repairs. And then she'd lost so much time taking care of Hannah.

"If I remember correctly," Sebastian either caught her hesitation and understood or serendipitously turned the conversation. "The tenants left when she died."

"Close," she told him again. "I was *not* ready to run a boarding house full of people I didn't know. So I had the estate attorney handle getting them out."

Sebastian's brows shot up.

"Not like that!" She held up a hand. *Why did it feel so awful that Sebastian thought badly of her?* "It wasn't that harsh! They knew Aunt Abbie was older, and she told them repeatedly that they would have to find somewhere else to live when she died. She told me she was leaving the house to me about three or four years before she passed. I gave them five months to find somewhere to live and all of them were out within four. So no one actually got evicted."

Sebastian was nodding along and Maggie was relieved.

"Because it was all handled by the estate attorney—" she opened the door to the back room, "—I don't know who was in this room, and I don't know where they went. But they buried that strange box of jewelry under the floorboards in here."

CHAPTER FIVE

Sebastian didn't like the feeling in his gut as Maggie pulled the box out of the empty closet. She'd put it back into this room, *out of sight?* She clearly didn't like it either.

He didn't know what it was that made him feel this way, but it was the same visceral premonition he got right before a fire flashed over. It was like the sinking sensation when they were standing on a roof and he yelled, "Let's get out of here" moments before it caved in. Sometimes he yelled too late.

That was the feeling tugging hard at him now.

It wasn't any kind of psychic intuition. It was just about having been on the job long enough for the back of his brain to sometimes put things together before the front of his brain did. He looked at Maggie, who sat on her knees in her nice business suit and set the box between them.

The old room had been emptied except for a nightstand and a dresser. Old wallpaper lined the walls with puffy roses that had faded to a pale pink over the years.

He'd always wondered how Sabbie had housed grown men in such frilly rooms. He flipped the lid open and looked again at the jewelry. Though nothing in the box looked like something the older woman would have picked out—she'd always worn work pants and men's shirts when he'd seen her—he reminded himself that what he knew about women in general could have fit in a box this size. "Is any of this maybe your aunt's?"

"I don't think so," Maggie told him, rocking back a little bit. She shrugged as if she truly had no clue what the box was, or why it was here.

For a moment his tongue got stuck. He'd told her she looked nice when he walked in the door. Had that been a good thing or a mistake? He reminded himself that it didn't matter. She was with Rex, and he'd been too slow. He'd asked her about wanting kids, thinking that if she didn't it would help him slough off this useless crush he was carrying around. Instead, she'd made it grab him even harder.

But Rex was a fellow firefighter, part of the brotherhood. So there was no making a move on Maggie.

"No!" Maggie interrupted his pity party. "This can't be Aunt Abbie's. She had a box of jewelry that was given to my cousins as part of her will."

Sebastian nodded absently, still trying to make heads and tails of what he was seeing. There was a small handful of necklaces. The one with the diamond. Two looked cheap, like something you'd win at a county fair. The bracelet and the anklet—not just a large bracelet apparently. He wondered if Maggie wore anklets, because they looked sexy.

But as he peered into the box a little more carefully, he thought she was right. The mix was odd.

"I don't like it." Maggie's words mirrored his own thoughts. "It feels weird."

She didn't mention Kalan's comment, but they had to both be thinking it.

Sebastian was now very curious. The rumors about Sabbie had been wild and too varied to believe. Some said she was hiding cash under the bed. Others whispered that she'd been dirt poor or that she was in love with one of the boarders. Sabbie would tell anyone who asked that she'd never been married, and she liked it that way, but the rumors flew that her true love died in one of the wars, and so on.

"The jewelry she gave my cousins was only a small handful of necklaces. A couple of rings—one of them had a jade that was a couple of carats. But nothing crazy, no crown jewels." She laughed a little and seemed as though she reached her hand out to touch him. But then she pulled it back. When she waved toward the open box and spoke again, she sounded a little strained. "But it was nothing as expensive or as cheap as some of this stuff. All the things Aunt Abbie left were clearly out of fashion. There was maybe one jade necklace I would wear, if I had to attend a ball or something."

For a moment, his mind cut to the annual Firemen's Ball and how she would look in a green gown with a jade necklace. Then he quickly reminded himself that she would look that amazing on *Rex's* arm, not his. And he reminded himself again that he was an idiot for not asking her out when she first got to town and had still been single.

So he forced his mind back to reality and the boyfriend she had. "Did you show Rex?"

She shrugged again, though it wasn't about not knowing the answer. "He saw it at the station house, same as you."

"Did he say anything else?"

"Only that Kalan shouldn't have scared me like that." Her jaw tightened and he could see she didn't like the implication that she was frightened over nothing.

Then she dropped a bombshell.

CHAPTER SIX

"I thought someone was in the house the other night …"

Maggie let the words hang between her and Sebastian. She knew Rex would brush her off, but if Sebastian did too, she would finally let it go.

Instead, he looked at her as though she was nuts. "You called the police?"

Maggie shook her head and explained. "What would I tell them? There wasn't an open door or window. Nothing was moved. Honestly, it might have just been the house creaking." She hated admitting that she was in her thirties and still being kept awake at night by the sound of an old house.

"You told Rex?"

She tried not to let her lips press together, or let Sebastian see how she really felt right now. Because lately she hadn't been able to even go to Rex. She'd been his babysitter, not his girlfriend. Surely, the cracks in her relationship were already showing. Probably everyone saw them by now.

She liked Rex— but that was the problem. She liked him; she wasn't in love with him.

She'd moved to town and he'd asked her out right away. He

was charming, with his dark Italian good looks and ready smile. She was hoping to make friends and meet someone and maybe she'd said yes a little too quickly. They'd barely begun dating when Hannah had come along. And maybe that's when she'd known it wasn't going to work, because Maggie had fallen in love with Hannah ... not Rex.

"Should we take the box to the police?" she asked, wondering if the PD would even have time to do anything with it. The box was the only evidence she had and it was just a stupid box in an odd position. Hardly worth the officers' time.

"If we take it to them, they're going to keep it," he told her.

She wasn't ready for that. Besides, it wasn't really hers. If it was innocent, someone had left it behind. "So how I do find out who it belongs to?"

Even as she asked him, she caught a glimpse of the time. "Crap! I have a client on the way."

"Then leave me here. I can get photos of the pieces and see if anyone in town knows who they belong to."

"You can just do that?" That would not happen in LA. "Never mind. Yes, do it. Maybe someone can help. Thank you."

She was beyond grateful. She needed an extra pair of hands —or ten. She loved Hannah, but this wasn't working. She was nowhere near the number of clients she'd projected to have at this time, and her savings would only take her so far. Maggie was growing concerned about admitting defeat. Sebastian's offer was a godsend.

"Do you have a spare pencil?" He'd already used a pen from his pocket to lift the first piece out and spread it out on the floor. As if he thought he shouldn't touch it. His concern heightened her discomfort.

She would feel better after she returned it to the owner. "You don't want to touch it?"

"I'm just thinking if we can get a fingerprint off of any of it, we might find the owner." He didn't sound too hopeful, but he wasn't leaving his own prints behind, she noticed.

Maggie was popping up to grab him the pencil when she heard a car pull up out front. Her client was early or she had yet another unexpected visitor.

"Go meet your client. I've got this." Sebastian waved her away with a reassuring smile. He must have seen her anxiety and it made her heart melt.

She had to break up with Rex. Even if this was just a silly schoolgirl crush, her heart shouldn't be flip-flopping for one man when she was dating another.

Grabbing a pencil from her supply room, she turned back to hand it to Sebastian, only to smack into him. His broad chest in the soft t shirt stopped her like a wall.

She was simply grateful that she hadn't poked him with the sharpened end. That would have been even more embarrassing.

"Oh, I'm sorry." He jumped back quickly, as though he'd been the one not paying attention.

Sweet guy, she thought and held out the pencil, though she could still smell him in the air between them now. "Here."

She scrambled away as her front door creaked open behind her.

"Dear? I know I'm early ... Oh, I just love what you've done with the place!" Mrs. Miller was all of four foot eleven and her personality and forwardness filled up any space she didn't take up physically.

Maggie just smiled and nodded. She'd barely rearranged the furniture, not having the funds to replace it. And she wasn't a fan, but she pasted on her best smile. "Mrs. Miller! I'm glad to see you. Don't worry about being early."

The older woman nodded and took Maggie's hand in one of hers. She used the other to wave at the brightly welcoming foyer and front room. "Now, let's get down to the nasty business of writing this will."

"Wills are a good thing," Maggie reminded the woman as she squeezed Mrs. Miller's hand.

The older woman settled herself into one of the plush chairs across from the large oak desk. Just as Maggie was opening her mouth to ask about how Mrs. Miller might need to divide her estate, the older woman opened the conversation with something entirely different.

"I don't know if you heard ..." She leaned forward as though to share a secret. "But just outside of Lincoln, they found another body." The bright blue eyes looked truly worried, and she reached up and fidgeted with the stone on her necklace.

"I didn't know," Maggie said. She hadn't been in the area for long. A *body* was bad. *Another body* was worse. She felt her brows pull together but Mrs. Miller kept talking.

"They're saying the Blue River Killer is starting up again."

CHAPTER SEVEN

The more Sebastian handled the jewelry, the more his stomach turned.

He worked diligently while Maggie met with Mrs. Miller. He wasn't exactly sure what Maggie was doing for the older woman. He only knew that Maggie was a lawyer, and that her sign out front said: estate law, prenups, divorces, contracts.

He didn't think anyone around here was going to need a prenup, but he didn't tell Maggie that.

When she came in to do her station volunteer work, he'd found excuses to chat with her, and found that he liked her more than just a little. Seeing her every week was something he'd looked forward to, until she'd begun taking Rex's daughter during A-shift.

Sebastian told himself again it was a sign that they were serious and that he needed to get his head out of his ass. Nothing good could come from wanting a woman who was with someone else.

Besides, he wasn't anything special. She talked freely with all the guys. He'd gotten the impression—the way her voice sometimes tightened—that she wasn't all that confident her business was going to bring in enough money. So he didn't want to interrupt her now.

The old, scratched wood floor was too dark to be a good background for the pictures. So he headed into the room she'd converted to an oversized supply closet and found a few reams of white paper sitting lonely on a mostly empty shelf.

He picked up one of her pens and thought about taking it. The monogrammed "Magdalyn Willis, Attorney at Law" might have cost her something, so he put it back. The beautiful gold script was all Maggie.

Back in the room, he got down to business. Photographing the jewelry went much better with the white paper as a background. By the third piece, he admitted what he was doing. He was photographing evidence.

Evidence of what, he didn't know. But the more he examined the jewelry, the more he realized Maggie was right. No one person would want this odd collection. And which of Sabbie's boarders would want so much jewelry?

Who would collect such odd pieces, and then hide them in a cigar box under the floorboards? Sebastian didn't like any of the answers that came to mind.

When he was done, he scooped the jewelry back into the box without touching a piece. Using only one fingertip, he flipped the lid closed.

With nothing left to do, he needed to head home. As he snuck by the door Maggie had left ajar, he waited for a moment, watching her work. He thought about popping in and telling her he was leaving. But her serious expression and the words "my will" made him realize he shouldn't be listening. So he simply crept out the front door and pulled it closed tightly behind him.

His thoughts rolled, turning back to the box.

He'd known Sabbie. Hell, they all knew she had boarders in

and out of the house for years. Some had stayed a long time and others had rotated through in a week or just a few days.

The guys at the station had always worried—an older woman running a boarding house for men she often didn't know. Men often no one in town knew. But Sabbie had stayed safe and strong. She ran the house with an iron fist and a side of freshly baked cookies right up until the night she passed in her sleep.

Heading home, Sebastian figured he should take a nap, which was his usual routine. Starting the next morning he had a twenty-four hour shift. He needed to be alert the entire time. But he found he struggled to fall asleep this time and, an hour later, he was online.

He started by searching "boxes of jewelry." Which was possibly the stupidest search he could have tried, unless he wanted to buy a new, elaborate jewelry box.

The next thing he tried was finding a list of Sabbie's boarders. There was no way Sabbie would have kept this jewelry, let alone stuffed the box into the floorboards in a room she was renting. It definitely belonged to one of the men who'd come through.

So if he could figure out who they were, he might be able to figure out which one had left it.

Three hours later, Sebastian had only three names, spanning the last fifteen years of renters. That was not nearly enough, he thought, given the number of people he knew had stayed at the boarding house.

There had to be a better way, he thought. Then he realized the better way was simply to ask Maggie. Surely, Sabbie had kept records.

And seeing Maggie again wouldn't hurt. He didn't like that she thought someone had been in the house. Between the noises and his growing concerns about the jewelry, Sebastian was fighting that churning premonition in his gut. He decided he would keep a closer eye on Maggie. Rex wasn't doing it and someone needed to

Could he just subtly watch over her and still keep himself in the box that was 'just her friend'? Sebastian wasn't sure, but the alternative wasn't an option anymore.

CHAPTER EIGHT

M aggie shot up out of bed, her bare feet hitting the rug before she even realized she was awake.

Her blood rushed in her ears and her heart pounded.

With a concerted effort, she forced her breathing to slow, hoping she could hear something besides her own fear. Her toes curled into the plush rug she'd laid out beside her bed so her feet didn't hit the cold wood every morning.

She should have worn something other than a silly night shirt.

Thump.

There. She heard it again.

Oh dear God, there was *someone in the house.* Surely that wasn't a sound the house made on its own.

Without moving her feet, Maggie snaked her hand out and curled her fingers around the Louisville Slugger she'd set beside the bed. She'd found it in one of the rooms while cleaning last week. Had one of Abbie's tenants left it?

There was no telling. Maggie had cleared drawers of the antique chests to find real silverware, old letters, and receipts from purchases made twenty years ago. There were instruction manuals for appliances no longer in the house.

The baseball bat had been a boon.

Now she was grateful as she held it in her grip, aiming it down the stairs in front of her almost as though it were a broadsword rather than a bat. She had no idea what she was doing with it.

Slowly, so as not to make the floors creak, she stepped cautiously forward. What she wouldn't give to have Sebastian here.

Oh hell. Why was she thinking of him?

Thump.

Another knock came from downstairs and made her ribs squeeze and her fingers clench tighter.

Whoever it was, was trying to be quiet. Or, she told herself, maybe it wasn't a silent human, but a noisy raccoon.

It was entirely possible this was just some random wildlife that had snuck in. The property bordered on woods. Though the boarding house was relatively near the middle of town, Redemption had done a good job of staying green. Strips of lush trees, bushes, and woods buffeted many of the neighborhoods offering shade and walking trails.

Right now, however, Maggie was wishing for the trees to be gone. How she would love to see clearly out the back of her yard and into her neighbors', to make eye contact with another person who should have been there.

As the next noise made her jolt, she felt the anger flare. She'd had enough of this. Forgetting her bare feet and her unorthodox grip on the bat and her ridiculous nightshirt, Maggie bolted forward.

She thumped down the stairs, making more than enough noise for anyone to hear her coming. Her goal was speed. In her sheer pissiness, she'd forgotten her safety and was ready to duke it out with whomever might have snuck in.

Even as she hit the bottom step she heard another noise, this one toward the back of the house.

She whirled around the stair post and chased the sound, ready to throw down in defense of the home that still didn't quite feel like her own. As she skidded to a halt at the back of the house, the cool night air wafted over her, the gentle breeze knocking her back.

The back door stood wide open.

Holy shit, she wasn't just imagining things. The noises weren't just the creak of an old house, someone had actually been here.

She looked around the hallway, bat still choked up and ready to swing. *All* the hallway doors stood open.

She kept them closed normally, and if any were open, she closed them on her nightly lock up. Maggie didn't know why. It was just part of her regular routine, like checking the bolts on the windows. There were so many windows in this house.

Now, she reached out and gingerly closed the back door with one hand. Her fingers shook as reality set in while she tried to work the bolt. Only as she felt the heavy lock slide home did she realize that she might have bolted something inside with her.

Sucking in a breath at her own stupidity, she cautiously turned and headed toward the front of the house. She peeked into each of the bedrooms, looked into the living room and through the arch to the dining room. Maggie couldn't see into the kitchen but she wasn't willing to get too far from the front door. It could wait.

She padded softly into the foyer. The porch lamp sent a soft glow through the frosted glass of the front door giving her some light to see by.

Did a shadow move in it?

Her rage sparked again. No one had any right invading her

home. With one hand still on the bat, she rapidly undid the bolt and threw the door wide.

Maggie stepped boldly and angrily onto the front porch and smacked right into a broad, hard chest.

CHAPTER NINE

He'd heard the noises inside and wondered what was happening, but Sebastian was not prepared for Maggie to barrel out the front door and right into him.

He lifted his arms to hold her back but even as he started the movement, she wrapped both hands tighter around the bat she was holding and hauled it back.

Yanking his own hands skyward, he jumped backwards—maybe a little too far back. The floorboard at the top of the steps gave a little with his weight and he thought he was going to tumble down the porch stairs.

Thank God he was sure footed, because his sneaker slipped and he thumped down a step but he managed to remain upright. He did this while calling out, "It's me, Maggie. *It's me.* What's going on?"

De-escalate the situation, his brain was thinking, even though it was also thinking that Maggie had been plastered to him just moments before. And that she was wearing only a pink nightshirt with a Tweety Bird on the front. Tweety did not match her glower. He pressed, "Maggie?"

She held the tip of the bat out almost as though it were a

sword or a gun, keeping him at the end. "Someone was just in my house."

Holy shit, that explained the wild look in her eyes. And here he was on her doorstep, looking awfully suspicious at three 3am. The press of her lips and narrowing of her eyes indicated she thought exactly the same thing. "Why are you here?"

She'd jabbed the bat at him forcefully enough to make him dip backwards just a few inches to avoid getting a punch into the sternum, and damn if he didn't find the fire attractive. "You're not going to like what I have to say, Maggie."

Her eyebrows shot up and she jabbed at him again. Luckily, this time he was too far away. "Don't tell me what I will and won't think."

She had a good point. "I will tell you why I'm here, but can we first check the place out? Make sure no one's still here?"

He watched as she thought through her options then lowered the bat. She looked up and down the street, probably checking for her prowler, before stepping backwards. "Okay."

Though she didn't exactly invite him in, she didn't slam the door in his face either, and Sebastian slowly walked into the foyer. "Let's check each of the rooms."

He watched as her adrenaline turned to laughter. The bat now hanging loosely in one hand, the tip thumped into the hardwood floor. She waved her other hand loosely to indicate the house. "There are so many rooms, it'll take an hour."

Though she was exaggerating, she was right. He'd heard the place had six bedrooms for renters. He'd seen for himself that there was a den, two formal living rooms, a dining room and her office. Sebastian was about to find out for himself. "Let's give it a shot."

Fifteen minutes later, they'd done a cursory sweep of every room. He tried to keep his brain on the task at hand and off her bare legs. He was trying not to notice the way her nightgown occasionally hitched up or that she wasn't wearing anything underneath it ...

Pushing his brain back to the task at hand, he immediately thought of smoke and accelerants, but he'd seen all the corners and all the doors. Aside from the house itself, there were no fire hazards here. He'd seen the large upstairs bedroom with the attached bath that Maggie claimed as her own. The covers of the high antique bed had been thrown back haphazardly and he imagined the plush rug still held the footprints of her delicate bare feet.

Sebastian tried not to think about it. Instead, he walked heavily toward the back door and asked her if the noise matched what she'd heard.

"I think so. I mean, the back door was open and it sounded just like that."

"But you didn't see anyone?" He was just clarifying, but her eyes darted to the left and her jaw clenched tight as she said "no," as though she didn't like admitting that it might be nothing.

"It's not nothing," he told her. But even as he tried to reassure her, she turned a glare his direction. She was still seemingly unaware that she was only in a thin night shirt and that Tweety Bird was grinning at him.

"Why *are* you here at three in the morning Sebastian?"

He'd known this was coming, and there was no really good answer but the truth. "I saw the lights flipping on all over the house ... so I got out of my car and ran toward your door."

She only needed a sharp rise of one eyebrow to get him to confess the rest.

"I was watching your house." He sighed, "after what you said —" *and what he'd found*, but he didn't say the last part out loud, not yet.

Her look of sheer surprise didn't surprise him. Watching

over her was probably the dumbest thing to do. Then again, she'd had a problem and he was glad he was here now.

Her expression turned worried. "Why were you really watching my house at three a.m. Sebastian?"

Okay, she wasn't going to let it go.

He wanted to remind her that her prowler had gone out the back door and he'd been knocking out front, but she would figure that out on her own fast, if she hadn't already.

"Because I didn't like what I saw," it was a stupid answer, but he wasn't quite ready to tell her what he'd found online.

"About what?" she wasn't going to let him sidestep.

He admitted half of it. "When I left the other day, I saw footsteps around the side of your house. They followed the flower bed and they went into the back woods." He pointed at the wall as if to indicate the yard outside. At the time it had seemed silly to think they were sinister. "I told myself they were yours. But last night I remembered that I've never seen you wear work boots."

CHAPTER TEN

M aggie felt her blood start to rush again.

She didn't need this—as if having a break-in tonight hadn't been enough. She wanted to yell at Sebastian, "Why didn't you tell me there were footsteps in my yard?"

But it would just be rude, because honestly, she wouldn't have said anything either. Sebastian had thought they were her prints. And why would he think anything else?

Taking a deep breath, she fought to calm her racing thoughts. Her first clear idea was that she should thank him. The connection between the footprints and that he hadn't seen her in work boots was the only reason she knew the other sounds she'd been hearing were truly concerning and not just her wild imagination.

The second clear thought was that her nightshirt hit mid thighs ... maybe.

She looked up to see he was staring at her oddly, as though he knew she was about to lose it.

Was he staying? Was he going? He didn't look like he was done talking. Lord help her if he had other bad news. Well, she wouldn't face it in this ridiculous nightshirt and no bra.

"Do you mind if I go change?"

He shook his head *no*, but then followed her up the stairs. For a moment Maggie wondered if he was going to stand in the doorway while she got dressed.

But Sebastian Kane stood respectfully in the hallway with the door closed and waited without a peep. She knew this man well enough that thinking any different was about her and not him.

Her breath whooshed out of her lungs and she realized she finally felt safe knowing he was just beyond the door. Still, she didn't want to linger. She couldn't leave him standing in the hallway for the rest of the night. Maggie quickly pulled jeans out of her closet and a comfy t-shirt out of her dresser drawer— well, Aunt Abbie's dresser drawer.

Though it was barely 3:30 in the morning, she was fully dressed for the day now. No hair, no makeup, but that's what a man got when he showed up on a woman's doorstep in the middle of the night.

Sebastian smiled at her when she emerged, though whether it was for reassurance or because he was just happy she hadn't taken longer she didn't know.

He motioned down the hallway with one hand. "Should we go sit at the table and talk there?"

Maggie nodded and led the way down the steps. Even before they hit the dining room, she turned back and said, "We have to call the police."

Though he readily agreed, something about the too-quick nod made her wonder. She didn't have long to wait. He started talking as soon as she was seated.

"I don't think the footsteps in the garden are the worst of it."

Holy crap, she thought. Bracing her hands on the table, Maggie leaned forward and tried to untangle what had happened tonight.

Despite the fact that he was here at the same time as the prowler, she realized she trusted Sebastian implicitly.

Reaching out, he took her hand in his, probably offering a gentle kind of comfort. Did he know he sent a bolt of awareness up her arm? She fought the sigh that wanted to go with it.

"I don't know how to say this Maggie ... But I think Kalan might have been right."

"What?"

Her jaw fell open despite the fact that Maggie knew exactly what he meant. She was just so surprised that her reactions were getting away from her. At the time, everyone at the station house had told her Kalan's idea was nuts. Now, she was more concerned that Sebastian agreed with her.

Rex had brushed her off each time she asked if it was possible. She'd become convinced she was imagining things and definitely overthinking it. Maybe Rex had just been too busy to pay attention.

The last thing Maggie needed tonight was to confirm her own deep fears. Why would the box have been hidden unless it was a secret? So at the very least it was contraband of some kind.

"You really think it's a serial killer?" she blurted the words out, dreading the answer.

"I don't know about that," Sebastian replied calmly, as though he knew he was the eye of her hurricane tonight. "But Kalan made a good point. Who would keep such a random assortment of jewelry like that?"

He'd echoed her thoughts. No woman she knew would hang on to that collection or let it get so tangled.

"It's weird, for sure. And it belongs to someone who used to live here." Sebastian made the statements calmly, still keeping himself together in a way that Maggie envied.

She was holding on by a thread, but his next words made her breathe easier.

"The idea that it's a serial killer's trophies is a bit far-fetched. But, given the oddity of the collection, and the fact that it was shoved under a floorboard—probably with the intention that no one find it—makes me think it was stolen."

Maggie nodded. It was probably a stalker, or something one of the boarders had stolen. Maybe shoplifted things they had nowhere else to hide.

She was just starting to breathe easier when she decided it was time to ask Sebastian a question she probably wouldn't like the answer to. "Do you think the prowler is related to the jewelry?"

"I don't know," he answered with a loose-limbed shrug.

Maggie liked that about him. Lots of guys felt they had to have an opinion on everything, but Sebastian was more than willing to admit when he didn't. He was confident enough in who he was that he didn't have to show off.

But when he spoke again, she realized she was right: she *didn't* like his answer.

"I think the question is, what else might the prowler have been here for?"

CHAPTER ELEVEN

From the look on her face, Maggie did not like what he'd asked. Well, that made two of them.

"Oh, hell." Maggie shook her head as if everything was crazy. "It could be anything! There was so much crap in here that I already cleared out ... and I'm nowhere near finished."

Sebastian nodded along in an attempt to be reassuring in a shitty situation. "I'm assuming you haven't made an effort to search under the other floorboards?"

"Oh, dear God, no." Then she suddenly leaned forward, her rich auburn brows pulled in a tight frown. "Do you think there are more?"

"I don't know." Another crappy answer, and he just wished he had something better to say.

"If I have to check every squeaky floorboard, it will take years!"

He'd meant it that he would help. It was five shades of stupid, putting himself in such close proximity with a woman he had an active, serious crush on. But he wasn't going to leave her alone while someone broke into her house ... especially with her in it.

He was opening his mouth to re-volunteer his home improvement skills when she reached into her back pocket and pulled out her phone. Maggie announced, "It's past time to call the police."

Sebastian nodded solemnly and watched as she hit buttons. When he realized she was looking up the non-emergency number, he rattled it off for her. At her surprise, he said, "The PD is right next door to the fire house." As though that explained everything.

With a smile—finally!—she hit the buttons then paused and looked up at him. "Are you staying?"

His heart stuttered in his chest.

"As long as you need me." Sebastian fought to say the words calmly, though inside he was reminding himself this was about a prowler and not about desire.

Maggie had already proved she could hold her own the way she'd raced around the house with that bat, ready to take all comers. But no one should be worried about prowlers in the night alone. She'd need time to sleep, and he could help with that.

She offered him one small nod as she hit the button and he listened to her side of the conversation as she explained her middle-of-the-night adventure in a measured voice.

One of the upsides of the small town was that the police arrived right away. Sebastian saw the light bobbing through the backyard as one officer headed around the house to check for prints or other evidence. The other had already knocked at the front.

Maggie opened the heavy wooden door and said, "Hello."

He heard the voice before he saw the woman. "I'm officer Marina Balero." She shook Maggie's hand in a standard introduction, but turned to him and offered only a tight, "Sebastian."

Well, that was embarrassing. From the micro expression that flitted across Maggie's face, she hadn't missed it.

Marina didn't let any of their history get in her way, though. *Typical Marina.* "You had a break-in?"

For the next twenty minutes, they sat at the table and he and Maggie took turns explaining what happened, while Marina took copious notes.

When it was his turn, Sebastian admitted, "I saw the lights go on, one at a time, all over the house."

"And why were you watching her house in the middle of the night?"

Oh yeah, he'd known this had been coming. It was going to be bad when he explained it, but having his ex doing the questioning? He didn't even know how or what to tell Maggie. Despite his feelings for her, they weren't dating, and he suspected that Marina saw right through him.

The best he could do was not turn an embarrassing shade of red as he explained about the footprints, adding the date and time of day when he'd spotted them.

Marina next turned to what Maggie had heard from inside the house. He let Maggie explain how they'd swept each of the rooms and found nothing.

"Is there anything else I should know?" Marina asked, her eyes scanning the two of them as though they should start admitting to an extramarital affair. Neither of them was married, though probably everyone in town knew Maggie was with Rex.

Taking a deep breath, Sebastian said, "Actually there is."

Something about his tone must have grabbed her. Her eyes snapped up to his.

But this wasn't his to tell. He hadn't been here when the box was found. "Maggie?"

"Follow me." Maggie stood up and he watched his ex and his

41

current wish head down the hallway to discuss more of the disturbing events of Maggie's last week.

Maggie led the way to the back room, where she opened the closet and pointed up toward the shelf. The box was pushed so far back that even he couldn't see it. Maggie reached up on her tiptoes and pulled it out.

As she did, his mind put a few pieces of information together. The prowler had opened all the doors downstairs, Maggie said, possibly even this closet. But he hadn't found the box.

Sebastian began thinking out loud, narrating for Marina as much as to organize his own thoughts. "If he was looking for this, he would have noticed the floorboard where it was originally hidden is torn up."

Maggie still hadn't fixed it. Sebastian made a mental note to get on that right away.

"You think he was looking for this box?" Marina glanced between the two of them, still a bit in the dark.

"Who knows?" Maggie held it out, but Marina put a hand up, reached into her back pocket, and pulled out blue nitrile gloves.

Yeah, Sebastian thought, *the police definitely needed to know about this.*

Placing the box on the top of the antique dresser at the side of the room, Marina used a single blue-tipped finger to lift the lid. "Jewelry," she said, stating the obvious. Then she looked up at Maggie. "Is there anything special about it?"

"Just that it's odd," Maggie replied. "Who has dime store jewelry and expensive diamonds in the same box?"

Marina tipped her head as if to agree. Then she pulled a pen from her pocket. Using the tip, she attempted to untangle a few pieces, just as Sebastian had done.

"I have photos of the pieces," he volunteered, then immediately spoke again, preempting her because he knew she would ask. "I didn't touch it. I used a pen. But I didn't get it all untangled, so some of the pictures are a mess of several pieces."

"So it's been disturbed?"

"Well, yes," he said, but how would it not be? "It was disturbed when Maggie pulled it out from where it was hidden. It was shoved between the boards, sideways, so it wasn't preserved anyway."

Marina nodded but kept pushing through the pieces as if inspecting a meal for stray peppers.

Sebastian pulled up the pictures on his phone just as she scooped her pen under the ankle bracelet and slowly pulled it out.

Her expression stilled, and even Maggie caught the look. She asked, "What is it?"

"I can't say for sure," Marina uttered the words too quickly, tilting the pencil and letting the jewelry slide back into the box. She closed the lid carefully.

It was clear she wasn't going to tell them. Her jaw clenched a little bit. No one liked having information withheld, but Sebastian understood. Though he wasn't a law enforcement officer, being a firefighter he understood a lot about the privacy clauses that governed both their jobs.

He wasn't allowed to walk onto a scene and tell the homeowner it was arson, even if it was clearly arson. And Marina wasn't allowed to say anything just because she had a suspicion.

Marina made it clear she was done as she radioed the other officer for an evidence bag. While she waited, she asked again, "Is there anything else you remember that might be pertinent?"

They both shook their heads, and he was relieved the long night was coming to an end. Marina bagged the box and carried it gingerly at her side. That worried him. *What was so special about that box?* But he knew better than to ask.

Marina thanked them both, and let Maggie know she'd be

looking into the break-in. It was standard and trite and he got the impression that Maggie wasn't expecting much as she walked the two officers down the hall and thanked them.

But as the officers headed out the front door, Maggie blurted out, "I heard a rumor."

Her hands clenched into fists at her sides, worrying Sebastian for the umpteenth time that night. He was learning to read her signals and he didn't like this one.

Sure enough, she blurted out, "I heard that the Blue River Killer was active again."

Once again Marina Balero went dead still.

Oh, shit, Sebastian thought. There was no reason for her to react that way, unless ...

CHAPTER TWELVE

The following morning, Sebastian headed into Spill the Beans for his usual day-off coffee. If he woke up and felt like he needed the activity instead of the sleep, he'd get dressed and walk over.

Today, he was here because he hadn't yet been to bed. He'd left Maggie to climb into her own shiny antique bed, but he hadn't shaken last night off enough to sleep himself.

Lucille ran the coffee shop, having converted it from a deli when her father passed. Such a small town thing ... And Sebastian found himself wondering if Maggie saw it as quaint or backward.

He'd seen her in here, but that might just be because it was the only coffee shop in town. There were Starbucks' in Lincoln, and Scooters in Beatrice, but Spill the Beans was the only local option.

He'd grown up here. This place and the people made sense to him. He'd gone away for college, but not that far. Not any place as big as Los Angeles, and he couldn't help but wonder what Maggie thought of his small hometown and her intruder.

Wasn't that the whole point of moving to a town like this—

getting away from "big city crime"? Only, he knew it didn't work that way, and he hoped Maggie did, too.

Despite the fact that he opened the door to the shop and immediately spotted her tucked into a back booth with Rex and his daughter, he didn't want her to move away. She was trying her damndest to establish a business here, but locals weren't much for trusting newcomers, even if she was Sabbie's great niece and she'd been here for plenty of summers as a kid. Maggie was still "new," and trusting her with their wills or divorces would take time for Redemption.

As he moved forward in line, he hooked his shirt on the edge of the counter and put a small tear in the old white t-shirt. It was wearing thin, the FD logo on the upper left and across the back were severely faded, and he wasn't quite sure why he'd worn it. Maybe because it was soft and he wasn't fully in his head today. Maybe being a firefighter was who he was and he needed to remind himself of that.

He watched as Rex leaned down and said something to Hannah, giving the toddler another toy. Sebastian adored Hannah fiercely, but every time he picked her up he took a fresh jolt to his system. She was exactly the size of the Miller baby. *Tyler.*

He stepped forward in line trying to fight off the memories. Hazards of the job, he told himself. Live saves were rare, he told himself as he shoved his hands in his pockets to keep his sudden flash from the past from being obvious.

He'd be glad when Hannah got bigger and the weight and size of her didn't remind him of the toddler he'd carried alive out of the house ... the same one who'd been gone by the time Sebastian tried to hand him to his mother.

"Sebastian? Sebastian?"

He'd been moving forward in line automatically and hadn't realized he'd reached the front and that Penny had asked him what he wanted. "Oh sorry."

After placing his order, he stepped aside and waited.

"Bas! Bas!" Hannah called out, having spotted him even if Maggie and Rex were too caught up in each other to notice anyone else.

He would have gone over and said hello. He was okay, really. It was just always that initial jolt when he lifted her. He would get over it. Every one of them had a shitty story like that, and he was no different. But as he turned to offer a wave to the little girl, he saw Maggie's and Rex's hands were clasped tightly together.

Maggie was looking deeply into Rex's eyes.

He was the intruder. He waved quickly at Hannah and forced himself to step outside to wait. He didn't need to see that.

Or maybe he did.

Maybe he needed the reminder that Maggie wasn't his and never would be. Rex was a decent guy, and one of the brotherhood. Though, honestly, it was more like a 'cousinhood' until things got rough. He would need Rex at his back one day, and Maggie was severely off-limits.

Sebastian couldn't say he was impressed with the way Rex was handling fatherhood, but having never had a child of his own, Sebastian didn't think he was one to judge. When he heard his name called, he ducked back in and grabbed his drink from Penny, trying to ignore her over-eager smile.

Then he headed down the street, forcing himself to not look at Maggie and Rex again. They hadn't seen him even if he'd needed to see them.

The problem was, it was barely nine am and he had the whole day in front of him. Six hours ago, he'd been watching Maggie's house like a lovesick puppy. Five hours ago, Marina's eyes had gone wide and made him think the jewelry box Maggie had found was maybe a serial killer's trophies.

But Maggie had told him to go home and get some sleep.

She'd said she was going to bed, exhausted. But now she was in Spill the Beans with Rex.

He shouldn't be thinking about her. Sebastian knew that.

But he also knew he couldn't stop his own feelings.

So the question was, did she abandon her inheritance tonight and stay in a hotel? If she did, she would leave the house open to whoever was on the loose. Her prowler could get in and find whatever he was looking for.

Or did she stay and hold the fort against all comers?

And if she did, would Sebastian play the lovesick puppy again and stay up all night watching over her?

CHAPTER THIRTEEN

It had been four days since the break-in. Maggie couldn't say she was sleeping well. She was staying up all night with the baseball bat and then napping her way through the daylight when she could.

She'd spent too much of the time doing research. She should have been seeing clients and fixing up the house—she was already so far behind.

She'd seen several clients, though one had insisted on an eight am appointment. The older folks were coming to her, many saying that if Sabbie trusted her, they could, too. But it wouldn't be enough work to keep her afloat financially.

The combination of small town life and working in an office from her home was presenting challenges she should have foreseen, but hadn't. She'd thought it would be an easy commute, a welcome respite from her hours in traffic in LA. And it was that, but there were no boundaries. Work existed every waking moment ... or the obvious lack of it.

But once she'd finished up with Mr. Mackey's land division, she'd napped, made coffee, and pretended she was starting her day for the first time. Some of her research about the house and the area had been comforting and some of it had been absolutely petrifying.

Maggie had not heard of the Blue River Killer before Mrs. Miller had decided it was excellent gossip. From what Maggie found online, Mrs. Miller needn't worry as she was not the Blue River Killer's target demographic. The upside was that Maggie didn't fit the profile either.

This murderer pulled women and young men from nightclubs and apparently talked them into walking with him and maybe even getting into his car. There was never any sign of a struggle near the point where they were last seen. No one had been abducted from their own home. And none had been a red-headed lawyer in her mid-thirties newly arrived in Nebraska. This guy liked blondes.

Maggie had also been reading up on break-ins in general. She felt better knowing it was extremely rare for a burglar to come back to the scene. So when Sebastian had called that night and asked if she wanted him to stay, she'd been comfortable enough to say no.

If things got bad, she would head to a hotel. But she didn't really have money for a hotel. Redemption wasn't booming with legal needs, and if it wasn't for her volunteer position at the fire station and the friends she was making, Maggie would have considered packing up and moving.

Hell, she was considering it anyway. She'd already contemplated selling the house, though it felt a little unfair to do so. Maggie had definitely been her aunt Abbie's favorite, though there had been three other grandkids related to Abbie the same way.

If she sold the house now, she would feel compelled to split the money equally. But Abbie had left the house to her because she thought Maggie had loved the house. The problem was that as a child she'd loved its twisted servants' staircase from the kitchen. The slim space had always felt like it was just her size.

She'd loved the big backyard and the porch that wrapped all the way around the house. Here she'd had blackberries that lined the back fence and Abbie had let her scatter wildflower seeds along the sides of the yard.

But what she'd really loved was spending summers with Aunt Abbie. Without her great aunt and her childhood adventures, the place wasn't the same. The blackberries and wildflowers were still there, and so was the servants' staircase. Though it was still really cool, cleaning the place was a bitch. As an adult, it wasn't quite as whimsical.

She had only been here a few months, but it was past time to admit that it was killing her to keep it. The problem was, what could she sell it for? It was in disrepair, luckily falling into the "shabby chic" phase, but probably barely worth anything in a town this small with no real tourism.

Maggie rolled out of bed Saturday morning thinking that the next day was A-shift at the station. She was going to go in and do her volunteer work and not interfere with her weekly work schedule. Filing the reports, making the dispatcher's schedules and organizing the station house were at least tasks that were do-able. It felt good to be useful to the people keeping the town safe. She even looked forward to calling the medical cases from the week's runs and seeing if they were doing okay. If she worked on her own house today, she could hopefully count more things checked off, and at least not be even further behind this week.

She pulled on cut off jeans and an old t shirt worn thin in the wash. Maggie was confident she would still get too hot and sweaty doing the work, though. She pulled on sneakers and tied them into perfect bows, as if going slowly now would make her day run a little more smoothly.

She hadn't heard any noises the past few nights. Though she'd woken up once around two am the night before, she had heard nothing but the wind and she'd managed to roll over and get back to sleep. Maggie decided to count that as a win.

She procrastinated a little more by lingering over a bowl of oatmeal and starting a pot of coffee. Eventually, she headed into the room where the loose floorboard still sat sideways, leaving a gaping hole. She would have to fix that. She couldn't stand seeing it each time she walked in.

But Maggie still hadn't figured out the best method. So she wouldn't touch it today. She didn't need the frustration of going down the rabbit hole of Do-It-Yourself videos. Plugging in the steamer, she decided to attack the wallpaper.

One wall was mostly stripped when she heard a knock at her front door. *Who was knocking on her door at nine am on a Saturday?* Given what had transpired the other night, she was no longer saying hello and pulling the door open wide. On her tiptoes, she checked the peephole and smiled. She wasn't surprised to see Sebastian.

Now, she did throw the door open wide and stepped back as she said, "Good morning."

She didn't formally invite him inside. He'd become that kind of friend. Hell, anyone who showed up in the middle of the night when you had a prowler automatically qualified.

He didn't step over the threshold, but glanced at her up and down. For a moment she thought if she'd known he was coming over, she might have put some makeup on, or maybe not worn these shorts. The jeans were fraying with a few strings hanging down her thighs. Not her best look. But if you showed up unannounced, you got what you got.

Sebastian saw the coffee mug in one hand and the hammer in the other. With a grin he asked, "Weapon or home improvement?"

She laughed, "Home Improvement."

He hooked the thumb over his shoulder toward where his car was parked. Then he said maybe the best thing he could.

CHAPTER FOURTEEN

Sebastian walked the hardwood floor in a grid pattern checking for other squeaks. He shouldn't have shown up and offered to help. But it wasn't as if Rex could take the day off and do it. And Sebastian was finding it hard to stay away.

So he lied to himself about small town charm and being neighborly and he showed up on her doorstep. He'd now put the missing floorboard back into place. Patching the hole made the room look less sinister, and he hoped it gave Maggie a little peace of mind.

When he didn't hear anything this time around, he wanted to believe he'd gotten all the squeaky boards. *Only fifteen more rooms to go.* That would be a lot of time around Maggie ... if he could handle it. He looked across the room to find her peeling back the paper on yet another wall.

"Wow, that's impressive."

Her sincere *thank you* made him smile, probably a little broader than he should have. She was using a steamer and a wide scraping tool to pull off the layers in gooey sheets. It shouldn't have been attractive. *Damn Rex.* And damn himself for not asking her out sooner.

"Sebastian, come look at this."

"What is it?" He was afraid it was another hidey hole with another sinister surprise, but thankfully it wasn't.

"Look at this," she said holding up a layer of wallpaper she'd peeled away. She'd revealed the layer of white wallpaper with burgundy colored line drawings of French families playing in the countryside.

"There are a lot of layers on this wall," he commented. "I didn't know there was a toile under here."

Maggie raised one eyebrow at him, seemingly surprised he understood. His mother loved the stuff, that's how he knew what a toile was, but he didn't say anything.

"It's not that it's toile," she said, and pointed at several different spots. "Look closely. It has monkeys. This is *monkey toile.*"

"Is monkey toile even a thing?" He'd not seen it with anything other than people and a few birds before.

"I guess it is. Someone clearly manufactured it." She shook her head at the wall as though it were misbehaving. "It still has to go."

"If you want to peel the layers separately, you can frame a square of it to keep if you want."

"Look at you, Mr. Home Improvement," she teased and turned back to working on the wall.

He watched her stand on tiptoes in those short shorts, her legs stretching as she reached up high. Her shirt pulled up when she moved her arm over her head, revealing a slice of smooth skin at her waist. It was all making Sebastian a little crazy.

Rex should be here, not him.

He understood that Rex couldn't be here and he wasn't going to encroach on a fellow firefighter's girlfriend. But Maggie needed a hand and a spare set of eyes on the lookout. If anyone saw him looking at Maggie's ass, well, he'd have to figure out something to say for that, too.

In an effort to shift his thoughts, he shifted the conversation. "How has it been here at night?"

He'd driven by himself at least once each night, wanting to keep her safe, and also trying to respect the choice she'd made not to have him stay over. She'd gathered plenty of information, and she convinced herself—and mostly him, too—that she was safe enough. Her burglar had gotten inside the house and hadn't found what he wanted. He'd been actively chased off and he shouldn't have reason to come back.

"I'm doing better," she said, as she kept working. "The police are driving by a little more. I've heard them passing at different hours some nights."

He didn't comment that she might have heard him checking on her, too.

"Have they gotten back to you?" He was curious what the results were from all the jewelry in the box.

"Nope," Maggie shook her head, seeming happy. "I figure that has to be good news. If that box was full of serial killer trophies, someone would know, and we would have heard before now."

Sebastian nodded along. That reasoning made sense. Plus, he and Marina Balero had dated for almost six months—nothing hot and heavy, and when they had broken up it had been relatively amicable. He wanted to believe she would tell him if there was something he needed to know.

He hadn't heard anything either, which was another relief. But he didn't say this to Maggie. She would wind up asking about the obvious history between him and the officer. He wasn't ready to volunteer his past.

They worked together through periods of easy silence and bursts of conversation. He learned all kinds of things about Maggie and it bothered him that the information all made him like her more. He wanted to find something that would make him back off. But this was, once again, having the opposite effect on him.

She'd been on the dance team in high school and always wanted to be a lawyer. She was a little frustrated with the slow speed at which her business had been growing in Redemption, but she countered quickly. "I knew this was a possibility, but I told myself it would happen faster. I was here when I was a kid, but I'm not really a local. So I guess I don't have that advantage of everyone knowing me and trusting me right off the bat."

He'd agreed. People were just a little insular that way. Even though they liked Maggie, it would take a while before they brought their business to her. It wasn't like she was selling hardware at a discount either, she was offering personal services like contracts between friends and partners, wills and prenups. Maybe he could talk Rex and the others into promoting her business as a thank you for her volunteer work.

At lunchtime, she insisted on buying him a sandwich. Then he tagged along to the paint store—like a friend, and not like a man who desperately wanted a woman he couldn't have. Sebastian wound up providing commentary on paint colors.

She raised a delicate eyebrow at him once again, a look he was coming to appreciate.

"Do you just do everything?" she asked.

He finally confessed to why he knew these things. "No, but my dad is a master carpenter—he's done construction and contracted houses—and my mother is an interior designer. So I know things. Ask me about your color palette and whether you want modern, farmhouse, or cool beach tones."

At least he'd made her laugh, and the sound diffused through his system. Rex was an idiot.

Sebastian stayed with her as late as he could, hanging out and working until Maggie decided her day was over. She fed him soup that she'd made and frozen earlier in the week. Then she thanked him profusely, until it was clear that she was ready to be home alone for the evening.

There were no hugs, just a friendly goodbye, no matter how much he would have loved if there was something more between them. But as he got in his car and pulled away, Sebastian still couldn't quell the uneasy feeling that had grown steadily throughout the day.

CHAPTER FIFTEEN

Maggie sat across from the chief, trying to keep her hands from fidgeting and showing her nerves. It was like being called into the principal's office as a kid, only she knew better than to squirm now.

She pushed her hands between her knees and tried to sit calmly, as though that would hide her irritation. Rex sat next to her and leaned back in the chair. His butt slid toward the front edge, his hand on his forehead and, as irritated as she was, she felt surprisingly sorry for the man.

"I don't know what's going on with you two," Chief Taggert said, but he shook his head as though he didn't want to know. Turning to look directly at Maggie, he said, "We love having you here. We need you as a volunteer. And I was happy when you came back on A-shift."

She nodded. She already knew that, and she knew it was because they had volunteers on the other two shifts already. He'd been willing to let her trade shifts to babysit Hannah in a domino effect to keep both his volunteer and his firefighter when Rex suddenly inherited his daughter. But now, things were supposed to have gone back to normal and he was as frustrated as they both were.

"Rex," Taggert turned to her now-ex-boyfriend, his hands clasped together on the desk. "I can't have your child dropped off here."

"I know. I told the sitter that, but clearly I can't control what she does." He sounded so defeated that Maggie wanted to help, but she couldn't always take up the slack.

Rex's new babysitter had made it through only one and a half shifts. *Not even that,* Maggie thought. The older woman had come in today with Hannah and her stroller and a fully packed bag. The firefighters had all smiled and said hello and Maggie had thought how nice it was to be on this end of things for once. But then the woman had pulled Rex aside and apparently explained that her daughter had gotten a horrible diagnosis, and she was leaving town ... right that moment.

Maggie had heard part of the conversation. "I understand," Rex had assured the woman. "I'll find another sitter for Thursday."

Though Maggie hadn't heard the rest, it had become very clear when the sitter left and Hannah didn't. Rex had to explain to the chief that his child was in the station and he suddenly had no childcare for her.

It had been hard enough finding this woman. Maggie didn't know what he would do.

The chief wasn't done. "Either someone takes your daughter —quickly—or you take a sick day and I call in a sub."

Rex hated taking sick days, Maggie knew. In fact, he picked up most of the spare shifts that he could. Since Hannah had arrived he'd worked exactly zero extra hours.

It was costing him, especially now with the child care on top of the loss of income. He'd been paying child support, but now he was paying everything. The last Maggie knew, he'd heard nothing from Hannah's mother.

The chief looked back to Maggie. And she understood what he was silently asking. She was the easiest fix to the situation—even if she didn't like it.

So she turned to her ex. "Three hours. I will take her for *three hours* until you find another sitter." She hated to have to be so harsh, but she had to get her business going or it was going to fail. There was also the issue of the house. "I can't keep her overnight. And if I don't get my business going, I have to go back to LA. Then there's no sitter and no A-shift volunteer at all."

"I thought you were doing fine."

"I am. But only if I have the hours to run my *own life*." Maggie tried not to grind her teeth, but maybe he just wanted to be sure she was okay. He was a decent guy, just in a shitty situation. "But if someone breaks in again, you don't want Hannah there!"

Wow, she thought, just those words coming out of her mouth were concerning enough. Rex nodded. She held up a hand to the chief who was looking alarmed. "Nothing has happened since last week. I'm doing okay. The police are sending patrols by. I don't think my burglar is coming back. But if he does—" she turned back to Rex, "—and Hannah was in the house with me, I would never forgive myself."

He wouldn't either. She knew that much. If anything happened to her, he'd blame himself and his circumstances with Hannah and his ex. But it wasn't his fault, and Maggie wasn't his girlfriend anymore. She said the words again. "Three hours."

"Thank you. Really. I appreciate it."

She looked between the two men who seemed to believe that that fixed everything, but it messed everything up. Her volunteer work was cut an hour short, but the chief seemed to think it was worth it to get his firefighter back and not have to call in a sub.

Heading out into the main room she found Hannah

squealing and running around. She was playing with Sebastian and Kalan. Apparently one of them was chasing the other two, but Maggie couldn't figure out quite which way it went. When it calmed down, she packed the little girl into her stroller and gathered Hannah's things along with her own, making it look more like a camping trip than a walk home.

As she said goodbye, knowing the guys were watching her, and thinking ... well, whatever they thought about her doing all this for Rex and Hannah, She heard the Chief's phone buzz and her heart sank. Sure enough, thirty seconds later the alarm rang and the men scrambled into action. She heard the call—both trucks. It could be nothing, but there was every chance that Rex wouldn't even be done with this call in three hours, let alone have another sitter lined up to get his daughter.

She tried to put her best face forward to the little girl. None of this was Hannah's fault, but Maggie felt only resentment as she pushed the stroller through the bay doors and down the sidewalk. As the trucks rolled and bounced past them, Hannah waved and squealed and Maggie looked up in time to see a few of the guys waving back to her.

They hit the park and played until the small bag of snacks ran out. She counted the cars that went by, suspicious of everyone and everything and hating being out in the open. But Hannah loved the park and the silver sedan wasn't evil, just someone she didn't know. When they were done, she pushed the stroller the five blocks back to her own home, her stomach twisting the whole way.

She'd texted Rex multiple times but got no word back. So Maggie fed Hannah dinner and they watched the sunset out the front window.

Even as Hannah squealed at a pair of squirrels running up and down the big tree in the front yard, Maggie looked at her watch. It had been five hours and there was no word.

Were the guys safe? The fire must have been bigger than just a small call. They were called out for more than just smoke alerts and medical emergencies, though they got those, too. Sometimes wildfires came close to town, and their crew was added in with the smoke jumpers and stations from Lincoln or even Omaha.

They were as safe as they could be, but it wasn't a safe job.

She checked her phone again as the front yard grew dark and she grew more and more worried. As she pulled Hannah away from the window, Maggie saw the silver sedan go by again.

CHAPTER SIXTEEN

Maggie had slept on the couch in the living room the night before. The crick in her neck wasn't doing her any favors nor was the maybe four hours total sleep she'd gotten during eight different attempts.

Stretching her arms up, she felt the pull of angry muscles. Maggie tipped her head side to side, glad that Hannah wasn't here. Having a toddler would have only made the night worse and heightened her paranoia.

Rex had shown up and fetched Hannah about thirty minutes after Maggie had finally given up and put her to sleep. He'd managed to text a few minutes before he was on his way but it wasn't much warning. Still Maggie was glad to have Hannah with Rex where she belonged, even though it had meant Rex missed part of his shift.

He hadn't been able to find a babysitter at all. Maggie quashed her guilt. She felt bad that she couldn't help him out, but she was concerned about having Hannah overnight *before* she'd seen the silver sedan go by at both the park and her house.

So she'd stayed up late, fully dressed and sitting on the couch. She clutched her high-powered LED flashlight and sat in the dark, watching out the small slit in the front curtains. Maggie had hoped she would be able to see if someone came on her property. She was hoping the streetlights were bright enough she could catch the license plate if the silver sedan went by again.

It hadn't.

She'd given up around two a.m. then woken up numerous times throughout the night to various creepy noises. She'd shown the light into the front yard once and the back yard three times. If anyone had actually been on her property, the powerful beam had scared them off.

In the morning, she'd headed outside and checked the grass for any new evidence. There had been no new footprints, but there hadn't been any new rains either and Maggie honestly didn't know what she was looking for. She thought about calling Sebastian and telling him about the silver sedan—just so someone else would know where to start looking if something happened to her.

But the sun was coming in through the sheers and the fears of the night before began to recede. So, after she'd eaten her oatmeal and had her coffee, Maggie got dressed for the day and called the police station. She was hoping for a little bit of good news to tip her world back to upright.

She waited on hold two different times as she was passed from department to department. Finally, Officer Balero answered the phone. "Miss Willis—"

"Maggie, please," she offered. Despite the strange tension lingering between Sebastian and the officer, Maggie liked her. Maybe she'd find out whatever that bit of gossip was later. "I was hoping to get my box of jewelry back. I've been looking through my aunt's records and trying to find who the tenants were. I'd like to return things to their owners."

"Oh," Marina seemed surprised by the request and it took her a moment to respond.

In the space before she answered, Maggie felt her stomach twist—a feeling that was becoming far too common in her life.

Her best case scenario was simply that they wouldn't return the box. And though she was trying to find the owners, she really didn't care about the jewelry itself. Right now, she didn't know who it belonged to. If she found out who it belonged to, he could go to the police and request it back himself.

But that wasn't going to happen. Marina's next words stunned her. "We don't have the box anymore ... Nor any of the jewelry."

"What happened to it?" Maggie blurted out the words before thinking. That was not her usual style. As a lawyer she'd been carefully trained to think before she spoke. But she felt she was blurting out so many things these days, because the world was moving both too slow and too fast.

Her brain tumbled over ideas as if she were running too quickly downhill. Maybe it had been lost. She'd always heard about evidence going missing. If that was true, she didn't care, but it was the tone and the officer's voice as she gave the information that had Maggie's tension ratcheting up again.

"The FBI has the box."

"The FBI? Why?" Again, she blurted her thoughts.

"They took it as evidence—" Marina seemed to cut off the last word, as though she were going to say more before thinking better of it.

Maggie wasn't having any of that. Though she wasn't a courtroom lawyer, she'd also been trained in tenacity. She'd harbored hopes that one day she and the officer might be friends. This was putting a damper on that, as her tone came out harsher than intended. "Evidence of what?"

Silence reigned from the other end of the line.

Maggie tried a tactic she knew when waiting out a client, one that let them off the hook. Legally they could say later that they'd never told her anything. "Okay, if I'm wrong, tell me *no*.

The FBI took my jewelry box as evidence because they think the jewelry in it links to a crime."

Silence stretched again and Maggie waited, hoping the officer would say something to put her at ease, but nothing happened.

Maggie pushed a little harder, not liking where this was going, but needing answers. "They took it because they think it's related to the Blue River Killer."

Again, Marina Balero didn't speak

Holy shit.

CHAPTER SEVENTEEN

"Kane! Come around to the front with me."

The chief motioned for Hernandez to take Sebastian's place on the fire hose. They were soaking the final corner of a home that had been almost fully engulfed just hours before. Only the front of the home had survived, making it look a little surreal from the street view.

He operated a stepwise hand-off with Luke. The power of the firehose could get away and cause more problems if the exchange wasn't well orchestrated. When Hernandez was successfully in his spot, Sebastian headed toward the wet and dirty front yard. It had been a long night to say the least.

At the front entry, he waited as his boss slowly placed a foot, and then his whole weight, on each of the steps from the front porch. It looked as though the area had remained untouched by the fire, but they both knew looks could be deceiving.

Firefighters all learned early on to be rule followers, for their own safety and that of their brothers. So Sebastian followed rank and waited until the chief turned around and motioned for him to follow. Only then did he pull his mask off and breathe open air.

"I need your head in the game on this one," the chief told him, as he opened the front door, a silly gesture given that the back half of the house was mostly gone.

Sebastian wondered what the chief had meant about his head being in the game, but he nodded in agreement. It had to mean that all his distractions and worry about Maggie had been showing. As it ran through his head quickly, he took a brief moment to decide what to say.

Rex was another firefighter that the chief was having trouble with. Though it wasn't anyone's fault, and they all knew it, it might help if the chief knew what was going on. Sebastian spoke up. "Before you go in … I don't know how much of this Rex knows, because he's been so swamped lately, but Maggie's had a burglary at her home."

"She told me all of it a while ago," Chief answered as though to ask if there was anything else.

That was good at least, Sebastian bought. "So you know about the jewelry box?"

Now his chief frowned at him. Maybe she hadn't told him *all of it*. "She found a box of jewelry shoved under the floorboards and it looked very suspicious. It's been given to the police."

"Interesting." The chief drew out the word as though the story had finally become pertinent. "Do they think the two are related?"

"We don't know yet," Sebastian said. "But that's where my head has been. I've been trying to help out."

The chief nodded at him and Sebastian fought the flush that wanted to creep up his cheeks as though his father had caught him crushing on some high school girl. He stumbled through the words to cover it up, and probably did a crap job. "You said to get my head in the game. It is, but that's where it's been, and I thought you should know since she's our volunteer."

The volunteers were considered part of the team and this was a job where being distracted could get you killed and though it hadn't been comfortable, Sebastian was glad he'd brought his boss fully up to speed.

Though Sebastian was ready to head inside and investigate, the chief turned back to him and offered up, "That might have something to do with why she and Rex broke up and why she's not watching Hannah anymore even though the new babysitter quit. It's been a cluster."

Sebastian tripped over his own thoughts at the information. *They'd broken up?*

That was the last thing anyone should have said to get his head in the game. So with sheer force of will, he turned his thoughts back to the building. "Well, now that everyone's up to date. What's going on in here?"

"We're looking for any obvious signs of arson." The chief opened the door and gingerly headed into the room. "Can't get into the back half of the house yet, but I'm curious if anything might be visible here."

Sebastian nodded and stepped inside. The carpet squished under his feet and he lifted his mask back to his face taking a hit of cleaner air. His nose had tickled at the telltale scents.

Every firefighter was trained in recognizing the signs of arson. Investigators would be brought in for more detailed analysis if the situation warranted. Often the insurance companies paid their own investigator after the fact. So he and the chief were just the first wave of inspection right now.

The chief was of course the most highly trained local investigator—except for Sebastian. Last year, he'd won a coveted position at Quantico training. Now, he was on his way to being name district's official arson investigator, a position the chief now occupied. It was a question of whether the chief handed him the role or if Sebastian would have to wait until the older man retired.

Sebastian had even considered throwing his hat in the ring

for chief. That meant working toward his next promotion now, and there was no time like the present.

Together they scanned the area and for a few moments, neither said anything. His thoughts were focused on the sound of the water buffeting the last wall in the back of the house, the words of firefighters issuing commands through the slightly staticky comm at his shoulder.

Sebastian tried to see the place with unbiased eyes as he and the chief each came to their own conclusions before sharing. But to Sebastian the burn trail across the carpet was clear. Someone had lit the fire in this room and it had snaked along the trail and into the back half of the house.

The chief broke the silence first, since this didn't require much discussion. "It's pretty clearly accelerant."

Sebastian pointed into his boss's line of sight, his big glove making the gesture almost too obvious. "It's a shitty job. I don't know if they thought the fire would cover the evidence. It could be they're an idiot for not hiding their own tracks. Or maybe this was blatant, and they wanted us to know."

CHAPTER EIGHTEEN

Maggie had been awake all night. She was exhausted, wired, and mad at the world.

At one am coffee had seemed like a good idea. But at seven, as the sun came up, it was clear she'd been making bad choices. She hadn't been in danger of falling asleep; she was far too concerned about every noise and every car passing on the street.

She had not seen a silver sedan again, which was a relief. However, a police car had cruised her street three different times. She knew this, because every time she heard an engine, she dashed to the window. Each time a tree tapped on a window, she ran frantically around the house looking for intruders.

So she sat with her fifth—or seventh?—cup of coffee and watched the sun come up out her back window. The sunrise was gorgeous, though maybe if only because it indicated that her night was over. She was a wreck.

The entire night was a stunning reminder of what a shitty job she'd done of making friends.

When she'd first moved to Redemption a few months ago,

she'd thought she could reconnect with her childhood friends here. That had been a pipe dream, because she knew adults didn't really work that way. And it hadn't happened. Maggie wasn't a local, she was a summertime visitor at best. Instead, she'd been raised in Los Angeles and still carried the city vibe.

She didn't fit in. And asking if there were women's clothing shops and then not shopping at them because they weren't her style didn't help. But she desperately wanted to fit in, to make a home here. It just wasn't happening as fast as she'd like. She'd spent days with the tight clench in her chest worrying her that she'd always be an outsider.

So when Rex had asked her out, she'd instantly said yes. She liked him and hoped for more, and she'd fit in easily with his circle of friends. Maybe she was also trying to prove to herself that Ryan and Celeste were not her fault. That finding her groom in bed with her best friend a week before the wedding was on them and not her. To add to the horrifyingly cliched betrayal, her father insisted that she go through with the wedding. It had been far too expensive to let something so miniscule get in the way.

That was how she'd come to believe that her parents' marriage had not been a faithful one, a harsh blow for any adult who'd grown up with other ideas. She'd been too young when her mother died to see it, but now …?

Looking back, Rex had seemed a safe bet. Maybe because she knew she'd never really fall for him and he couldn't hurt her. Maybe because the circle of his friends had made her feel as if she might belong.

Now, she was confident he had retained the friends in the breakup.

And Maggie was back at square one, only now she was on her own with a serial killer looking for things in her house.

She needed help. The two people she could pick up the phone and call were Rex and Sebastian, not that Rex could do anything. Revealing the glaring absence of a friend circle even more, both men worked the same shift at the fire station. So for a minimum of one day out of every three, she had no one.

A-shift had been on duty yesterday and last night. And Maggie had no one to call since she'd learned that the FBI believed her stupid jewelry box might be associated with the Blue River Killer. At least it looked like the police had stepped up their drive by checks of her house, but she still felt incredibly exposed.

Sebastian had volunteered several times to stay over and Maggie was ready to take him up on it. Screw what the neighbors thought.

Let them believe she was sleeping with a firefighter. Her business might take a hit, but it wasn't like it was thriving anyway. And she'd still be alive later to give it another try or move back to LA with her father ... a thought that churned her gut as much as the jewelry box.

She was already calculating the loss of income. Her brain churned through possibilities like a brush fire. One option was to sell the house and move away and ignore what that would look like to her cousins. Yes, the house had been willed to her because Aunt Abbie knew she loved it. But if a serial killer was breaking in, wasn't that plenty enough excuse to get the hell out of dodge?

Still, she didn't want to leave.

She was exhausted from staying up and running around like a fool every time a light passed by. She'd tried to read, but she didn't dare turn on the TV for fear that it would mask any noises and the killer would be standing in the doorway before she knew he was even in the house.

Though it was daylight and she was breathing easier, she still couldn't go to sleep. She had three clients, starting at nine. *Thank God.*

It had originally surprised Maggie that the town's older

residents were the ones turning up on her doorstep. She'd fully expected her clients would be closer to her own generation but, two days earlier, Mr. Muskogee, had been very clear. "Sabbie told me you were excellent. So here I am!"

It seemed the vast majority of her business roster had been handpicked by Aunt Abbie. Even before she died, she'd been drumming up business for Maggie.

Sitting on her couch, and contemplating the sorry state of her life, Maggie started to cry. Tears rolled quietly down her cheeks and threatened to drop into the mug of coffee that had gone cold in her grip. She missed Abbie fiercely, but she could hear her aunt's voice in her head.

Abbie would tell her to buck up. She'd say, "You've got a baseball bat and your brains. What else do you need?"

She needed friends! She needed a home, and Redemption wasn't it, not yet. Los Angeles wasn't a safe haven to flee to. There was nothing. But the Abbie voice was right. Even through the tears, Maggie smiled.

So she headed to the kitchen and poured her coffee down the drain, got dressed, and waited for 8:04 to roll around.

She'd been at the fire house often enough that she knew exactly when to call. He'd be done with his shift, and probably out the door, but he wouldn't quite yet be home.

God forbid, they had a call that had run them over. But 8:04 am was her best chance to catch him. So Maggie tried to read the newspaper and avoid yet another cup of coffee.

She hoped her makeup hid the dark circles beneath her eyes and the tension at the edge of her mouth.

At 8:03, she gave up waiting and dialed.

CHAPTER NINETEEN

Sebastian did an about face in the middle of the sidewalk when he got Maggie's call.

His duffel bag bounced at his side with the quick movement, but he enjoyed the stutter in his chest at the sound of her voice. He tried not to linger on the wonderful knowledge that she and Rex had broken up. As tempting as it was to ask Rex if it was okay if he made a move on her, ultimately he figured it was probably better if he asked Maggie herself.

Anything he said to Rex was just a courtesy so his job would move smoother.

The problem was that the hitch in her voice didn't sound like an eight am booty call. She sounded *scared*, but she wasn't willing to tell him anything over the phone.

Though he'd just passed the intersection where he'd take a left to go to his own house, he turned and headed back, taking the other direction and heading straight toward Maggie's. So what if the neighbors saw him double back?

He was maybe seven minutes away, just a handful of blocks to wonder *what could possibly have gotten Maggie so riled up?*

Once he'd agreed to come over, she basically hung up on

him. Sebastian picked up his speed, not willing to run the whole way but not quite willing to take a leisurely stroll either.

Halfway there, he realized he would show up on her doorstep sweaty and dirty. The only other option was to turn around, again, and shower at home like he'd intended to do in the first place. But he'd told her he was on his way, and hopefully he could shower at Maggie's. She might take one look at him and send him home. He tried to surreptitiously sniff at his shirt and decided he didn't smell too horrible.

He arrived at the old house and jogged up the path, listening as the front porch floorboards squeaked beneath his feet. He could fix those for her, he thought, but more importantly, he needed to solve this morning's dilemma first. Even before he got close enough to knock, the door opened and there stood Maggie.

She was in another business suit, one that showed she had a flair for fashion and also an understanding of small town sensibilities. Sabbie must have warned her.

She looked amazing, and he wanted to say so, but a closer step revealed dark circles under her eyes artfully covered with makeup. He saw the twist at the edge of her lips and the expression that didn't smile at seeing him.

"Come in." She said it almost formally, waving a hand to gesture him inside as she stepped back, her heels clacking on the hardwood. She motioned him to the living room, but Sebastian held his hands up in surrender.

"I was on my way home to shower after shift. You don't want me to be sitting on the furniture."

Her laugh was a brittle sound. "I don't want the furniture at all … but you're right, I'm stuck with it for a while longer."

He'd wondered about it. It didn't look like "Maggie" to him. The ornate wood pieces were stuffed and padded and buttoned within an inch of their life. He wasn't even sure it suited Sabbie, but it seemed to be part of the inheritance. He stood in front of the couch and waited for Maggie to sit down.

She didn't. Her hands laced together in front of her, fingers twisting nervously and spiking his worry.

Maggie was competent and fierce. Instead of hiding in her closet with a phone, calling 9-1-1 when a burglar had broken into her house, she'd headed down the steps waving a baseball bat and chased him out.

But now ... she looked nervous and paranoid. Even her voice had a small tremor to it. "I called the police and asked about the jewelry box."

Sweet Jesus, he thought as she told him what she'd learned. He really wanted to sit on the edge of the couch and drop his head into his hands, but he really was too dirty. So he shifted from foot to foot, trying not to look as nervous as Maggie already did.

She explained that she stayed up all night. "At least I didn't have any prowlers ... at least not any that I know of."

"You could have called me," he chastised her before thinking better of it. People said that all the time. How could he make her know he meant it?

"You were at work," she replied quick enough to let him know she'd considered it.

He hoped she'd call even if he was at work next time. "I can lose a shift here or there."

"I wouldn't want you to." She was shaking your head, but he pinned her with a return glare.

"Apparently someone in this house was a serial killer or at least related to one in some way ... You've already had at least one break-in." He emphasized the words, and Maggie seemed to catch on.

He understood her hesitation, he'd seen it a lot in his line of work. Each thing that could get brushed off, explained away individually, wasn't that bad. It was a coping mechanism. But when everything was strung together, it was hard to ignore. He let her digest the information he'd basically held in her face.

"Okay." She nodded, though what she was agreeing to, he didn't quite know. Maybe just that she would make decisions giving the circumstances the weight they deserved.

He stepped a little closer, probably beyond the boundaries of what he should do as a friend. He picked up her hands where they were clasped in front of her and separated her intertwined fingers. Taking her hands in his, Sebastian gave her something to hold on to. She gripped him tight.

"Alright, Maggie, let's make a plan."

She nodded quickly, and he kept talking.

"You're dressed, so I'm assuming you have clients."

"Yes. At nine."

"And I'm assuming you're not moving them."

This time she almost pulled her fingers out of his grasp as she shrugged and looked away. Her words were soft. "I can't afford to."

He understood. His salary was fine, but it was nothing to write home about. Firefighters were definitely not overpaid. So he merely nodded along. "When do you finish for the day?"

"I should be done by noon or one, depending on how long my meetings take."

With his mind racing beneath an exterior that he hoped projected a calm he didn't feel, he looked her in the eye and started a plan. "I need a shower. Can I use yours?"

"Of course." She pulled her fingers from his and waved her hand behind her, gesturing up the staircase behind her, as though he could obviously just take any of the rooms up there.

But he wasn't done. He liked the feel of her, so he regrasped her hand. "All right. I'll get out of the shower in a few minutes, and I'm going to be here while you have your clients."

Maggie nodded one more time, clearly at the end of her rope

and seemingly grateful that he was taking over some of the decisions.

"While you work, I'm going to search the rooms. I know you did already, but I want another pair of eyes on it to see if there's anything else—any other loose floorboards, items hidden in the back of closets."

She might not have been looking for hidden boxes and trap doors, loose floorboards and hidden stashes. He would.

Sebastian watched as she perked up. Research seemed to be her thing. *Probably what made her a good lawyer,* he thought.

She spoke in full sentences, a little more chutzpah behind her words. "I've been going through Abbie's records, trying to figure out who her boarders were. At first, I only found a couple. But yesterday, I found a much bigger box of records. I just haven't started going through it yet."

"When I get out of the shower, you'll point me in that direction. When I get done with the rooms, I'll start going through the records. Then," he said, "we'll get you some sleep."

And he would see if he could maybe find a name in all of Sabbie's mess.

CHAPTER TWENTY

Sebastian showered in the bath attached to the upstairs room that Maggie wasn't occupying.

He wasn't the kind of guy to parade down her hallway in only his towel. But the steam from the bathroom forced him out into the room itself to change. Wherever Maggie was, she wasn't sneaking a peek.

He reached into his bag and pulled out the roll of clothing. He always carried a change of clothes with him—typical firefighter thing. Climbing into his old, soft jeans and faded t shirt, he realized he might have some explaining if her new clients found him in her house while she worked. People were picky about pre-marital sex, not that he was having any right now, but it wouldn't do Maggie any favors if things looked like she'd had a sleepover and didn't even have the sense to hide it.

At least Maggie's clients seemed to be Sabbie's old friends. They would hopefully say "What a nice boy. Helping the new girl out."

Sebastian headed back downstairs, his hair still dark and wet. He hoped it would dry before her clients showed up, but there hadn't been a hair dryer and he couldn't remember the last time he'd used one anyway. So he hadn't done anything with it.

At the bottom of the steps, he turned the corner and saw Maggie curled into the corner of the sofa. She couldn't be asleep, the position looked as uncomfortable as the furniture did. It seemed she was trying to catch a few minutes of rest without messing up her suit.

Stepping forward softly, he tried to stay quiet, but hit one of the many squeaky floorboards. There was no sneaking around here. Maggie popped up, startled, but she settled when she realized it was just him. Something about the way her gaze traveled over him made him think maybe his hair was getting a little shaggy.

"Let me show you where she kept her records." Maggie stood, heels tapping on the hardwood floor as her hands smoothed the fabric of her slim fitting pants as though there was maybe a wrinkle to be found. His thoughts traveled but he reminded himself that wasn't why he'd been invited here.

"I'll help look for now, but my clients tend to show up early. They tend to be older."

He knew. He knew this town.

Sebastian also knew the population was finally skewing younger. He'd been in many people's homes and he knew who was a hoarder and who had OCD. He knew who was struggling to pay rent with seven kids and who was secretly rolling in it. Firefighters didn't see everything, but they saw a lot. And they fielded medical calls at four am for many of the crowd who were making up the bulk of Maggie's new clientele.

He wasn't surprised that nine felt late for them.

He also wasn't surprised that Maggie handed him a piece of printer paper she'd drawn on. A basic layout of the house clearly showed the ground floor as well as the upper floor. He fought a grin, art was apparently not one of Maggie's skills. Neither was architecture.

Firefighters read blueprints. They needed to go into businesses and homes, knowing where the load bearing walls were could save a life. So could understanding where a closet was likely to be, because children hid in them. Maggie's sketch was missing a few key elements, but he could see where she'd made notes.

"All the rooms with the checkmarks are rooms that seemed to have, at least at one time, belonged to one of her boarders. She had three when she died."

"I thought she had five bedrooms? Six including hers."

Maggie shook her head. "Six for the boarders, though only five occupied them."

He looked down the hallway, there were only five doors not including the communal bathroom.

"There's another in the shed out back ... it's converted. Plus the two upstairs."

"One of those was hers—now yours." He pointed to the drawing.

"This one was hers. Where you showered." Maggie pointed. "I'm staying across the hallway."

Both of the rooms were large and had their own bathrooms attached. Maybe she just hadn't brought herself to take over her aunt's room yet.

He looked back at the drawings. The other portion of the upstairs was a game room / sunroom / library. Maggie didn't seem to have touched it yet either.

"Here's where I've looked already." She motioned to the spots of pink highlighter she'd made on some of the rooms. Art might not be Maggie's strong suit, but organization was. He fought a smile as she kept talking. "And here."

She was pointing to a third, smaller room. "This is the upstairs office."

He tried to ignore the feeling of her standing so close, and the change in his own reaction now that she was single. That didn't mean she wanted him, though it meant he could ask. Forcing himself to pay attention to the diagram was harder than it should be. "She had an upstairs office?"

Maggie tipped her head and gave him an odd look. "I think it was designed as an office … Abbie used it to …" the words trailed off and she waved her hand as if to conjure the correct word. "*Office* is far too organized a term for anything she might have done."

That meshed with the Sabbie he'd known—head on straight, always practical, but always scattered.

"You're welcome to go through anything there. I'm assuming there's more than what I found. No," Maggie corrected herself. "I *know* I haven't been through all the papers yet. I'm assuming there is more information on her boarders."

"Did she register any of her paperwork with the city?"

Maggie raised her palms and offered a full-sized shrug.

She looked better than she had when he'd arrived and his chest squeezed. Maybe it was because he was here. Sometimes all you needed was to know that you had backup.

"I'll look into it," he told her.

"Thanks." She started to walk away, but she turned back, her tone changed. "Really. I can't thank you enough. You don't owe me any of this, but I appreciate it so much."

Her eyes darted away, as though it was tough to admit it was better not going it alone. Without her looking him in the eyes as she so often did, he reached out and touched her shoulder, to aim her back toward him.

"Maggie, I don't mind." He almost added, *that's what friends are for,* but he didn't want to give her the idea that *friends* was all he was interested in. Instead he said, "This is a big deal. It's definitely concerning. Don't ever think that you're overreacting. But we've got this."

Then she shocked the shit out of him and threw herself into his arms, hugging him tightly. It was so easy to hug her back. He felt her pressed against him, her arms wrapped around his waist.

With one hand, he tugged her closer, while the other snuck up into her hair. He would have kissed her, but this wasn't the time.

It didn't matter anyway, because just then the doorbell rang.

CHAPTER TWENTY-ONE

Maggie was just finishing up with her last appointment that morning, when she heard the knock at the door from where she sat in her office.

Her first reaction was to jump up and answer it, but before she could, she heard footsteps in the hall. *Sebastian was here.* The thought soothed her far more than was appropriate, and she wondered if the shy firefighter knew she was fighting a raging attraction to him?

Maggie kept her eyes on her client and continued the conversation. At least they should be wrapping up.

The older man's goal was to split his property and give a piece to each of his children to build on. But it had taken Maggie a little more time than she'd planned to help him understand what the city ordinances were.

"So the property lines will go here, here, and here." He said it with authority as he pointed to a rough sketch he'd drawn on a napkin before arriving.

Maggie replied the best she could. "I hope so. Ultimately the surveyors will make that decision. But you can request it of them."

"This is going to take longer than I thought it would," he complained.

"I know. It's a longer process than most people think, but that's mostly because the city needs to sign off on everything when property lines change."

Though he still seemed cranky, he understood. Maggie nodded, though she was listening to the conversation in the front hall with half an ear. She could have sworn she'd heard "FBI."

She both wanted to and didn't want to shove Mr. Gentson out the door. The stubborn part of her refused to shortchange her client simply because someone was at the door. It was worse that it likely wasn't some random visitor. Her heart thumped a little harder, afraid she'd heard correctly.

"So you have this—" She pointed to the documents she'd printed for him and reminded him what each one was. Then she watched as he reluctantly signed two of them. She took the check from him and slid it into the drawer, having left it on the desk while they worked.

A friend had warned her to take more than just electronic payments and that had been very smart advice. She'd had more clients insist on handing her checks or cash than anything else.

More of the conversation in the hallway filtered through. Though she couldn't make out the words, it sounded like Sebastian was holding someone at bay verbally.

"What else can I do for you today, Mr. Gentson?"

"That's it, ma'am. I just needed to get this ball rolling."

"I'm glad I could help. I'll let you know as soon as we hear anything back." She tried to keep her smile in place, and she was glad he was here, but just beyond the door was something she didn't want to deal with.

At least he left with a smile. As he opened the door, Maggie suddenly became concerned about what he might hear as he headed out.

Sure enough, a man and a woman—both in stark dark suits —stood inside her front hallway. She must have heard correctly —these two couldn't have screamed *FBI* any harder if they tried.

Sebastian glared at them as though warning dogs to sit and stay. The agents only nodded to Mr. Gentson as he left, a confused look on his face. He managed a concerned expression for Maggie over his shoulder.

"I'm okay, Mr. Gentson. You have a good day." She closed the door behind him and turned, even before she was facing the two newcomers, they were holding out badges toward her.

"FBI. Omaha," the man announced.

Maggie made a point of leaning in and checking their badges against their faces, though she wasn't sure what the point was. Once she realized everything matched and that she wouldn't know a fake if she saw it, she decided to play the kind hostess.

"Come on in." She motioned everyone into the living room, then watched as the two agents followed her awkwardly while Sebastian brought up the tail position, almost like a sheepdog unwilling to let them turn and escape. She appreciated that.

With a firm hand, and an irritation level that matched them interrupting her first chance to sleep in over thirty hours, she motioned them onto the uncomfortable couch. Then she quietly lowered herself into the matching ornate chair and waited.

The two agents looked to each other, one of those passing glances of understanding that didn't require words.

It was Watson—a blonde woman whose hair was scraped back into a bun and who could only have looked more like a TV version of an FBI agent were she wearing dark sunglasses inside the house—who spoke first. "It would appear that you already know why we're here."

Maggie wanted to nod. She wanted to tell them how angry she was that it had taken this long for her to be told what was going on. Instead, she offered only information. "A week ago, I handed a jewelry box to officers at my local police station. I had found it hidden under a floorboard. The tangle of jewelry inside seemed odd. I also had a burglary … actually just a break in. I can't be confident they took anything."

The two nodded but, once again, didn't say anything. She could feel Sebastian's presence behind her, and she wondered if he had those big arms crossed and was offering her brute muscle as a backup. It probably wouldn't intimidate the agents, but Maggie appreciated it. Shame she couldn't turn her head to look without losing her authority play.

"Since you're here," she continued almost rudely, "I'm assuming the jewelry in the box *was* associated with the Blue River Killer."

The two agents looked to each other again, and Maggie felt her stomach drop. Then Watson spoke and it got worse.

"Not exactly."

CHAPTER TWENTY-TWO

Maggie swallowed hard. Agent Watson's words could not indicate anything good.

Sebastian had reacted, too, walking out across the room and grabbing the chair that matched the one she was sitting in. He picked it up, rather than risk scraping the floor, and pulled it over to sit next to her. He made it look as though the piece was as light as a folding chair and not the massive beast Maggie knew it to be.

For a moment, she thought he might reach out and take her hand again, he was close enough. Instead, he sat there, leaning forward, elbows resting on his knees, hands clasped in front of him. Something about his expression let Maggie—and the agents—know that he meant business.

It was Decker who began speaking this time. "What I'm about to tell you is sensitive information. I'm sharing this with you because we're going to need your help putting the pieces together."

Maggie nodded, she considered it more of an acceptance that he had said the words than an agreement to do what he suggested. She was still pissed that she hadn't been told what they'd found before now. She was well aware they weren't legally obligated to tell her anything other than if she was in direct danger. It didn't mean she couldn't argue about it though.

"I'll be honest, agents. It's very concerning to me, as a citizen, that it took this long to get back to me. My evidence was turned in a week ago. You clearly know there's a link between my jewelry box and very serious crimes, yet no one told me about this before today."

Watson let a quick expression betray her, but when she opened her mouth her tone was neutral. "You *were* told about it before today. You were the one who told us about the connection."

"No, ma'am," Maggie countered sharply, her lack of sleep adding to her irritation. "It's a connection I surmised on my own. When I called the police station to ask for my jewelry back, they would only tell me that the FBI had confiscated it. I merely put *obvious pieces together*." She emphasized each of the last three words.

"Yes, ma'am. I understand." Watson nodded, walking back her earlier irritation.

Maggie didn't mention what information Marina Balero had exchanged with her, because the fact was Marina hadn't explicitly said any of that. Maggie found herself very grateful that she'd given the officer a way to answer without having to say the words.

Sebastian remained silent, but still sat beside her acting like he would take out anyone who pissed her off. It took a moment, but Agent Decker picked up the thread. "The reason you haven't been contacted before now, was because we were still putting pieces together. We received the box in our possession only three days ago and our analysts have been working on it nonstop, given what we found inside. We can't act until we have certain information, but Agent Watson and I were dispatched here as soon as we were given the go ahead."

As a lawyer, Maggie understood what laypeople often didn't, that law enforcement was very strictly bound in a lot of cases. She was still irritated, though. Her safety, after all, was at stake. She thought so, even if they didn't.

She waited them out, hoping to get the agents to cough up more information, but it was Sebastian who offered a stern look and prompted them. "Well then, tell us what you found."

It seemed legal concerns were on agent Watson's mind as well. She turned to face Maggie but gestured toward Sebastian. "This man introduced himself to us at your door. I'm assuming that you're accepting of his presence here. And that you're okay with him hearing the information that we're about to give you."

She watched as Sebastian almost rolled his eyes, but legally they needed her permission to say anything personal in front of him.

"He's a friend and he absolutely can stay and hear anything you have to say," she offered her explicit agreement.

Watson nodded. "Three pieces of jewelry appear to belong to victims of the Blue River Killer."

Maggie felt the words like a sharp pop to her chest. She'd thought she was ready, but she wasn't.

Her brain scrambled and her thoughts went simultaneously in two directions. One concern was that she had been right—the FBI had managed to confirm what she suspected all along. But the second thing? *Only three?*

There had been close to seventeen pieces of jewelry tangled in that box. Her stomach churned harder now.

"Yes, ma'am. Only three so far. But that is what makes this case so concerning." Watson looked to Decker and he told Maggie the rest.

"Two other pieces in the collection—"

Maggie almost shuddered at that word.

"—appear to belong to Blue River Killer victims as well, though we've not yet been able to get confirmation from the families. One of the victims is still considered missing, not confirmed dead. So we're stuck waiting on that."

These were all things she and Sebastian couldn't repeat in public until the families were told first. She might feel sick to her stomach and she might have a creepy jewelry box and a break in, but she wasn't a murder victim or even missing, presumed dead. That was something to be grateful for.

Maggie took a deep breath to stabilize her wildly swinging emotions. It only partly worked, but she nodded at them to continue. There were still many more pieces to account for.

But the agents weren't making that any easier.

"The problem is an additional four pieces of jewelry appear to have belonged to victims of the La Vista Rapist, who has been operating in Omaha for the past seven years."

CHAPTER TWENTY-THREE

Sebastian had tried to keep his mouth shut, but it had been very difficult. The information they were hearing was more than enough to make him want to put his fist into a wall or at least whisk Maggie away to somewhere safe.

The agents were talking about all of this as though it didn't affect her, but it was Maggie's jewelry box—Sabbie's tenants—in question, and they were in Maggie's home.

Still, he'd not been prepared for that last bit of information. It had stunned him and broken whatever dam was holding him back from joining in. "Are you suggesting that they're the same person?"

He'd heard about the La Vista Rapist. The entire firehouse had been alerted by the police. They were all on the lookout for any cases that bore similarity to the ones happening in Omaha. The city wasn't that close, but it wasn't that far away, either.

He even had some case-specific information, because firefighters interacted with medical patients as first responders. Knowing what might identify a serial case was critical information. But he couldn't tell Maggie that.

He'd have to ask around. At least, as of right now, he didn't know of any cases where the La Vista Rapist had ventured outside the bounds of West Omaha.

He had so many questions. Though he tried to keep an eye on Maggie and gauge her reaction, he was also watching Watson and Decker.

The agents looked at each other once again. Though they both had excellent poker faces, that move was their tell.

This was about to get worse.

"It's plausible that they are the same person."

There was a heavy pause and Sebastian waited for the gut punch.

"It's also possible that they knew each other."

This time it was Maggie's turn to lose her cool and blurt her question. "You think they know each other? Like they are friends and this is *some kind of a high school pact?*"

It was Decker who took a deep breath and put his hands on his knees, as though the conversation were somehow turning more casual. Sebastian knew it wasn't.

"There's scientific data showing that if a room has a hundred people in it, and two of them are sociopaths, they'll find and acknowledge each other in the first five minutes."

It took Sebastian a moment to put together why that information was pertinent. "You think the two were operating separately and then *found each other.*" He was tempted to use air quotes.

"Anything's possible," Watson added as though covering for a gaffe her partner made. Decker hadn't said anything of the sort. "It's possible they were childhood friends. It's also possible they are not sociopaths."

"It's hard to believe anyone with a conscience would do these things," Maggie stated, disgusted tone bleeding through. Sebastian ached for her.

Watson answered that question, too. "There's a story that no one hated Jeffrey Dahmer as much as Jeffrey Dahmer." She offered only a brief pause before she filled in, "We don't know the motives for the crimes. And though we have profiles on each perpetrator, the information doesn't necessarily answer these questions. The profiles are often broad and vague until we get more evidence."

How they didn't have enough evidence on the Blue River Killer was beyond Sebastian. The killer had been operating for close to thirty years now, and seventeen bodies had been confirmed victims. More were suspected. That should have been enough.

Watson was talking again, and he pushed himself to pay attention.

"That 'more information' is likely in this house."

Sebastian felt his heart sink and watched as Maggie's posture visibly slumped. He wasn't going to make her ask. "What is it that you want?"

"We need to search the house."

"We've been searching it," Sebastian countered, as though that would make them say, *oh, okay, I guess you're on it then.*

He was considering what to do. Maggie needed sleep. She also needed a house that wasn't possibly full of serial killer and criminal mementos.

Just who had Sabbie been renting to?

Maggie stood up abruptly, hovering over everyone else in the room. "I haven't slept in over thirty-six hours. You're welcome to come back tomorrow morning and search the entire place."

"We need to begin as soon as possible," Watson stated, still sitting as though she understood that letting Maggie stand and dominate the conversation was making Maggie feel better.

Maggie shook her head. "I could have been informed when the FBI claimed the box, that there were circumstances the FBI was investigating. I could have been warned that my safety might have been in danger. You chose to wait three days. In fact—"

"We were forced to wait until the evidence cleared." Watson interrupted, but Maggie wasn't having it.

"Yes. I understand. And you need to understand that now you'll need to wait until you get my consent."

Sebastian hid a smile. Lawyer Maggie was on the case.

"We can come back with a warrant." Decker stated it as though it was friendly banter, instead of the threat they all recognized it as.

"You should have come with one in the first place," Maggie smacked back.

For a moment, Sebastian wondered if they knew what they were up against. But then he remembered she had a sign out front. If they didn't catch that she was a lawyer, then they weren't very good agents.

She softened her tone. "I will happily let you search my house. But I haven't slept since I woke up *yesterday*. You interrupted a meeting with a client rather than calling ahead and asking me when it would be a good time. And now you spent almost an hour here when I was supposed to be catching up on sleep because I. Was. Up. All. Night."

She was repeating herself, but even no-sleep Maggie was magnificent and formidable.

The two agents looked to each other again. "Why were you awake all night?"

Maggie lost it. "Because people have been breaking into my home! And I've had the same car pass my house multiple times!"

Sebastian felt his head snapped to stare at her. *Why hadn't she told him?*

It hit him quickly. Maybe she hadn't told him because he'd been working. He didn't have the kind of job where you called up and told someone that, knowing they'd be home by dinner.

Maggie rattled off information about a silver sedan. He

noticed that Decker had pulled out a notebook and was jotting down information as quickly as she spoke. "License Plate?"

"I didn't get it. The times I saw it, I had my friend's daughter with me. I was babysitting. And I wasn't in a position to leave her and run out and chase the car down the street … I haven't seen it since."

"You've been watching?" Watson added in.

"Yes. I've been watching."

Sebastian suspected her stern tone was part of what caused the conversation to wrap up. They needed to come back with a warrant. Maggie suggested that she wasn't being rude but that she wanted the paperwork as a matter of course. She asked them to grant her at least six hours of sleep.

At last, they left. Sebastian closed the door behind them.

He expected to turn and have Maggie fall into his arms and pass out. Carrying her up the stairs and tucking her into bed would feel wonderful after this crazy morning.

But Maggie didn't fall or crumble at all. Her shoulders didn't slump, and she didn't sway. She simply watched over his shoulder out the window until the agents closed their car doors and left.

Then she pinned him with a glare. "We have work to do."

CHAPTER TWENTY-FOUR

Maggie was beyond dog tired, but there wasn't going to be any sleep. What she'd planned had been snatched away.

The FBI was coming, and they were going to search her house. If Maggie was lucky, they would wait the six hours she requested, but there was no guarantee. If they knew what she had in mind, they would come back sooner.

The search they were intending to do had just pushed Maggie's agenda forward.

"You need sleep," Sebastian told her, his warm hands resting on her shoulders and making her want to do what he said.

"I have to document the whole house before they tear it up."

"Document?"

"Photograph every room. Copy all the papers."

He frowned at her. "Are they going to take Sabbie's paperwork?"

Maggie nodded, "And everything they find that might be pertinent. I don't think I can fight it, it's a murder investigation —well, actually an ongoing multiple murder investigation. I don't want to fight it. I want them to have the evidence they

need to find this guy—" or both of them, she thought. "But I
need copies of those documents for myself."

Maggie sighed. Aunt Abbie had been horrible at paperwork.
This was going to be a mess.

Luckily, she had Sebastian on her side. "Then, point me in
the right direction."

"First, I have to change." She was not going to rummage
through drawers and closets and boxes of old documents in her
suit. Sebastian, always on his game, asked where he could start
while she was changing.

"We need photos of every room, from many angles. Be sure
to get every item on a tabletop or a shelf."

"Like documenting a house for fire insurance."

She hadn't thought of it that way. "Yes!"

"I'll start in the living room then."

She emerged a few minutes later, more comfortable in her
jeans and t-shirt. She had her hair up and her sneakers on but
hadn't washed off her makeup. It was a little much for
rummaging around but she had to get started.

Sebastian finished the living room and they headed up to
Abbie's office together. She had to prioritize in case the FBI
came back sooner.

While Maggie had hoped to find neat stacks of paperwork
that she could feed through the photocopier, she'd only found a
few slim stacks that worked. She let Sebastian carry the box
down to the office and copies those. The rest she started
photographing.

Between the two of them with their phones, they'd managed
to make pretty short work of all the paper inside, and even
catch the backside of several things. Abbie's accounting system
had been just as terrible as her renter's documentation—notes
written on the backs of receipts and more.

Maggie pulled out a napkin with one line about a rental
agreement, a date, and two signatures. "Well, that won't hold up

in court." She sighed and snapped a photo anyway. The date was old enough that no one was going to come after her for anything, at least.

At least Maggie now had pictures of the box and everything in it.

Sebastian asked, "Do we organize it and put it back in nicely?"

All Maggie could say was, "If they check it, our fingerprints will be on everything. And I'll tell them the truth, that we'd been looking through the house for over a week and checking all the records. She didn't have it organized. I don't see any reason for us to make it neater than she did."

So the two of them haphazardly shoved the contents back into the box. Maggie thought it looked exactly as it had when she found it, and they put it back where it had been originally— in the back of the closet.

"Did you put it back for a reason?"

Maggie looked around the room. "I'm not trying to mess up evidence. If it's important that it's in here, then we should leave that information for the FBI."

Just as they confiscated the jewelry box, the Feds were very likely going to confiscate lots of items from her home. She could only hope they didn't stab the furniture and check the stuffing. She didn't have the funds to replace it.

It was then that Sebastian tried again to convince her to get some sleep.

She shook her head. "The office has other papers, her drawers are full of crap," *That I should have cleaned out before.* But when would she have done it? She was renovating and watching Hannah! "And we need to check every room."

"I checked this morning. While you were working."

Maggie nodded. "But did you photograph it? We need evidence, not memory."

He looked to the ceiling and put his hands up as if to say, *No, of course I didn't think of that.* But she waved him off.

"That's not on you!" The last thing she wanted was to make this man feel anything other than as safe and appreciated as he made her feel. "When you were checking everything, you were just trying to keep my house safe and the FBI wasn't on the way to ransack it."

They spent more time wandering each room with their phones. They stuck together, bouncing ideas off each other in an easy manner that once again made her regret saying yes to Rex. But Sebastian hadn't asked her out. Could she nudge him that way? Maggie tried to pay attention to something other than his backside as Sebastian showed her how he checked the floorboards in the closets.

They photographed the placement of all the furniture. They opened drawers in the old boarders' rooms and took pictures of any contents left behind. When Maggie found a drawer full of letters, she opened each of them up and photographed both sides of the pages, as well as the envelope. It was tedious work, but this was her property, and she had the feeling it wasn't going to be her property after the FBI came through. She'd be lucky if she ever got it back.

As she put the last letter back into the drawer as she'd found it, she turned and spotted Sebastian's fine ass in the air as he checked the floorboards in this closet.

He seemed to know she was watching and spoke loud enough for her to hear. "This is how I tested them earlier and didn't find any secret doors. I'm just photographing now."

Having finished with the letters, she got pictures of the two mismatched socks and a very old cigar she found in the other drawer, Maggie headed over to the closet to join him.

"Is there any attic access?" She looked up.

"Not from the ground floor," he told her and for a moment she felt stupid. Then she remembered she hadn't slept in a long time. He didn't look at her like she was being an idiot and she was grateful.

"What about the back wall?" she asked, wondering if it was equally stupid. "Isn't that where you always find a secret panel?"

This time, he shrugged and turned back to the closet, tapping on the wall and checking for seams. He pushed on it and nothing happened. Once again she felt silly.

But, three rooms later, the wall on the back of the closet gave way.

CHAPTER TWENTY-FIVE

Sebastian hadn't thought anything would come of Maggie's suggestion to try the backs of the closets. Finding something under the floorboards was strange enough.

But as he looked into the closet, he realized the wallpaper didn't line up. He hadn't noticed before, maybe he'd become immune to what people did with their homes over the years.

The design was floral and incredibly busy—easy to miss the odd seam—but when he pushed, it gave. He pushed a little more. It took a few minutes to realize it wasn't anything like a trap door with a hinge, simply a loose piece set into place at the back of the closet.

He pried and the piece fell into his hands. It was a piece of plywood that had been wallpapered. As Sebastian examined it, he realized it wasn't even the same wallpaper design, just very close. Also, none of it was the same as the walls; the house was old enough to be made of lathe and plaster.

Interesting.

But when he looked back to what he'd revealed, his stomach dropped. Immediately he looked over his shoulder, double

SAVANNAH KADE

checking when he was already certain. This was the room with
the loose floorboard.

"Sebastian?" Maggie asked. He wished she didn't see this.

Nails had been driven into the wall in between the studs.
Individual pieces of jewelry hung from each nail. Longer
necklaces hung from a single nail. A bracelet hung from another
but, below it, another nail held another bracelet, indicating the
nails were built in as the pieces were added.

"This is more of the same collection, isn't it?" Maggie asked
warily, as if she didn't even have it in her to be surprised.

Sebastian nodded. The FBI was going to have a field day
with this.

"I'm going to take pictures," she said it in a flat tone, but he
could tell she was as disturbed as he was. "I'll take some with
and without flash."

Maggie had immediately become an archivist.

"Don't touch anything," he warned, though he figured she
knew that.

The way the jewelry was hung up—each piece on its own
peg—said something even more disturbing than the box they'd
found. This jewelry was special.

The box had been the discards.

Sebastian would have liked to believe that at least this stash
was the work of one of the two criminals and the box was the
other. Unfortunately, he couldn't delude himself. Pieces from
both serial cases had been found in the jewelry box. He
wondered what the chances were that the feds would find
evidence linking both from this set of jewelry.

As the flash went off behind him, he moved to the side and
tried to reason his way through what they'd found.

He wasn't a detective, nor an agent, but he did know a little
something. He understood that criminals changed their M.O. as
they evolved over time. It made sense to him that the La Vista
Rapist might become the Blue River Killer, but the timelines

didn't work. The Rapist started up after the murders had. And the Blue River Killer didn't sexually assault his victims.

Given his own limited knowledge, Sebastian was relatively confident that they were two different people. Which meant they were working together. There was no way for this jewelry to be good news unless it was just a glut of evidence ... enough to catch the men responsible.

Maggie's flash glinted off something as she moved from side to side. Sebastian held his hand up. "Hold on."

"Don't touch it," she told him, reiterating his own earlier warning.

He wanted to grin. But there was no grinning as he stuck his head closer to the hole and looked down into the floor. Reaching into his back pocket for his own phone, he aimed the light downward.

"There are photographs in the bottom."

"*What?*" Maggie said, leaning forward, the two of them trying to share the small closet space.

As much as he enjoyed being up close and personal with Maggie, being shoved together over sick crime scene trophies didn't qualify. He caught a better glimpse and warned her. "Don't look. Just hand me a phone to take pictures."

He'd only caught a glimpse of the images, but it was enough to turn his stomach. Sitting back on his heels, he asked Maggie if she had enough photos.

Then he set the board back in front of the jewelry, not pushing it back into place, but covering the hole.

"We'll have to walk the FBI through the house and tell them the various things we found," Maggie said, as a matter of course. "And we now have to confess that we were documenting everything before they came. Because if we had known about this before they arrived and didn't tell them ...? I don't know how to explain that. And I won't hold up under a polygraph."

He nodded but swallowed hard, his thoughts running in a different direction.

Initially, he'd been disturbed by Kalan's comment that it might be a serial killer. Kalan was a smart guy, but he was also constantly watching Forensic Files at the station house. So it had been very easy to believe that he was simply overshooting. Now, Sebastian was relatively confident that Kalan—though joking—maybe subconsciously recognized something about the jewelry box.

When they'd done everything they could with the new find, they headed through the rest of the rooms, luckily not finding more. If there was anything else, he was content to let the feds deal with it.

"It looks like whoever it was, was staying in that room."

"Why leave it behind, though?" Maggie asked. "Why not take it with him?"

Sebastian shrugged. He had no good answers for that.

Every room was now cataloged and Maggie looked dead on her feet. He tried again to convince her to sleep the remaining few hours.

"I don't think I can sleep," she said. "And I can't even take any medication, because the FBI could be back at any time."

"We still have almost four more hours," he said. It had only taken a few to go through the house. They'd gotten very fast at snapping pictures.

"That's if they honor my wishes," Maggie reminded him.

"Then it's all the more important that we get you whatever sleep we can now."

Though she nodded in agreement, she was still protesting. "I'm too dirty to lay down on the bed."

They had gotten a bit dusty in their searches. Many of the rooms hadn't been cleaned and some of the renters had vacated as long as a year or so ago, maybe more.

"We need to change," he agreed, looking at the dirt scuffs on his knees. There would be little doubt what he'd been doing. "If the FBI shows up and we're filthy, they'll figure us out."

"It's not illegal," Maggie told him. "It's my house."

"I know, but it seems like poor form."

"Do you have another change of clothing?"

"Maybe." At one point, he'd found four full changes of clothes he'd been carrying in his bag. If he was lucky, he'd find another now.

Reaching into the duffel, he dug through Redemption Fire Department shirts, tons of spare socks, towels for his workout, swim trunks and goggles for the pool, and more. Eventually his fingers, closed around another roll of clothing at the bottom of the bag. "Got it!"

In a few minutes, they both looked roughly the same, but cleaner. He managed to convince her to sit on the couch with him. Convinced her to lean her head on his shoulder. And it only took a few moments before he felt her sinking into him. Slowly, finally, getting some of the sleep she needed.

If only his brain wasn't spinning with the find in the closet. It was all too close to Maggie.

CHAPTER TWENTY-SIX

Maggie woke up alone on the couch. The crick in her neck from a couple days ago had returned with a vengeance and now her back was sore to go with it.

Sadly, she was lying directly on the couch—not on Sebastian, which was where she remembered falling asleep. He must have eased his way out from underneath her. Bummer. It would have felt just as good to wake up on him, too.

Slowly she stood and stretched, and though she knew the stretch was necessary, she regretted doing it. Her neck hurt.

The sound of footsteps pushed through the heavy sigh she gave at waking up, but they came from her right, not down the hallway. She frowned until she saw Sebastian come around the corner from the dining room.

"Hey," he grinned at her and if he'd called her *sleepyhead* she would have taken it. "I hope you don't mind. I got into the kitchen."

"I don't mind at all."

She wondered what he'd done in there, taking pictures of her pots and pans, or mostly, *Aunt Abbie's* pots and pans that had been left to her. Maybe the interior of the oven—but, no, they'd already photographed the kitchen for posterity. And as she got closer, she realized it smelled *really* good.

"You cook?" she asked.

"Decent." He offered only a shrug, but the decadent smell disagreed. Then he asked, "You?"

Maggie guessed he was being polite. If he'd been in her kitchen, then he already knew the answer was 'not unless she had to.' "I'm great with a crock pot and I can microwave a mean pizza."

She tossed the words out but then watched as he cringed, clearly believing pizza did not belong in the microwave. Maggie spied cutting boards, plates, and knives across the countertop. "What did you do?"

"I hope it's okay," he didn't really answer.

She motioned as if to say *anything is fine*. Anyone who wanted to feed her, particularly anyone who wanted to look that good doing it, was more than welcome. "I'm easy," she said, then realized that might not have been the right thing to say to a man she had just fallen asleep on top of.

Sebastian only grinned then pointed at the counter.

A plate of bruschetta was laid out with toasted french bread covered with chopped tomatoes, peppers and black olives. He'd grated cheese and drizzled it with something dark.

"You had balsamic vinegar," he answered her confused look. "So bruschetta seemed like a good choice."

She didn't know she had balsamic vinegar.

"I found fish fillets in the freezer. I put those in the oven."

Ah, she thought, she'd smelled that too.

"And I found frozen peas."

Maggie almost grimaced. He'd pulled food out of her freezer, because it was really the only place she had actual food. "It looks fantastic."

"I hope you didn't have plans for the fish."

"I eat whatever, whenever." She hoped to let him know that

she was grateful he'd cooked for her, but maybe she'd let him know she wasn't really capable of feeding herself anything other than frozen foods and the occasional soup.

She motioned him to the dining room table—yet another ornate, antique piece, that someone, somewhere would love to own. That person just wasn't her.

They were mostly through the meal when the knock came and Maggie dragged herself to the front door. Sure enough, Watson and Decker had returned, warrant in hand.

She stood, politely blocking their entry, dinner napkin still in her hand. She could tell Sebastian had come from the table, too, and now held guard behind her.

Maggie didn't have any way to fight the search this time and she didn't want to. She didn't want her home torn up, but she understood that there was pertinent information regarding very dangerous criminals here. That evidence needed to go to the people most likely to catch the killer. That was almost definitely the FBI.

Though Watson made a small move as if to come in, Maggie held them at bay. "I'd like to read the warrant first."

She wasn't rude enough to do more than scan it. A few minutes wouldn't change anything for their search. Her legal brain decided it was fine. So she nodded but held her hand up, still keeping them on the porch.

There were four agents this time, two unknowns, so she motioned to each of them. "Hello. I'm Maggie Willis and the homeowner and I'm a lawyer." She didn't normally introduce herself that way, but she didn't want anyone in the FBI thinking that they could get away with anything here. She shook each hand in turn. Then she laid out the rules. Not that she was making them, but she tried.

"If you need to get into any of the furniture, I'll show you how. But I prefer if you don't rip any cushions. I will be suing you for any damages." Given that they had the warrant, she wasn't sure her threat would hold, but she was certainly going to make it. "You're welcome to enter any room, or check inside any space, but before you tear anything up, please just ask nicely. Many pieces are antiques."

With that, she motioned them across the threshold and continued in her weird cross between hostess and legal monitor. "This is Sebastian Kane. He's a local firefighter and a friend of mine. He's been here off and on for a while. He knows the house pretty well. He can answer your questions too."

She moved them all down the hall, saying, "Come with me."

Maggie pointed out the room where they'd found the jewelry box and the floorboard under which they'd found it. The FBI was definitely going to pull up the floorboard Sebastian had finally so nicely repaired. It figured.

She had to come clean. "I appreciate you letting me have six hours. I needed the sleep, and I wanted to document everything before you moved it. With Sebastian's help, both got done. Thank you."

She next explained that they'd repaired the floor earlier, not knowing it would be evidence. "I know you'll search everything, but my aunt's office is upstairs."

She explained that they'd photographed it all and, no, they hadn't messed it up, it looked that way before and she would gladly show them a picture. Maggie added that they were welcome to take it if they thought it was helpful. She was confident they would.

Turning, she made sure she caught the attention of each of the four agents. "I will want an itemized list of everything you take. You're welcome to all of it—I want this guy caught—but I need to know what's missing and what's not when you leave."

They nodded. From anyone else, it would sound weird and too strict, like she was hiding something. But she was a lawyer. They all had to know that they didn't serve warrants on lawyers without getting the rundown.

Then she took a breath. "While we were documenting we re-checked everything. We weren't looking for secret stashes before. I only found the jewelry box because the board was loose. But this time, we found this …"

She motioned their attention to the back of the closet and watched as Watson and Decker shone their lights and shoved their heads into the space.

Maggie talked them through. "We were checking all the closets and this panel was loose. Once we recognized it was cut, we popped it out. We haven't touched anything other than the panel itself."

She watched as they shone the light up and down and she heard Watson's voice say, "Holy shit, Decker. Do you recognize that?"

CHAPTER TWENTY-SEVEN

I t was hours later that the FBI agents left. Sebastian was exhausted from dealing with them and Maggie had to be, too.

The agents checked the rest of the house and didn't find much that Maggie and Sebastian hadn't already pointed out. There were a few items in drawers that they thought might be interesting. They confiscated everything in the dresser from the room that had the jewelry box, but that wasn't surprising.

Maggie hadn't protested at all, only asked again for her itemized list. Watson and Decker readily complied.

Though she was spouting legalese the whole time, Maggie was perfectly compliant. They took her aunt's box of records, but that was expected. Sebastian was grateful that Maggie had thought to photograph all of it so that she didn't lose the information. It probably would have been better to have her hands on the papers, but it would have looked suspicious if she hadn't let the FBI take it.

When the agents were gone, he turned back to the dining room, where he and Maggie had abandoned their meal. Though his own plate was mostly clean. Maggie's, on the other hand, had a quarter of the fish on it, and half a piece of bruschetta. He'd made the mistake of thinking they would welcome the agents inside, then sit back down and eat while the house got searched. It hadn't worked that way.

Maggie had wanted to trail them around, keep track of what they did and found. And Sebastian agreed—it was fascinating watching them. They searched in ways that the two of them hadn't.

Though Maggie had looked under the sofa for things that might be shoved under there—drugs, cash, who knew what? The feds also looked under every dresser and piece of furniture. They checked every floorboard and tapped at the ceiling of every closet looking for access upward.

"Do people hide things there?" Sebastian had asked.

Watson and Decker had both nodded in response. Decker added, "You'd be surprised. Also, in a lot of cases, they create links between the two rooms. This might go directly up to another closet. Old places like this—with a servant staircase?—there are a lot of hollow walls."

The feds had found a hidey-hole next to the base of the servant staircase. It was Watson who pointed out that the cabinet there was too shallow and had to have something behind it. She pushed on the back of it until the whole thing popped out. Unfortunately, there was nothing back there.

When at last they were gone. Everything was still in one piece. They hadn't slashed any of the upholstery, but every bit of furniture had been moved.

Turning to look at him, Maggie held her hands out toward the mess. "At least I didn't lose anything I didn't expect to."

He nodded, wanting to take her into his arms and comfort her, but that wasn't his role here. Besides, she'd just broken up with her boyfriend. So he filled the gap between what he wanted and what was appropriate. "They took longer photographing and removing the jewelry from the closet than I expected."

"I watched, they didn't touch anything. It was impressive." They'd watched as special evidence bags were brought in and everything in the hidden compartment was removed with tweezers and gloves.

Though the sofa had been left in the middle of the room, Maggie plopped back onto it, making Sebastian wince. That was not a couch for flopping onto.

She curled her lip and reached around to her back. "The crick in my back from earlier has returned." Her sigh was weary.

Sebastian held out a hand. "It's getting late."

It was dark. And, though he'd been watching where he could, he hadn't seen the silver sedan she'd described. But who knew what they'd missed?

It was over for now. They both needed sleep and he needed to know she was safe. "Come stay with me tonight."

Sebastian felt her fingers slide into his as he realized he might sound like he was offering more than ... well, not more than *he* wanted, but more than she might want. "I've got a guestroom."

An expression flickered across her features making him wonder if she wished for something more than the guest room. He pushed a little harder. "You need a good night's sleep somewhere you feel safe."

But Maggie shook her head at him and pulled her fingers back. *Damn.*

"I need to stay here. I don't want to leave my home empty."

If he went home, he didn't doubt she'd have another night watching the window. She needed to rest. The nap had not been enough.

But he only nodded and didn't argue. "Do you want me to stay here?"

The relief at him asking showed on her face and he wondered how stressed she actually was about staying here alone. She nodded quickly and asked, "Do you need to get anything?"

He laughed. "I do. I've managed to go through both changes of clothing I carry with me. Unless you want me wearing swim trunks and goggles in the morning, then yes."

"Why don't you go now? While there's still a little bit of daylight and I'll stay here and put the furniture back together."

Sebastian refused. "Nope. The furniture can wait till tomorrow. I'm taking you out for a real meal."

"I have to put the furniture back, I have a client tomorrow."

Maybe she was too tired to look at it clearly? Sebastian shook his head. "Can you move your client?"

"I—"

He knew she needed the work, but … "You've slept only four hours in the last two days. Are you really going to be good for your client by morning?"

"I can be," she said it as though she was trying to talk herself into it.

"I'm sure you *can*. But *will* you? How long is it going to take to put things back? We have to at least put back the foyer, the hallway, the living room, and your office." He'd said *we* and he wondered if she'd caught it. "Can we do that and get you a good night's sleep and get you ready for your client by tomorrow morning?"

She sighed. "No. But maybe if I bump him till noon."

He waited while she called and told the couple that she'd had a mild family issue. Sebastian felt the sigh of relief through his whole body as she said, "thank you," and he knew it wasn't going to be a mad dash or another sleepless night.

"Is it just the one client?"

"Unfortunately, just the one."

This time when he took her hand, he didn't let go. He pulled her out the front door and down the steps to the street and put her into the passenger side of his car. When he slid in across from her, he could see she was tired, but the half a meal she'd eaten in the early afternoon wasn't enough. "The next question is, where do you want to have dinner?"

Maggie only shrugged.

"How about pasta?" he asked. Thinking about the kind of Italian food that could lull them both into a night's sleep worthy of a carb-coma.

But there was something about the way she smiled at him that made him wish she wasn't actually thinking about pasta. He would stay at her house tonight, but how long would he make it before he just blurted out what he really wanted to say?

CHAPTER TWENTY-EIGHT

On Sunday morning, Maggie found herself alone again for the first time in two days. Sebastian had headed home early to shower, repack his bag, and show up for his shift. As a volunteer she wasn't due in every time A-shift was on duty.

Somehow she'd managed to not blurt out her feelings the whole time, even though things stayed pretty low key. She wasn't sure if she was proud of herself or ashamed.

When Sebastian asked, she told him that she was good by herself. It had been both the truth and a bald-faced lie.

She *was* good by herself. Maggie went to the grocery store—something needed after she and Sebastian had eaten everything she had. He ate twice as much as she did but feeding him was a small price for in-home security, especially from someone she enjoyed spending time with.

When the groceries were put away, she tackled her aunt's office, organizing what remained after the FBI confiscated everything useful. Maggie would have loved to use the office for herself, but she would have to sort everything to make the space usable. So she only lined up the remaining papers and put them in drawers.

Then she made herself a decent meal as if to prove to herself that when Sebastian wasn't here she could cook for and feed herself.

Even when she'd finished eating, it still wasn't noon yet. Knowing she wouldn't sleep well that night, she tried to nap. Though she managed to fall asleep and catch a few hours, she hadn't been able to stay asleep. She'd slept much better with Sebastian here the last two nights, but she was still running on a deficit. As the sky had grown dark that evening, she considered what to do with the long night in front of her.

She wasn't going to sleep, that was certain.

She fielded texts from Sebastian and reassured him that she was fine. The real problem was that she *was* fine—fine enough to take advantage of some good internet and bad curiosity.

With the information the FBI had given her, Maggie began researching both the Blue River Killer and the La Vista Rapist. She poured over old reports, missing women and a few young men, bodies found, reports filed, basically anything that pinged when she searched. When that overwhelmed her, she found more scholarly articles on serial predators and how they operated.

Even what little she'd found was enough to convince her that the two perpetrators were separate people. Which made it even more concerning that both their trophies had wound up in her home ... and in the same box.

She didn't know yet what the closet meant.

Maggie had set up in her living room, ready to check the front window at each passing engine. She had her phone at the ready to take pictures and record the license plate if she saw the silver sedan again. But though she was several hours into the night, the only thing to go by had been the Raylan family's minivan.

Next, she pulled up the picture files on her phone. She and Sebastian had messaged them to each other as a way to preserve the full trove in two different places. So she had copies of everything he had taken and he had hers.

She flipped through, looking for something unique about the victims, some thread. Not that she thought she'd find what the FBI hadn't, but she wanted to know what had been here ...

She pulled up pictures of the victims on her laptop, their faces large on the screen, smiling in family photos or senior yearbooks. It didn't get her very far, but it got her far enough. Another car passed by, revving its way down her street. Maggie fought a shudder, but she could already tell the engine was too loud to be the sedan. Sure enough, she'd pulled back the curtain to see the taillight of a motorcycle and she felt her stress drop back down from the spike.

Whoever it was who had killed these people and raped these young women was still out there. The smiling senior photo of one victim made Maggie's heart drop: the necklace in the picture matched the necklace that they'd found in the back of the closet. The young woman was from Beatrice, a small nearby town just south of Lincoln.

Maggie hadn't known about the predators because she didn't live here. It had been a number of years since she'd spent a summer with Aunt Abbie. But the locals understood what the killer was doing and, according to the news, they were afraid.

Maggie knew it was well past time to stop reading. She reassured herself that the FBI was checking on her. And she reiterated the words they'd given her: they didn't think he would be back.

The FBI had very openly and visibly searched her house and confiscated everything they could find. Whatever her prowler had been looking for, it wasn't here anymore. That should be obvious to anyone watching the place.

She told herself that if the FBI was confident, she was confident. But it was another lie.

Still, she pulled up another article and reached into the big bowl of popcorn she'd made. This was not popcorn kind of entertainment, Maggie just needed something to eat that would help her stay awake. It turned out it wasn't the popcorn, but what she read that was doing an excellent job of it.

The Blue River Killer was called that because he left his victims in shallow water. The first had been found in the Blue River, though the Platte River closer to her had also seen a few. It didn't take long to find more journal articles written on him. Maggie also found the locations where he'd killed. The pattern to his killings began to make a disturbing amount of sense. Her own home wasn't dead center, but it was certainly an option. The feds had to have been searching for him near here long before now.

They simply hadn't gotten to checking out Aunt Abbie's boarders ... or they had and, for whatever reason, dismissed them.

Maggie's eyes felt bloodshot. Her brain was stuffed full and her heart hurt for the victims left in these predators' wakes. She'd had enough for one night. Looking up at the clock, she saw it was just after two a.m. Sebastian hadn't texted for a while and she was getting sleepy.

Closing up her computer, she headed upstairs to comb through Abbie's remaining records. But, an hour later, it was clear the FBI had taken everything of value. Maggie was left with a stack of papers on her desk that resembled trash more than anything else: receipts for restaurant dinners, dry cleaning tabs from a decade ago, old flyers for a county fair. Maggie almost swept if off the desk and into the trash can. But she couldn't. Abbie had saved it.

It sure looked like trash and Maggie wondered how much she owed Aunt Abbie ... The woman had left her a house that, despite the dire need for modernization was more than serviceable and worth far more money than any of Maggie's cousins had received. She left the crap on the desk. She would have to decide what to do with it—probably toss it—but she wouldn't decide in the middle of the night.

Back at the couch, she wished she had a cat to curl up with her. Could she do that? Abbie had often had a house cat or at least a feral one that she fed. Maggie sighed, she was getting tired or bored. Her mind was wandering. Since she wasn't getting a cat in the middle of the night, she pulled up the pictures of Abbie's records on her computer.

This was hard to research, too. Abbie's paperwork was as much a mess as everything else. Nothing was in order. Rental contracts from thirty years ago were filed with one from last December.

It might have been the last one she wrote, Maggie thought, but she pushed the nostalgia aside and pulled out a notepad and pen. She began keeping track of names and dates. As she plowed through the pictures, a few odd facts emerged.

CHAPTER TWENTY-NINE

Sebastian stood at the front of the house, the heat of the flames could still be felt through his thick gear. They lit up his view and a good part of the neighborhood.

Next to him, the chief stood surveying the damage, hands on his hips. He wasn't happy. He also wasn't in full gear but did have his mask on to breathe clean oxygen. The whole neighborhood was rolling with smoke and ash.

The two men watched as A-shift dampened the blaze. They didn't have to talk.

House fires were rare. Abandoned buildings sometimes caught fire. Camp sites caught fire an inordinate amount of time when people failed to follow necessary protocol. Wildfires sometimes started with lightning strikes or fireworks run amok.

But this? Two house fires in a small town within a week was odd.

The first house had at least been empty when it had gone up. It had been for sale. That had triggered an investigation by the insurance company. Though, from everything Sebastian had gathered when he and the chief had gone back to check the place out, the family had lost money in the blaze. The area was relatively nice, though not one of the up and coming places in town, and the sale of the house would have been worth more than the insurance was paying out.

Sebastian had heard that the staging company was also going after the insurance to recover everything they'd lost. All the furniture and fake family pictures, kitchen supplies, everything they'd added to make the home look lived in and welcoming to prospective buyers had been destroyed, too.

This house though ... it was smaller, more rundown, and lit up like a fucking firecracker.

Chief motioned him to move back and they stepped further down the street. Their comms would keep them in touch with the others, but this allowed them to take off their masks and speak a little more freely. They definitely had to watch out for neighbors listening in.

The street was overrun with lookie loos. They weren't drivebys gawking. They were neighbors, bringing water bottles to the family or treats for the family's two dogs. One of the dogs had already been walked away to a neighbor's where he could be taken care of.

That was the kind of community Sebastian wanted for himself. His apartment building didn't have it, but he hoped one day to get himself a fixer-upper.

"We won't know till we get inside ..." the chief started, letting the phrase trail off.

Sebastian understood. They'd have to find evidence if it was or wasn't arson.

"Older house," Sebastian mused. "Could have been the wiring."

"They should have seen something or smelled something first," the chief countered.

"I don't know," Sebastian shrugged. They should have, but

should didn't always mean people did notice. Or they'd noticed but dismissed it—either thought it wasn't that bad a smell or decided that they'd just fix it later. He wasn't ready to rule out faulty wiring.

He spotted Luke coming up the street toward them. That was odd. The firefighters stayed put. Each had his position and leaving it would rearrange how the team worked. It must mean Luke had something to say.

"Hernandez." The chief greeted him with a neutral tone, letting him know he was free to talk, but unexpected.

Hernandez glanced towards Sebastian, but again the chief nodded. The movements were simple conversation between people who worked together as a unit consistently, sometimes in life and death situations. They all understood the nod to mean that, whatever Luke had to say, he could say in front of Sebastian.

"I didn't put anything together before," Luke looked between them. "But I'm getting a little concerned about the locations of the fires."

"I don't understand," the chief said, now curious about what one of his newest firefighters was bringing.

"When I was a kid," Luke added, "We moved around a lot. It was my mom, my dad, me, my three brothers. Then my dad left when I was seven."

Chief nodded. Sebastian understood. Luke hadn't made a secret of his family history, and he was wondering why it was getting repeated now.

"I've lived in each of these two neighborhoods. I've ..." He didn't finish, but shook his head as if shaking off something disturbing.

Interesting, Sebastian thought. Two house fires, barely a week apart. One firefighter had lived in both places.

The chief took a more cynical approach. "You moved around a lot. But the people who live in these neighborhoods move around a lot more, too. It's probably not just you who's lived in both places."

"True," Luke said, and Sebastian wondered if maybe there wasn't something more. There was. "This house—"

He didn't point. They'd all been trained not to do that. Not to draw attention.

"—belonged to a man my mother once dated."

"But not anymore?"

"No. He moved out of town years ago."

"Do you think an arsonist is targeting you?" The chief asked, finally becoming pointed to what Luke was maybe hinting at.

"No." The answer was firm and clear. "I used to play with the kids in the family that lived in the other house. If someone were targeting me, there would be much better places to hit. I just think it's odd I've had a connection to both of the houses."

Sebastian was soaking in the information. It probably had nothing to do with Luke personally, but the idea opened up a new line of thought ... especially if this was another instance of arson.

"Anything more?" the chief asked.

Luke shook his head. "I just wanted to report it. I didn't want it coming up later and you didn't know. If there's anything you can ask me—anything I know that can help—I'll do what I can."

But the chief dismissed Luke, and he headed back down the street to join the brigade.

"We should definitely take advantage of what he knows," Sebastian said. "If this is a hit, then we should be asking *Who else moved around this neighborhood, like the Hernandez family?*"

It was an angle he and the chief hadn't entertained. Whether the chief had thought of it before, Sebastian didn't know, but it was certainly a new angle to him.

Their chat done until actual investigation could commence —which probably wouldn't even begin until tomorrow—the two of them headed back down the street, not far behind Hernandez.

Luke joined back on the line, aiming the water at the base of the flames. A second team watched between houses, aiming to douse any flying sparks before they could take hold. They'd already wet the houses as much as they could, but nothing could be counted on with fires.

The homes were packed in relatively tightly here, and several neighbors were more than a little worried, standing on their own front lawns as the neighborhood glowed with loss.

As he stood back and surveyed the damage, Sebastian surreptitiously checked the crowd for watchers, anyone who didn't belong. He didn't even know yet if this was anything more than faulty wiring or a too-old appliance, but he had his eyes open for an arsonist coming to admire his work.

His thoughts turned and he wanted to message Maggie. He hoped she was asleep, it was the middle of the night after all. Though she said she'd be fine—and he believed she'd be safe—he didn't think she'd be comfortable.

But there was no time.

He left the uneasy feeling behind and hoped he'd get back to the station in time to catch a few hours of sleep before shift end, because it looked like he and the chief would have to come back here tomorrow.

Something told him they'd find ample evidence it was arson. He hoped he was wrong, because the more he learned the less he liked leaving Maggie alone.

CHAPTER THIRTY

Maggie was grateful that Sebastian had made it home—well, back to her house—by ten. He'd gone to his apartment, showered, changed and came immediately to her place.

Would she have the presence of mind to say something to him today? To maybe ask him out? He wasn't moving too fast, but maybe that mean he wasn't interested.

He looked good, if tired, and instead of offering up herself she offered him breakfast. "I make a mean scrambled omelet."

"What's that?" he asked, giving her the side eye.

"It's when I try to make an omelet and then I give up and scramble it halfway through, but it tastes just as good." She'd even found hash browns she could make in the oven.

They'd eaten together quietly at the table—Maggie having a sensible breakfast, Sebastian acting as though he hadn't been fed at all in the last twenty-four hours. The guys ate meals at the fire station, but it was well known that the better the meal they sat down to, the more likely the bell would ring.

"You look exhausted," she told him. "I'll show you what I found in Abbie's records later."

"Why not now?"

"There's a lot of it, and you need sleep."

"I do," he agreed, then added, "and I've got to go back later and check out an arson."

"Well, if you're staying here ..." she hoped he was. He'd said he'd be back and then he'd shown up. But they hadn't explicitly stated that he was sleeping at her place now. "You can go to sleep in your room."

She could call it *his room*. It should be his after two straight nights of him sleeping in that bed.

"You look relatively tired, too."

Maggie had never dated a man willing to tell her she didn't look her very best. But then again, she and Sebastian weren't dating, to her disappointment. Though she'd managed to snag a few hours before he got off work at eight, her dreams had been wild and crazy, from running from faceless menaces in the dark, to finding bones in the water, or getting tangled in gold chains.

It didn't take any kind of therapist to figure out what they meant.

"I did my best. I got some sleep," she told him, then switched topics. "Will you be back before dark?"

"Absolutely." He looked her in the eye to let her know she wouldn't be alone another night and her anxiety settled. "Arson investigations work best in daylight. Trying to find evidence in the dark is a bitch."

"Then go sleep now."

"What about you?" He was already standing, taking his plate to the sink, rinsing it and putting it in the dishwasher, yawning as he did it.

"I want to sleep tonight. So I'm going to check out the backyard."

She could see him pause. With one hand on the counter, he

frowned at her from the kitchen to where she still sat at the table, finishing the last of her eggs.

"The feds checked out the yard."

"I know," she said. "But it's not their yard. They haven't been visiting and digging up the flowers here since they were eight. They might not notice if something was amiss."

"It's a good point," he conceded. For a moment, he looked like he would offer to join her. Then he yawned again though she could see he was trying to fight it.

"You go to sleep."

With a nod, he walked past and her eyes followed as he made his way slowly up the stairs, looking more exhausted with each step he climbed.

Maggie finished her last few bites of hash browns, put her own dishes into the dishwasher, and headed straight through the kitchen and out the back door. She hadn't been out here since the FBI had come through. The grass had mostly sprung back. When they'd left, she'd been able to see footprints everywhere.

Now it looked as if the yard was righting itself. Maggie checked everything she could think of. She gazed down into the flower beds around the house. Abbie had ringed the whole place with three feet of mulch and a variety of plants that bloomed at different seasons. It was a bitch to weed all of it, but Maggie loved that it looked somewhere between manicured and wild.

The open space of the yard was plain grass and Maggie had hired someone to mow it. She was getting ready to pay the fee for them to weed the gardens, too. Turning away from the cultivated beds, she peered along the fence where her wildflowers bloomed. Some of them were several feet high.

Now, she examined it with a different eye. She headed to the fence and pushed some of the unruly plants aside, as though she might find jewelry and evidence littering the dirt. The only other thing she could think was to dig holes and see if she could turn anything up. A metal detector would be better, and she didn't have any tools on her.

Heading toward the back, she looked to the blackberry bushes that lined the back wall. She walked along that border too, though nothing jumped out at her as being out of place.

As much as Aunt Abbie loved her gardens, she hated change. These bushes were the same ones Maggie remembered from when she was little. The newest things in the yard were the flowers she herself had added as a child, and that had been quite some time ago. Even inside, Abbie hadn't replaced any of the old wallpapers. The best she would do was refinish a floor now and then. From the looks of it, that hadn't happened in a long time either.

The old gate was exactly as she remembered it, though when she was a kid, the latch was almost at her eye level. Now, it barely passed her waist. Lifting it, Maggie swung the gate open. The creak and whine of the hinges indicated it too hadn't been maintained. She closed it behind her and re-latched it though she didn't know why.

The back gate opened to one of the stretches of woods that ran through the town. There were walking trails back here and houses on the other side of the trees.

The other neighborhood wasn't quite so far away that Maggie couldn't see through to the other side if she looked. But if she wasn't looking, it would be easy to pretend she was lost in the woods, as she had when she was little.

Now, knowing what had been found in her home, it was easy to imagine that someone had come out the back of Aunt Abbie's boarding house and cut through the yard. As long as they'd made it across the grass undetected, they could have cut through the trails and wound up almost anywhere in town.

Though it was late morning and the sun was shining brightly, casting little diamonds of light along the ground,

Maggie suddenly felt as though she knew that *this* was what the killer had done.

Her prowler had gone out the back door—and not the front —then disappeared ... *just like this*. Maggie was becoming more and more convinced she was right.

A chill climbed up her neck despite the bright day. She spun around, looking all directions, feeling suddenly as if someone was watching her.

CHAPTER THIRTY-ONE

Maggie stood for a moment looking first one direction then the other down the path, debating what she should do.

She'd only wandered a few feet from the back fence. Though she was in a thick stand of trees, her own home was still visible. When she tipped her head or paid attention to the light, she could see through to the houses on the other side. But Maggie was just as confident that they wouldn't see her.

She turned a full circle, alert to anything unusual, but found no one actually watching her. It didn't change the warning sensation that crawled the back of her neck.

Taking stock, Maggie asked herself what weapons she had. The answer was *none*.

But there was no one visible to need weapons against. And neither of the two predators she was dealing with seemed to strike in the woods or at daytime. Also, she had her phone on her.

Despite the sensation crawling up her neck, she was perfectly safe.

Sebastian knew where she was. She'd told him she would be

in the back yard. It was an odd feeling, planning how to best be careful if something happened to her. She wanted to make sure they knew where to start looking. But she wasn't even in either target demographic, and she was pissed.

The elderly clients—who were her only clients right now—were likely already gossiping that she had FBI agents in her home. That wouldn't help her practice that wasn't even off the ground yet. Someone had broken into her home and they might not have taken anything she could find, but they'd stolen her sleep and her sense of peace.

And if she had a way to add to the FBI's evidence? Well, she was going to take it. So, rather than turn back, Maggie let her anger fuel her forward.

Her home—and thus this strip of woods behind it—was relatively close to the center of town. The front opened onto one of the more traveled streets, just off the main drag. She could turn left or right.

Before she went one foot further, she turned on the location system on her phone. She opened the app she had and messaged a link to Sebastian. If he woke up before she got back, he'd see the message from her and be able to find her quickly. That was being smart. Then she made a random decision and headed to the right.

Following the trail, Maggie kept her eyes peeled for any suspicious movement. Her ears strained for any unusual sounds. But the movement she saw was birds and squirrels and a single raccoon. The sounds were muffled by the same traffic she heard on the street, no different from an average day in Redemption.

She passed by the backs of various houses and realized likely none of them even knew she was back here. Maybe in the winter, when the trees were bare, the sightlines would be clear, but now, when it was dense and green like today? No one would see her unless they knew exactly where to look. And maybe not even then.

It disturbed her more to know that she could have accessed any of these homes easily from the trail. All she would need to do is cross the back lawn and go into the back door. She would bet many of the residents left their doors unlocked.

Then again, she hadn't, and she'd still had someone in her home. So maybe she wasn't any smarter or safer than anyone else.

Turning again to look down the trail that stretched in front of her, she thought back to the map that one intrepid reporter had made and posted online. None of the murders had occurred in Redemption. Only one victim had been a Redemption resident, and that had been a handful of years ago. The young man had been staying in Lincoln at the time.

She walked a little further, surprised at how many homes in Redemption backed up to this woodland. She'd known the trail was long. but it was warm today and she was surprised she hadn't seen anyone else. No joggers. No moms with a stroller. No one.

Maggie passed into a different neighborhood and was now at the backs of playgrounds built on the lawns behind apartment buildings. If she followed it much farther, she would reach the industrial complex at the edge of town.

It had been almost an hour since she'd gone out the gate and it was past time to turn around. Heading back, she thought through the things that were known about the Blue River Killer and the La Vista Rapist.

For a wild moment, she entertained a ridiculous fantasy in which one of the boarders was the rapist and Aunt Abbie herself was the Blue River Killer. It took less than thirty seconds to get to the point where Maggie was almost laughing out loud. Abbie hated houseflies but couldn't kill a spider. The victims had been relatively young and seemingly innocent, not the kind of people that made Aunt Abbie angry enough to even curse at them. Maggie couldn't imagine her sweet and sour Aunt as an actual murderer.

Besides, another body had turned up missing since after Abbie had died. DNA evidence said it was the same predator. So Maggie dismissed the absurd idea.

Even if she was laughing at herself, light hit her eyes from the right hand side.

Something glinted.

Maggie turned to see what it was.

CHAPTER THIRTY-TWO

Sebastian followed the moving dot on his phone, grateful that Maggie had messaged him the link. Otherwise, he would have been terrified.

The La Vista Rapist took women from their homes. Some prowler had already been in Maggie's house while she was there, and it made him doubly nervous.

He hadn't told Maggie what he thought of this—that maybe the prowler hadn't been after the box of jewelry but had been scoping the place out. He didn't want her to worry more. She already wasn't getting enough sleep.

Having him staying here should keep her safe, but it was still far too easy for anyone to find out what nights he was out of the house. Waking up and finding her gone had been petrifying.

Luckily, he'd found the text before he fully panicked. Hitting the link, he'd headed out the back door and was now following the trail she'd left behind. According to the dot, she'd turned around a while ago and he was about to run into her.

"Maggie?" he called out,

"Sebastian!" He heard her from far enough away for her

voice to sound small. But she was up ahead, exactly as the system said and he breathed easier.

As she emerged around a corner in the trail, appearing healthy and sound between two trees, he let out the breath he hadn't realized he'd been holding. She was safe, happy, and motioning him to come forward. "You have to see what I found!"

He didn't have the time. The chief had called him in for the follow-up on the house and he needed to get going. He'd only come out here to be sure that Maggie was safe and let her know that he was leaving. But he didn't say that yet.

"What did you find?"

"Look." She'd come all the way up to him, reached out for his hand, and was now pulling him along. He wished she was holding his hand for some other reason, but he would take the feel of her hand in his for what it was. Something about their fingers laced together simply felt *right*. When was he going to say something? Would it ever be the right time?

He couldn't go on wanting her, but if he made her uncomfortable … who would keep her safe?

"Come with me." She turned and tugged him back the way she'd come, but didn't explain further. He didn't have time, but he didn't say no.

She took a short side path and they emerged near a paved boat ramp and small parking lot. A rickety looking dock jutted out into the water. She was pointing at the river. "The lake is here."

He frowned. Had she not known it was back here? "It's a tributary of the Platte River."

"I know." She turned to look at him, her eyes bright with wanting him to catch on to something he wasn't catching. She gave him a hint. "It's a public dock."

"Okay?" He let it hang in the air like a question. Still not understanding.

"It took me about twenty-five minutes to get here from the back gate. Well, give or take, because I passed it the first time. I needed to be coming from this angle to really see that the water was right over here. And I had to take a side path." She pointed back behind them to where it joined up with the main trail that went on until the woods ended.

They walked further, down onto the old blacktop, near the water's edge. And he confessed, "I'm missing the point."

He needed to get back.

"The point is," she explained gently, "You can walk out my back gate, and come here, and get in a boat." She waved her hand toward the water again. "A boat that you've docked and kept here."

"It's always been that way." He was still missing something.

"Exactly. You could leave by boat from this dock anytime day or night, and no one would really notice. It's always been here. In fact, there are more docks than just this one around town, right? But this one is a quick walk from my back gate."

"Oh shit." He saw what she saw now. It wasn't a guarantee that it had happened this way, but it was even more plausible that the killer had been a boarder in Sabbie's home. While he lived there, he could easily have walked out the back gate, come here unnoticed, and taken a boat he had tied up.

"How much do you want to bet that the city doesn't charge for the boats kept here?" She looked at him as if she knew she were right.

"I'm not taking that bet. We don't even keep track of who has a boat tied up at the main dock. The town is too small for the city to bother with it. There's never been an issue."

She looked a little surprised that he knew that.

"We had a boat at the main dock catch on fire about seven years ago. No one claimed it. And there were no records to track down who it belonged to." But now that her eyes narrowed at him, he wondered if maybe the boat hadn't belonged to the killer and he'd had to get rid of evidence.

Maggie was talking again. "All of the victims' bodies were found in the water. How easy would it have been to take a boat from here?" She waved her hand again a little too excited. "He leaves the scene from the water, not the land."

Shit. She was making too much sense given what he knew of the cases.

"It explains how he vanished without a trace from the scenes. I wonder if the FBI has thought of this?"

"I can't imagine they haven't." Surely the FBI hadn't released all the information they knew, but the information she was spouting convinced him that she'd spent all night up reading. She hadn't had this knowledge when he had left for his shift the day before.

"It's not mentioned in any of the newspaper articles I found," she confirmed his suspicion. "So either the FBI is sitting on the information, and they have managed to keep it quiet for *years*, or the FBI doesn't think this is the case." The irritation in her voice didn't suit the danger of the situation, he thought. She should be more on guard, but she was just angry. Still, now wasn't the time to point it out. "Also, I need to show you what I found."

Shit, he thought again. This time he tugged on her hand, pulling her away from the scene and leading them back home. The new information was concerning in the reverse: If the Blue River Killer could have come and gone from Sabbie's easily to kill someone, then he could just as easily come back in the middle of the night. It made too much sense with the prowler she'd had. He'd gone out the back door and probably over the gate in his speed.

But what Sebastian said was, "The chief called me in, so I came out to let you know that I'll be on scene for a couple of hours."

"Why are you called in?" she asked, genuinely curious.

"I'm a trained arson investigator." He watched as her eyes lit up, having forgotten that she didn't know that. Everyone at the station did. "I was trained at Quantico." He added that last bit then felt dumb, as though he'd been trying to impress her. "So, the chief and I are the preliminary task force here. And we're concerned that we've got a serial arsonist."

"Are you *kidding me?*" She yanked her hand out of his in order to put both fists on her hips and stare at him. *"What the hell kind of small town is this?"*

He had to laugh. "I'm beginning to wonder that myself, though you have to admit both the Blue River Killer and the La Vista Rapist operated out of the Omaha and Lincoln areas. Not here."

"Okay. Valid point," she conceded. "But the arsonist is here."

"Yeah, we got one."

"And it looks like the La Vista Rapist and the Blue River Killer both have very strong ties to Redemption. In fact, to my own home." Again, she sounded more irritated than angry, as if the newspaper had been overcharging her or such.

Her dismissal of her possible danger petrified him. What if something went horribly wrong and she wasn't prepared? "Come on back. Let's get you locked in. I'll only be a couple hours."

When she didn't balk at that, he reached out again, taking her fingers in his.

Without the threat hanging over their heads, it would have been a gorgeous walk. But as he got back closer to the house, he couldn't shake the feeling that something worse was on its way.

CHAPTER THIRTY-THREE

S ebastian fought the urge to break the speed limit.

It was a gorgeous day and being on his bike again felt wonderful. In just a few months, he'd have to put it in storage for the winter. The arson investigation had quickly been handed over to the state, and now that he didn't have that occupying his brain, his only thought was getting back to Maggie and making sure she was okay.

In his mind, when he climbed on the bike, he'd told himself he was going *home*. It took effort to remind himself that Maggie's place wasn't his home, that this was only temporary until the killer was caught. Then again, the killer hadn't been caught already for close to twenty years.

He could only hope the jewelry box and the other evidence in Maggie's house was the break they all needed. In the meantime, pushing the speed limit wasn't the only urge he had to fight. It was getting harder and harder to stay with Maggie and not act on his feelings. The more he was around her, the more he liked her. He'd thought that, being in the house with her twenty-four/seven, she would begin to annoy him in some way or other, but it hadn't happened.

Until the feds caught the guy, or until Sebastian was certain that she returned his feelings, he didn't want to push. What if she said no? Then she'd be alone.

It would have been relaxing to peel off his helmet and feel the wind in his hair, to really enjoy the sunshine. But it wasn't safe and, especially as a firefighter, he wasn't going to drive around town illegally and unsafe. He'd already passed a handful of people that he knew.

Taking the last turn, he let the bike lean hard underneath him. He saw Maggie's house, still standing—not burned to the ground or some other bizarre torturous fantasy that had occurred to him while he was driving. The sight alone relaxed him, but he knew he'd feel better when he got inside and saw that Maggie herself was in one piece.

Just as he was ready to turn into the driveway, his muscles clenched and his pulse kicked up as he saw a silver sedan at the end of the street. It was older, dinged and just a little dirty—exactly as Maggie had described—and it was driving away from him.

Would the driver notice if he sped up and followed?

Did it matter?

Maybe it would be best if this person understood that someone was on his tail, someone willing to give chase.

Sebastian revved the bike and beelined down the street. At the end of the short block he hung a sharp right, following where he'd seen the silver car turn. He'd walked here yesterday with Maggie on the trail behind the houses in the strip of woods. For a moment, he lost sight of the car. But then, once again having turned right, Sebastian caught the car and made another sharp turn to follow. He was now aiming back toward Main Street.

At the end of the block, the sedan turned right this time. Sebastian pushed the bike harder, hoping no one would notice he was chasing a car. Following through two more turns, he managed to get close enough to memorize the license plate.

Surely this asshole knew he was being followed by now. Besides, he hadn't done anything wrong that Sebastian knew of. If the police stopped him or if this guy called it in, there wouldn't be much he could say in defense. So he hung another right and pulled to the side of the road, his heart pounding.

His fingers were clumsy as he punched the license in a text message to Maggie. Even as he started to relax, it occurred to him that he'd seen the sedan driving away from Maggie's house.

What if this person was leaving the house? What if Maggie was in trouble?

His pulse shooting up again, Sebastian took off, aiming back toward Maggie's.

A few minutes later, he pealed into the driveway probably grabbing all of the neighbors' attention as he did. He didn't care. He raced to the front door, one hand grabbing his helmet and holding it by the strap out of habit alone. Otherwise he might have tossed it on the grass in his haste to see that Maggie was okay.

Even as he reached for the door, it flew open.

"Are you okay?" Maggie asked, looking concerned but okay.

The irony that she was worried about him wasn't lost. But he couldn't speak as all the breath whooshed out of his lungs.

She was fine. She was in shorts and a T shirt. Her hair was up in a haphazard ponytail and his immediate response was to take her in his arms and kiss her. He reached for her out of sheer want, his body reacting without thinking.

But she frowned ever so slightly, and it was like the scratch of a record pulling him back to reality. He hadn't said anything, hadn't made a move on her before, and pulling her into his arms —basically assaulting her now—was not the answer.

"I'm okay." He managed the words she needed to hear.

"I saw the silver sedan." She pulled her phone from her

pocket and frowned. "You messaged me."

"I saw it too. I was chasing it and I got the plate."

She smiled now, wide and beaming, and again his heart twisted. He wished that was for him. "I got a picture of him. That's why I didn't get your message right away. I had my phone in my hand and I was sending it to the FBI."

"Good. I'm hoping if we just hand everything over to the feds they'll finally catch this guy."

Maggie replied, "Agreed, but I'll also do my own reverse online search."

Smart, he thought, still breathing heavily and only just now beginning to calm down.

He looked her up and down again. The running shorts weren't normal for her. She was barefoot. Even her ponytail was a bit of a mess—very un-Maggie-like—with dark red curls springing out in various places. He was curious now. "What were you doing?"

"Cleaning," she offered it with a wry grin. "House this big doesn't clean itself."

This was new to him. An image of Maggie as a domestic goddess had simply not occurred to him before.

"Somebody's got to clean," she sighed.

"I'm staying, I can help."

"I got most of it done while you were out." He noticed then that everything was shiny. She must have mopped and dusted everything, maybe burning off extra energy. Lord knew he had plenty to burn himself, but cleaning wasn't how he wanted to burn it.

He nodded and they stood there in the foyer, face to face, not speaking for a moment. As the silence grew awkward, Maggie looked at him oddly and asked, "What?"

He'd been staring at her.

"What is it, Sebastian? Something's wrong. Tell me."

He stood there, debating with himself. *Should he tell her?*

CHAPTER THIRTY-FOUR

S omething was wrong, but Maggie couldn't quite tell what. Sebastian's jaw was clenched and he wouldn't tell her what it was.

To change the subject, she asked, "How did the arson investigation go?"

"It was definitely arson," he answered, though the tension didn't seem to go away. "The paper will likely have already printed it. This person didn't do much to cover their trail. So they're either a newbie or making a point."

"You really do have a serial arsonist on your hands."

He nodded, resigned.

"Any leads?"

"Of course not." His jaw was still clenched. He was having this conversation with her but still thinking about the other thing he didn't want to tell her. Had he learned something about the silver sedan? Was he afraid of worrying her? Or was it something else entirely?

Not knowing was painful. Maggie stayed on topic though and asked wryly, "Is anybody missing any jewelry?"

Wouldn't it just be perfect if a serial killer, serial rapist, and serial arsonist all had ties to her home?

"At least it wasn't that," he said and offered a half smile, but he still hadn't budged from his position.

Changing the subject hadn't worked. He wasn't in any better of a mood and she still wanted to know. She went back to the direct route. "What aren't you telling me?"

"Nothing bad," was all he offered, but he didn't look at her.

"Then tell me."

He shook his head and shrugged as he sighed, clearly untangling something for himself, before he finally spoke. "I just don't want to burden you with something else."

Maggie almost threw her head back and laughed out loud at the idea. "Sebastian, you've *unburdened* so much already. Whatever it is, I can handle it. And I think I should know if it pertains to my safety."

He shook his head. "It doesn't." But again, he looked away and she saw his fingers curl, clenching into fists.

"Tell me," she pushed again, but he shook his head.

"If you don't agree, it'll ruin everything."

"Then I'll probably agree," she offered easily. They got along great, maybe too well. And she was beyond curious now what was going on.

"But that's just it, I don't want you to agree just so that I'll stay here."

Well, hell. There wasn't much he could have said that would make her more determined that that. "So, if I don't agree, you'll leave?"

"I won't leave. You'll *want* me to leave." Even as he said the words, she could see he was trying to swallow them back, as though he thought he'd already said too much.

But Maggie was still very much in the dark. She put her hands on her hips, going for intimidation. Not that it would work as he towered over her, but she tried. "Now you have to tell me."

He didn't have to tell her. He didn't owe her anything. *She owed him.* But she wanted to know what he was holding back and she was willing to force him to tell, if she could just figure out how ...

"You've been through too much already," he said, still not spilling whatever he was holding.

"I've had very threatening things," she corrected. "But aside from walking down my hallway with a baseball bat, I haven't actually been through that much."

"You broke up with your boyfriend recently."

"It was hardly traumatic. We should have broken up well before that," she said. "Trust me. I liked the guy, I really did—oh God, please don't repeat this to anyone—but that was all it ever was. In the end, he wasn't around, and I didn't miss him that much." She shrugged as she tried to explain a relationship that had been fun, then not, and never anything more. "I haven't been sitting here heartbroken, if that's what you're wondering."

Even as she said the words, she began to wonder what Sebastian might be suggesting. *Was his concern that she was still hung up on Rex?*

"Tell me," she pushed again, her heart pounding in her chest. Could he want what she wanted? Could she maybe fix the error of saying yes to the first man who asked her out? She should have waited for a better offer, for someone she really wanted to be with ... someone like Sebastian.

Still he shook his head.

"If you don't want to stay here, I can find someone else—"

"No! It's not that," he interrupted.

Well, that sounded good, she thought. It didn't really mean anything, though. This was so frustrating. She wanted him to kiss her and he was probably going to tell her he'd found more footprints or he knew the man in the silver sedan.

"Tell me."

He shook his head.

So she tried playing just a little dirty. It was either going to work out really well or be a phenomenally stupid move. She stepped closer and put her hand on his chest. "You can tell me."

Big Sebastian, who could face anything, looked terrified. But he blurted out the words. "I want us to be more than friends."

Her eyes went wide and her breath sucked in. It was exactly what she was hoping he would say, but she hadn't believed he actually would. She'd been waiting for this, but it was still a shock.

"I'm sorry," he blurted that out just as fast and stepped back. "I don't want you to think that that's the only reason I came, or that I'm staying because I think that you owe me something, or—"

The fingers she'd laid on his chest curled involuntarily. And it had the effect of stopping his words in their tracks.

Stepping closer, she lifted up on her tiptoes and said, "Me, too."

Her lips lifted to his, the shock of finally kissing him reverberated through her system as she pressed her mouth to his.

But Sebastian stood stock still.

CHAPTER THIRTY-FIVE

Sebastian had expected Maggie to tell him he wasn't welcome anymore. He'd been ready to beg her to let him stay until someone else showed up, maybe even Rex. Or he'd planned to squeeze his eyes shut and listen to her tell him how she liked him, a lot, but not in *that* way.

He'd been braced for a lot of outcomes.

But not this one.

Her lips on his shot fire through his system and he wasn't ready. The headiness of her wanting him had him frozen in place.

Until the touch of her left and he had nothing but air to make him wish for something he hadn't expected. His eyes blinked open as she stepped back.

"Oh. I'm sorry, I thought ..."

Hell, no.

He was not letting her think he didn't want her.

"If you thought I wanted you, you're right. I just ... I didn't expect you to want me, too."

She laughed, a soft sound that didn't ridicule his uncertainty, it only assured him. "I wish you'd asked me out first."

He would have reached out to pull her closer, but she stepped back.

"If we're confessing things, I wished you'd asked me out even when Rex and I were first going out. And that was horrible of me. Rex is a great guy who got a rough deal lately, though Hannah is awesome, but I was not a good girlfriend." She seemed to be explaining away things Sebastian didn't think she owed anyone. Besides, he was still hung up on the 'wish you'd asked me out first' part.

"You were a really great girlfriend, babysitting full time like that." He stopped himself right there. The last thing he wanted to talk about was her ex. Instead, Sebastian wanted to suggest she could be an amazing girlfriend to *him*. "Can I make up for just now?"

Those mossy green eyes blinked at him, confused until his hand slid around her hip and nudged her closer. As she moved willingly into his arms, he slid his other hand into her hair, hinting for her to tip her mouth up to his. The headiness of finally having Maggie in his arms washed over him and his movements were pure instinct.

This time, when her lips touched his, Sebastian let the fire take over. Every connection lit up, the feeling of kissing Maggie engulfed his whole world. Her lips parted for him and he didn't know if he'd done it first or if she had, but his tongue swept her mouth, an intimate invasion that felt right.

Her breasts pressed against his chest as she shifted upward, fusing their mouths together. No more light touches, no more tastes, Maggie had moved to devour him, and Sebastian was willing to return the favor.

His hands roamed and slipped beneath the edge of her t-shirt. Though he had traced every curve of her—the fabric was so thin—the touch of skin under his fingertips burst through him like wildfire. There was no containing it.

Maggie's touch roamed his shoulders, her fingers curling in

to pull herself up higher and letting him know that she was here for this as much as he was. He let her nudge him backward, until the wall was at his back and he almost slid down, just a little, to put them on more even levels. She was tall, but not as tall as him.

When Maggie pulled back with a small frustrated growl, his heart stopped cold in his chest. *What had he done?* But she grabbed his shirt in fistfuls and pulled him away from the wall.

He was more than willing to let Maggie steer him around. *Dear God, yes.*

She turned him, pushed him backward and he was looking in her eyes—her mischievous green eyes—as she maneuvered him back onto the stairs.

Oh. God. Yes.

Reaching back, he settled himself onto a step, and was more than rewarded when Maggie settled herself on his lap. "Is this okay?"

She was sliding forward, up his thighs, her legs straddling his.

"Very much." He maybe didn't get all of that last word out. He'd pulled her closer, sliding her the last few inches until she was settled flush against him. Until she could feel with no doubt that, yes, it was very much okay.

This time, his touch wandered down below the edge of the so-short running shorts. It was too easy to stroke her skin, right up under the edge of the fabric, to grab her sweet ass and try to move her even closer.

He wanted to peel all their clothing, toss it aside, and drive into her right there on the steps. And he also wanted, just as badly, to let her know she was safe with him. To turn this into more than just a fuck on the staircase. The ride they were on was careening wildly forward, and he wasn't sure he could stop it.

Maggie's soft fingers slid under his shirt, traced the edge of his jeans, and elicited a moan from somewhere deep in his soul. God, he'd wanted this for so long, and he didn't want to stop it.

She pulled back, her breathing as heavy as his. Her chest moved with each inhale, but her eyes stayed on his. Was she going to say they should stop?

Pulling her down, he kissed her again. She could stop them at any time, but he'd wanted to taste her again. Just this once.

Maggie leaned into him, almost toppling him backward. He was lost to everything except the feeling of her skin on his.

But then she jerked upright, and he placed the noise he'd just heard.

Tires squealing on pavement, just outside the front door.

CHAPTER THIRTY-SIX

Maggie jolted back at the sound. She was straddling Sebastian, her hair a mess from his fingers. Her own hands were still twisted into his t shirt. The two of them looked like they'd been doing exactly what they'd been doing.

Awkwardly, she scrambled off him and bolted toward the front window. Hearing the car squealing down toward the end of the street, she tipped her head to the left and almost pressed her face to the glass.

Sebastian was right behind her.

In any other situation, she would have been concerned about climbing the couch like a dog and having her ass in the air while she looked out the window. But not right now. She looked back at Sebastian. "It was a silver sedan."

"That's not good," Sebastian said. "Which means he was here. Probably sitting in front of the house. Even after I followed him earlier."

She looked to the man she'd been ravaging just a moment before. His clothes and his hair were still mussed. His expression was anything but—it was fierce, angry, worried.

He was strong and lean, and even upset, he looked like

something she wanted. Maggie shrugged at him, not knowing what to do about the silver sedan. She wanted to go back to what they were doing, but clearly they hadn't been paying enough attention.

Who knew if he'd even come to the door? He might have even peeked in the window and seen them. They'd been making out on the stairs in the front foyer. Thank God the window on the front door was frosted, but the living room window afforded a clear view.

Her attention had all been focused on Sebastian and the way he made her feel. And oh, how he made her feel. That one kiss had blown everything with Rex out of the water—just more proof that she'd not made a good decision up front.

Climbing off the couch, she turned to face Sebastian. That was when she saw the uncertainty in his eyes, too. As if he was wondering if that would be it: one flash makeout session on the steps and then never again.

She stepped toward him again, pushed up on tiptoe and pressed her mouth softly to his, fighting the urge to turn the gentle kiss into something more. Forcing herself to step back, Maggie realized her hands still twisted into his T shirt, as if she could hold him to her. "We should look up that license plate."

His own hand came up to cover hers, reassuring. "Can you do that? I thought only law enforcement had that ability."

She tipped her head. "Maybe. But at this point it's worth a try. We might not get a reverse search on the plate, but you know as good as anybody, that there's a lot on the internet."

She headed toward the back of the house, "I'm grabbing my laptop." And she heard Sebastian head up the stairs, presumably to get his. Settling in at the dinner table, she realized she was out of sorts in her running shorts and T shirt, with her computer at her overly formal antique dining set.

But she needed to work more than she needed to change out

of her house cleaning clothes. So she was already punching buttons as Sebastian powered up his own laptop next to her.

He was so close and he smelled of some kind of deep aftershave. She wanted to be doing a lot of other things with him besides internet research, but here she was. Maggie pulled out her phone and checked the picture she'd taken. Then she matched it against Sebastian's text. And, confident that they had the same number, she started typing.

First, she looked for sites where she could input the plate itself.

"Well, shit," Sebastian said, as he looked over her shoulder. Her screen had popped up. Sure enough, the plate belonged to a silver sedan.

"Looks like a Toyota in this picture," she pointed at the screen. Her own hadn't been clear, it wasn't her best photographic effort.

"I think it was." He looked up as though trying to remember. "I was more concerned with memorizing the plate, though."

"Actual DMV records should be harder to come by," she said. Sure enough, it was difficult to get a picture of the owner or even a name as to who the car was registered to.

"What about the VIN?" Sebastian asked, and when she looked at him oddly he said "Vehicle ID number, if you can get that from the plate, you might get the owner or even the seller from the VIN, maybe even a list of recent repairs."

He was typing on his own keyboard, looking up similar information. But after fifteen minutes with no results, she asked, "What about arrests?"

The more she thought about it, the more she liked it. She snapped her fingers as she realized it could work. He was grinning at her enthusiasm, but she said, "Arrests are in the newspaper. They're public knowledge. If we search and we search for a silver Toyota sedan, then if he got pulled over in the car … we should be able to find a name!"

Thirty minutes later, though, she was still looking. Sebastian was typing in short bursts himself but hadn't had any eureka moments either. They sat side by side, punching keys, scrolling through screens of data, and occasionally swearing.

"What about Blue River Killer suspects?" Sebastian asked as he hit keys again. Five minutes later, he said, "Look at this," and turned his screen to face her. "What about this guy?"

Maggie frowned. The picture didn't mean anything to her. He was older, brown hair cut short, but clearly turning white. She hadn't thought about him being old, but if he'd been killing for twenty years, he would have had to start as a teenager to be any younger than she was. This was probably the right age range for him, she realized.

So she looked a little closer ... but then she read his name and her heart twisted as she realized she'd seen it before.

CHAPTER THIRTY-SEVEN

Maggie clicked buttons frantically on her own laptop, her elbow threatening to bump his but she didn't care. "Remember I told you I found something?"

Sebastian looked at her with trepidation in his eyes, as though he was growing more concerned. He was right to be concerned.

"I went through Abbie's records—the ones we photographed. They seemed incredibly incomplete though it's plausible that the boardinghouse was just never full. I don't know which it is."

Sebastian leaned back a little in the chair, now thinking, no longer hunched over his own keyboard. "I don't remember. I mean, I was a kid for a lot of it. I can ask my mom."

"That would be great!" Maggie's thoughts twisted. She hadn't even considered that some of the locals could be references. They would know a lot about Abbie's boarders and maybe help sort this out. But then she wondered if she could get to meet Sebastian's parents herself. She had, after all, just had her tongue down the man's throat. The two of them had confessed that they were interested in each other, but ... where would that lead?

Unfortunately, right now, there seemed to be a killer associated with her house, which was definitely the more pressing issue. She waited a moment, while Sebastian went through the pleasantries with his mom. It warmed Maggie's heart that they talked with an easy camaraderie.

"Really?" he said, "Interesting. What years do you think it was most full?" He motioned to Maggie for paper and pencil. She pushed her notepad over toward him and he jotted down a few decades. Then he thanked his mom and hung up.

Setting his phone down, he rotated the pad around so she could read it upright. "This is when my mom remembers the place was hopping. Otherwise, she doesn't remember Sabbie keeping the place full. Sometimes she thought it was maybe just one or two people."

"And always men?" Maggie asked.

He nodded. "My mother always explained that it was an old-fashioned thing. There were boarding houses for men and boarding houses for women. But they were always run by women."

Maggie nodded. "So here's what I found when I looked earlier. This one particular man boarded here, repeatedly."

"He stayed a long time?"

"Overall, Yes. But he was in and out. He left for a while—months or even a few years—but he came back and boarded with her again. And he was always in the *same room*."

"Let me guess which one," Sebastian said wryly.

She nodded back, glad he didn't think she was silly. "He probably requested it."

This time she turned her laptop around to face him as she flipped through pictures and pointed to the ones that were important.

The third picture was one of Sabbie's crappy napkin rental agreements. "My guess is, by the time they signed this she felt she knew him, which is why they had this crappy rental arrangement."

"There's no name," Sebastian pointed out.

Maggie pointed to the photo of the napkin. "Right, nothing printed, but there are two signatures at the bottom. And this signature—" she pointed, then flipped to another image, "—matches the one over here." She flipped the screen again. "And this one back here."

She was having to remember where in the grouping each picture was. They weren't in chronological order, because Abbie's records hadn't been. Had she and Sebastian had time to go through them carefully, Maggie would have arranged them by date. When she had a chance, she'd duplicate the file and sort everything. Maybe it would reveal something else.

"The signature looks the same," she said, still pointing and popping through the images. "And the names on the first two are the same, as well. Merrit Geller—always in room number five."

Though she'd said it before, this time Sebastian frowned, and stared at her. "How would he always get the same room? Wouldn't he sometimes want it and someone would be in it?"

Maggie shrugged. "I didn't see any documentation where she moved somebody out of five for him. But if she occasionally ran at as low volume as the paperwork and as your mother suggests, Abbie might have been leaving that room open for him whenever possible."

"Which would indicate—" Sebastian offered, "that maybe she'd liked the guy ... At least professionally."

Maggie thought about it. What if Aunt Abbie had liked him more than professionally? She'd never married or had kids of her own, but to think that she'd never gotten involved with anyone would be ridiculous. It would be easy enough to have a romantic relationship with one of the boarders. No one would accuse her of having a man over when she wasn't married. They could keep it all hush-hush. And Maggie suspected that would have been necessary then. It would hurt her business to have an affair that people knew about.

Sebastian seemed to see what she was thinking. "If she was involved with him, he may have had special privileges."

Nodding along, Maggie flipped through the pictures again. "When we were photographing her records, I noticed a couple copies of a list of rules." She found one and pointed to the old mimeographed copy. "They had to be inside by eleven pm though. And they weren't able to leave before five in the morning. The Blue River murders are all estimated to have taken place late at night."

She was thinking out loud now. "Were all the men inside every night, did she check that?"

"Or—" Sebastian proposed, "did Sabbie just lock the doors at eleven? I mean, I've stayed at hostels before when I traveled. They had very similar rules, but they didn't corral you. If you weren't in by a certain time, you simply weren't allowed back in until they opened in the morning. It didn't mean you were always there."

"If someone was her favorite, he might have gotten a key."

Sebastian nodded along and Maggie didn't know if it worried him as much as it worried her that Aunt Abbie might have been involved with a killer. She'd loved her aunt fiercely. Even now, she missed Aunt Abbie more than anything, but—as she'd recently had the harsh lesson—other adults weren't the heroes they'd been held up as when she was a child. Even her parents hadn't come close.

It was looking more possible that her Aunt might have had some relationship with a murderer. The thoughts were turning in Maggie's head and she didn't like any of them.

Whoever had broken into her house had left no trace of a break in, even though she was certain she'd locked the doors. The police had assumed she was mistaken. Now Maggie was more confident that Aunt Abbie likely hadn't reclaimed all the keys. It had been stupid of her to move in here without remedying that immediately. Once again she'd been trusting and look what she'd gotten.

"Sebastian, I need to get the locks changed as soon as possible."

The dawning expression in his eyes indicated he'd put together the same problem she had.

He picked up his phone and was talking to someone in just a few seconds about getting her locks changed out. While he lifted that weight off her shoulders her thoughts tumbled randomly.

Was Merrit Geller the Blue River Killer? Or was he the La Vista Rapist? Or was he just a random boarder Abbie liked?

When a knock came at the front door, Maggie turned to look at Sebastian, but he was still on the phone. Craning her neck to see out the front window, she realized whoever was at the door was close enough she couldn't see them.

But in her driveway sat a police car.

CHAPTER THIRTY-EIGHT

Sebastian trailed Maggie to the front door. He, too, had seen the police car but not the officer.

It didn't surprise him though that Maggie opened the door and Marina Balero stood there. It did surprise him that she was alone.

"Officer Balero," Maggie said, and Sebastian could hear the question in her voice.

"Marina, please," she corrected, looking between the two of them, and offering Sebastian a "Hello … This is a bit of a personal visit."

Marina looked wary as though the two of them might turn her in for showing up on Maggie's doorstep.

But Maggie was generous with her wide smile and open gesture. Despite the wild kiss, Maggie didn't seem to have any issues with the officer being his ex. That shouldn't make him like Maggie even more than he did, but it did.

"Come in," Maggie led them all into the living room.

The arched passage into the dining room revealed the laptops set up on the table. If Marina had looked in the front window, it would have been obvious what the two of them were doing. Instead, the officer, still in her uniform, sat on the couch. Her hands twisted in front of her.

Definitely not an official visit, Sebastian thought. "What's going on, Marina?"

She took a breath and opened her mouth as if to speak. But she looked between the two of them to gauge the situation first. She must have found it acceptable, because she said, "There have been updates and I don't think the Feds or the department has been sharing them with you two ...?"

Sebastian turned to look at Maggie and found her looking back at him, one eyebrow up, confirming Marina's suspicions. "We haven't gotten anything."

"That's what I was afraid of."

"What's going on?" Maggie asked.

"The FBI has been hard at work. So that's really good news," Marina said it as though she needed to couch what she was going to say next. "They've been going back and re-interviewing victims. Re-examining the crime scenes and cross-checking dates. Everything is getting reopened now that the two cases are intertwined."

"What have they decided about that?"

"Everything and nothing. I wish I had something substantial, but I don't. The jewelry you gave them seems to say that the two are working together—"

"So they've confirmed there are two separate perpetrators?" Sebastian interrupted.

"That's the working theory. But, no, it's not fully confirmed." Marina answered.

It was the same conclusion he and Maggie had come to. So it didn't surprise him, but Maggie had more questions.

"What about DNA and evidence, wouldn't that indicate that it was two separate people? I mean, if they found the same evidence at the scene, they would have linked the two before this ..."

"Right, but if the two of them are working together, they may be primary or secondary on certain things. So yes, there are two people involved, but we don't fully know that the crimes are as separated as we originally thought. In fact, the discovery of the trophy hoard is clearly evidence that it's not."

Though they were both nodding along, Sebastian hated that it meant they still didn't have enough information.

Marina kept talking. "And when they look at the patterns and the dates, the overlaps in time now provide new information."

Sebastian looked to Maggie again and found her frowning at him, but Marina plowed ahead.

"The big concern is whether one or the other lived here at the boardinghouse for any extended period of time. The other possibility as that they were both in contact with a third person who was keeping the jewelry for them."

Now Marina turned to Maggie, her expression pleading. "I hate to tell you this, but they're going to be investigating your aunt."

"I figured as much," Maggie said. Though her tone was resigned, Sebastian saw that Marina looked relieved. "I mean, these things were found in her home. And she was the one who accepted or rejected the borders. Innocent or not, she was involved."

Though Maggie's voice was steady, Sebastian could hear the pain underneath. It was hard to lose your childhood heroes, or even to think that they might have made a mistake. Something told him there was even more at stake for Maggie though ...

"There are also some updates on the silver sedan," Marina told them. "I don't think anyone gave you those either."

"What updates?" Sebastian was curious now, not just confirming Marina's suspicions. The officers should have been watching the house, much the way he and Maggie were. But he'd been the only one chasing the car that had peeled out. And, if the officers had managed to tail the guy, why did he keep coming back?

"So the thing about the silver sedan," Marina told them, "is that we don't know that it's this perpetrator's car. Even if it is, we don't know if it's the same car they've had for years. However, there was a silver sedan mentioned in recent witness interviews in the case of the La Vista Rapist."

Sebastian turned to look at Maggie, stunned and furious. *Were the officers leaving the La Vista Rapist sitting outside Maggie's door?* He tried to ask a calm reasonable question. "Did they have it narrowed down to make or model or anything else?"

Marina shook her head. "Just 'silver sedan,' and it's only been associated with recent cases. So we're probably looking for someone who purchased a silver sedan between two and four years ago."

Sebastian was trying to figure out how they'd come up with that time.

It was Maggie who explained. "There was a two-year gap in the cases. They wondered if he'd moved away or quit." Then she looked back to Marina. "I'm assuming they're looking into reasons why he might not have attacked in the intervening years."

"Yes, and also why victims might not have come forward. It's entirely possible he was fully operational and no one reported it."

Sebastian nodded, he did understand that one. He was sympathetic to both sides.

"In the meantime, I thought you should be alerted to what we now know, so that you can stay safe." Marina pulled out her phone. "They have these suspects."

But first, she glared at the two of them, making sure she had their attention. "You can't do anything or hunt anyone down, because they're just suspects right now. The police haven't released this information and they didn't decide to give it to you. I did. If you do anything, it will blow back on all of us."

She glared again, then softened. "But given what you've seen and heard, I'm concerned that they might be coming back for their *trophies*—" the word came out on a choke, "I want you to stay safe."

She motioned with the phone, finally holding up the photo on the small screen. "Have you seen this man?"

Sebastian gave it a thorough look before turning to Maggie. She shook her head first, then Sebastian did, too. That neither of them had seen the suspect was concerning.

He added, "I can't be sure. I wasn't looking for *him*, and I didn't know what I *was* supposed to be looking for."

Marina nodded and lowered the phone. Sebastian thought she was putting it away, but instead she flipped to a second picture and held the phone up with another face he didn't recognize. Again, he shook his head. Maggie did the same. But the third photo she held up was Merrit Geller.

CHAPTER THIRTY-NINE

Maggie laid in bed staring at the ceiling. She was exhausted.

The information from Marina had been overwhelming.

It had been shocking to see the face of Merrit Geller on Marina's phone, but also comforting. They were on the right track.

When Maggie had excitedly shared what she'd already learned, they'd found out that another of the photos produced a name that had been in Aunt Abbie's rental records as well.

As the FBI had taken the records, Marina had not been privy to that information, but the three of them managed to put it together. As excited as they were, Marina was disappointed in the FBI. "They really need to be sharing this with you!"

Though Maggie and Sebastian had agreed, it didn't change anything.

Taking a deep breath, Maggie stared at the old plaster of the ceiling. It had been painted in 3D swirls with some odd brush. And she should have been falling asleep, but her brain turned next to Sebastian.

The locks he'd ordered arrived almost as soon as Marina

left. But it had been growing dark. So, while she owned new locks and doorknobs, she figured they wouldn't get installed until the next day.

Sebastian, however, insisted that she not go another night with doors that a killer might have a key to.

Maggie's brain rolled over. *Probably*. The killer only *probably* had the key to her home. But that was too much.

They had been only partway through the first installation—which, of course, had taken longer than expected—when Kalan called Sebastian. Though the other firefighter had originally been inviting Sebastian out for drinks, the invite was quickly turned the other way and within twenty minutes Kalan and two other A-shift guys were on Maggie's doorstep and ready to help.

Kalan had been shocked. "How many doors does this place have?"

Maggie would have laughed if it hadn't been going dark and she hadn't been learning how to install new locks on the fly. "Four external doors!"

"Whoa," Kalan had been shocked. "Obviously front and back ..."

He pointed from where he stood to where Luke Hernandez and Ronan Kelly were installing the one on the back door. The front and back doors were almost perfectly aligned at either end of the hallway running almost through the center of the house.

"But there's also one from the laundry room," Maggie told him. It discreetly let people out onto the back porch. "And there's a side door. I think one of the downstairs rooms was intended to be a den or an office and it opens to the side of the porch."

The front porch wrapped partly around the side of the house, and the back porch spanned the entire width of the place. Though they didn't meet up in a full circle, she still had a stunning quantity of inside and outside access.

"What is this part, Kalan?" Ronan called out from the back door.

"Why are you asking me?" the big man almost hollered it back, but his voice carried easily.

"Because, we figured you've been installing these things since you were three!" Luke almost cackled and they all laughed at a joke Maggie didn't get.

Kalan rolled his eyes. "While I have been installing locks since I was seven, it wasn't full doorknobs like this."

Maggie couldn't help asking. It was too much mystery to leave alone, and she couldn't stand to be on the outside of a joke. "Why do they think you should do this? And why were you installing locks at age seven?"

"I had two younger sisters and a single mother in grad school ... in Chicago. I got really handy at a really young age."

She could feel her eyebrows climbing. That was not the answer she'd expected. She'd just assumed he was from around here. So she asked what she hoped was a good question. "What was she in grad school for?"

"Her MBA." The pride in his voice said everything and Maggie smiled back at him.

As they wrapped up the installations on the first two doors, Maggie put her hand to her head and swore. "I have *five* external doors. I forgot about the upstairs balcony door!"

Her aunt's office had a balcony that opened over the porch in the back. She didn't use it much ... or ever. So she'd forgotten. But it did provide access into the house and it was keyed to the old locks.

The five of them began talking over each other, trying to decide what to do. Sebastian hadn't even bought a new lock for that door, because she'd forgotten it. She was apologizing and the men were debating.

"No one *should* be able to get up there, right?" Ronan asked her.

"They'd have to climb the posts to do it, yes. But if anyone did, the lock would be easily opened with the old key," she told him.

"If your prowler used to live here, he might know about the door and even an easy way up to it," Luke pointed out.

Even now, lying in bed with five new locks, it scared her to think that someone else knew other ways into her home ...

They didn't want to leave it. So Ronan had run to the store to get another kit and it made another hour of work. So she'd bought everyone pizza.

Sebastian had asked for a substitute for his shift the next day. Maggie had told him not to—she had new locks after all—but she'd still been grateful when he refused.

He was here. Across the hall.

Was he finally someone she could count on?

Rex hadn't betrayed her like Ryan and Celeste had. He hadn't ruined her memories like her father insisting that a little betrayal didn't really hurt a marriage. Aunt Abbie had remained a shining beacon in Maggie's memory when everything else had fallen apart. Maybe that was why moving to Redemption and moving into Abbie's home had seemed so appealing at the time. But even here, Rex had used her. She didn't have real friends, not yet. But would she ever fit in?

Aside from the man across the hallway, she was alone, and it was a stunningly sobering thought.

Though she pushed that awful thought away, her mind turned to the chaste kiss goodnight in the hall. She'd been shy again, not knowing what he expected or what might make their budding relationship blow up in her face.

Though the touch of his mouth to hers had rocked her world again, they'd gone through separate doors. At the time, Maggie had stupidly believed she would fall asleep as soon as her head hit the pillow.

Now, she'd been staring at the ceiling and the temptation to cross the hallway and see if Sebastian was awake was getting stronger. But there was no way to sneak through this house, so she stayed put. Besides, Sebastian had been tired, she didn't want to wake him.

Would she be going to him because she wanted *him*? Or would it just be so she wasn't so alone?

Maggie wanted to believe she was better than that, but her whole world had blown apart by her own inability to see others for who they really were. And now she was here, and it had been several months and nothing was really fixed.

She didn't know how much longer she lay there, wide awake and trying to ignore the sad and awful thoughts in her brain before she heard the door open across the hallway.

It was clearly Sebastian. She listened intently as his footsteps wandered down the front steps. And after that she lost track of where he went. Possibly the kitchen, maybe getting a glass of milk or something.

She waited for him to come back and it didn't take long before she heard him padding softly through the living room.

It wasn't a conscious decision, but when he hit the bottom of the stairs, she was waiting at the top.

CHAPTER FORTY

She watched as Sebastian paused at the bottom of the steps. His gaze slowly lifted and even in the dim light she could see the heat there.

Then again, she was wearing yet another stupid nightshirt—this one had Bugs Bunny on it—and maybe he could see up it from where he stood. She'd worn it specifically to keep herself from crossing the hallway and seducing him. Surely, she couldn't tempt a man in a Loony Toons nightshirt? But the look in his eyes said she could.

Slowly, he began climbing the stairs. He was wearing only plaid pajama pants and everything she'd wanted to see and touch before was on display. Well, not *everything*. The steps squeaked, protesting as he put weight on them, and the sound itself was suddenly sexy.

When he finally stood one step below her, and almost on eye level, she swallowed. Was she really going to do this?

Yes. She was.

Sebastian was the man she'd wanted for some time. He was flesh and blood standing in front of her, wanting her. The blaze in his eyes left no doubt of that.

She might be wrong, and they might fizzle and burn out, or he might rip her heart out of her ribcage, but it had been so long since she'd found a man who got better the more she got to know him. So long since someone could set her on fire just by looking at her. And she'd never felt this bone deep connection—this *rightness*—with anyone.

Sebastian didn't move. It took a moment to realize that he wasn't going to. No matter what he wanted, he wasn't going to push her, and damn if that didn't make her heat up even more.

Leaning forward, she kissed him. Softly at first, she nibbled at the edges of his mouth. Slowly placed her hands onto his warm biceps and held him there. She traced his jaw with little flicks of her tongue and felt his shoulders move as he groaned softly.

"You're killing me, Maggie."

"Why?" She whispered the word against his lips, then followed one carved cheekbone to his temple

"Because I want you ... so much. But—" He sighed again as she reached his ear and gently closed her teeth over the lobe.

"But what?" She felt him shiver at the soft touch of her breath on his skin.

"But I don't want to push you. It's so hard to resist. I don't want to ..."

She pulled back, her soft-focus world suddenly becoming crystal clear. "Are you going to think less of me if we do this?"

Some guys did. Clearly, Ryan had only liked chasing her. Being faithful hadn't been a priority.

"God, no. I'm afraid you'll regret moving too fast." Knowing that she had pulled back, he did the same. His eyes were clear in the dim light, a sheen that revealed he was looking over her shoulder. "I want more for us than a quick fuck, though I'm sure that would be amazing. So I don't want to push or move too fast. I can wait."

Maggie couldn't fight her smile. "I have wanted you for some time. It's not too fast for me, so you can stop resisting if that's really the problem." He was starting to smile now, the slow grin tugging at her heart. This man just got to all her parts. "But if you need to wait—"

She didn't get to finish the sentence because she yelped as he lifted her off her feet. Warm arms swept her legs up as he moved up the last stair. She was halfway to his door before she thought to be grateful that he hadn't chucked her over his shoulder in a fireman's carry. Her arms were already around his neck and she was pressing soft kisses to his shoulder as he carefully maneuvered through the slim doorway into his room.

"You are killing me," he whispered as he tried to carefully lay her down on the bed. But Maggie was holding on, her arms still twined around his neck, pulling him down with her.

With the bed supporting her, she traced one bare leg up his thigh, already regretting that he still wore his pajama pants. He groaned again, a musical sound of surrender, as he joined her, his full body pressed against her. There was no mistaking how much he wanted her.

He kissed her now, full on and heady, his mouth ravishing hers. Sebastian didn't hold anything back. They moved together as he lined himself up to stroke against her. He could have been inside her if not for her underwear and the stupid pajama pants. Those pants had been damn sexy just a while ago, now she hated them and wanted them off. She wanted to see Sebastian in all his naked glory.

But she didn't reach to pull them off of him. Her back arched with the feeling of him hitting the sweet spot. It was her turn to gasp out a noise between kisses. She was clinging to his shoulders, holding on for dear life and feeling the heat of his touch expand beyond where their skin made contact.

"Do that again," he told her. "Make that noise for me."

"Then move that way aga—"

He did.

She did, and she would have glared at him for grinning at her, but it felt so good and he did it again.

"I want you inside me."

"I want to go slow." He drew out the words as though he wanted to savor every touch, every kiss, every sensation.

"Me, too. We can go slow next time." There had damn well better be a next time, and another time after that. If this was what he did to her with his clothes still on …

Her words stoked the fire in him, and his hands moved. He slid one arm behind her to lift her and hold her in the right place. The other felt her skin, open palmed, moving softly from her knee up to the sensitive underside of her breast. Her hips rolled in response and he brushed his thumb over her nipple. The burst of desire only made her think he was still going too slow.

He did it again, and again, until she was moaning and pressing into his touch. Her hands finally found the drawstring on his pants and yanked until it came loose. Maggie traced that fine ass with her fingertips and pulled him closer, but he still wasn't close enough.

She wanted him enough that she wondered what she might blurt out. But she was far enough gone not to care.

He pulled the nightshirt up, his eyes following the edge of the fabric as it revealed more of her skin. She would have been self-conscious, but the heat in his gaze never wavered. He wanted her. It rolled off him in waves, and Maggie was willingly getting pulled under.

Just let it last …

Sebastian pulled back, giving her a moment of panic, but then his mouth found the spot beside her belly button and he pressed a soft kiss there. Her breasts lifted at the shock and she couldn't fight the small noises she made as his kisses slowly trailed up her body.

Her head rolled to one side, her limbs limp under the

onslaught of sensation. As her ear pressed into the mattress, sound magnified.

Maggie went still. *Had she heard something?*

Sensing the change in her reaction, Sebastian pulled back. He was clearly worried that something was wrong, and he was opening his mouth probably to ask, when they both heard it.

Sebastian found words before she did.

"That sounded like a door opening."

CHAPTER FORTY-ONE

Sebastian jolted, moving backwards off the bed, suddenly on high alert.

Was someone in the house?

They had changed every lock. Only he and Maggie had the keys—unless this was another firefighter? But that would mean someone had managed to duplicate the keys this evening while they installed the new locks. That didn't make any sense. Besides, Sebastian trusted the guys.

Though he knew he should be scared or alarmed, he was only angry as fuck.

Maggie scrambled up right, and he watched as she pulled her night shirt down, covering her gorgeous naked breasts and ending what should have been the singular most spectacular night of his life.

He yanked at the ties on his pajama pants, hastily making sure his pants stayed up, and jerked open the nightstand drawer. He should have been reaching for a condom, instead he was pulling out a nine-millimeter.

Maggie's eyes went wide. *Shit.*

He should have told her. Bringing a gun into someone else's

home was not acceptable without permission. But he'd brought it the other day, and things had just been busy. It was too late to do the right thing now.

As his hands automatically went through the motions of feeding the magazine into the butt of the gun and racking the slide, he looked her in the eyes and prayed she wouldn't be upset. "I should have told you I had it. I meant to, but ..." there was really no excuse, so he didn't offer one. "I have a concealed carry permit. I'm trained. And I'm not letting anyone get to you."

Hell, he should have gotten the gun sooner. He should have gotten two of them, and taught Maggie how to use it—if she wasn't already trained. There was a damn serial rapist *and* a serial killer associated with this house. But he could admit it still wasn't his decision to make. It wasn't his house.

He watched as Maggie seemed to decide it was a conversation for another time and bolted off the bed. As she ran into the other room, he shoved his feet into sneakers, trying to be as quiet as possible.

He could hear the invader moving around downstairs. Though Sebastian still hadn't yet figured out how that person had gotten inside the house, it was clear from the noises that he'd gained access relatively easily. Sebastian hadn't heard any glass break or locks give way ... then again, he'd been *occupied*.

Maggie appeared in her doorway as Sebastian stepped into the hall, her own feet shoved into winter boots. She'd zipped them up and looked disturbingly sexy with the fuzz that peeked at the top around her calves. In her hands, she held the Louisville Slugger and her phone. "Should we call 9-1-1?"

"If someone is here, yes." They began creeping down the stairs. Though Sebastian was in front he was pretty certain she had pressed 9-1-1 and was ready to send the call through if the noise was real.

Though they tried to move slowly and softly, the creak of

the old wood slats gave them away. At the first loud sound they made, the noise downstairs paused.

Then they heard the sound of someone scrambling away.

The sound of a door slamming into the wall echoed up the steps and Sebastian knew then—there was no mistaking it. This wasn't his imagination and it wasn't paranoia and he wasn't going to be able to sneak up on it.

Bolting down the stairs now, all semblance of attempting to be quiet gone—he held the newel post and swung around the bottom step. His eyes spotted movement and he caught a glimpse of the intruder disappearing through a door on his right at the end of the hallway. He could only hope Maggie had pressed the button and put the call through.

The old house was designed for a life before air conditioning. So, the bottom floor had a circular layout. Which sucked, because it meant until Sebastian trapped the man in a room, the intruder could always get away simply by running the opposite direction.

Maggie was right behind him, the two of them giving chase.

Sebastian sprinted across the back room, an old sitting room that spanned the length of the back porch and connected through to the laundry. Whoever this person was, they knew Maggie's house.

As he saw the laundry room door swing shut, he skidded to a stop, barely missing having the door crack his face. But his hand was on the knob and he threw it open and came to another screeching halt. There was a gaping hole in the middle of the floor.

A trap door had been thrown open.

"Holy shit!" Maggie exclaimed from behind him.

Though he wanted to look over his shoulder and check on her, she sounded fine. The old throw rug had been shoved out of the way, and the door was left open. "Did you know about this?"

"No," she answered harshly, "or I would have damn well locked it." He realized it had been a stupid question.

There was a cellar under the house. When the house was built, laundry machines were not an issue. This room connected into the kitchen and it made perfect sense to have cellar access here. It must have been converted later when they didn't need a place to store root vegetables but did need access for laundry.

Sebastian was about ready to jump down onto the old rickety wooden stairs and follow the perpetrator down into the dark. But as he moved forward, Maggie put a hand on his shoulder, holding him back.

"Wait!" She held a finger to her lips. "Listen." She pointed toward her feet.

Sebastian heard the noises under the floor and understood then. The house was built on a raised foundation, outside, there would be a small doorway that likely lead into the cellar. Whoever had entered had known about a trapdoor that Maggie hadn't.

Lord, the house itself was a puzzling conundrum of doorways and entries. *Would they ever be able to find and seal them all?*

Maggie pointed toward his gun and then down toward the sounds.

"You want me to shoot through the floor?" He tried to keep his voice low.

"Why not?" she responded. "I can repair my floor. We can't repair the lives these men have destroyed."

She was right, and it was her call. Before she was done with the sentence, Sebastian had fired three shots. He wasn't sure he'd hit anything, but they made the noise beneath the house begin to scramble even more frantically.

Doing their best to follow a perpetrator they couldn't see, Sebastian tried to aim to follow the sounds. But again, Maggie stepped forward and put a hand on his chest, holding him back.

"We don't know he doesn't have a gun, either. What if he shoots up?"

Sebastian held his arm out across her waist as though that would do anything, but together they backed away from the center of the room. Then they heard another noise near the edge of the porch.

He bolted toward the door and watched through the window as someone scrambled out from the crawlspace entry door. Cloaked in shadows, the man began fleeing across the backyard.

Sebastian flipped the bolts on the locks that had barely been in place for five hours. They were supposed to keep Maggie safe and instead they were holding him back.

As he threw the door wide, he heard Maggie right behind him as he began to give chase.

Turning around, he said, "Stay here, please."

But he wasn't surprised when Maggie shook her head no. "There's a rapist and a serial killer on the loose and you want me to stay in the house that they both know how to get into better than I do?"

Well, damn. When she put it that way ...

Reaching back, he grabbed her hand. Together they bolted across the backyard, through the now swinging gate, and into the woods.

CHAPTER FORTY-TWO

Maggie shook Sebastian's hand off as he would likely need both of them and she wanted her hands firmly choked up on her baseball bat.

It was also easier to run without holding on to someone else. But it was difficult to keep up with Sebastian.

He was already through the gate, but she was managing to stay close, glad she had zipped her comfy winter boots. She must look like a fool, racing into the woods, in only her night shirt and a pair of white boots with fluff.

Sebastian stopped at the turn, listening, and Maggie managed to pull up just short of smacking into him. But even as she got her feet under her, Sebastian was already pointing to the right.

She could see and hear someone up ahead crashing down the trail. Maggie and Sebastian gave chase. She wondered if Sebastian would just lift his gun and shoot, but as a lawyer she knew enough to know the shooter was responsible once the bullet left the barrel. If he hit a home or something else, it could cost him a lifetime in jail. Even if he shot the person running away, if that person wasn't the La Vista Rapist or the Blue River

Killer that would also spell massive legal troubles. Sebastian was keeping the gun down at his side, ready, but not aimed.

Smart.

The toe of her boot caught on a tree root, and she almost went sprawling but managed to catch herself and stay upright.

"Are you okay?" Sebastian turned and looked over his shoulder, ready to help her.

"I'm fine. Go!" she nearly yelled it. She wanted this guy caught. Whether or not he was one of the predators, this asshole had broken into her home. He'd known a way to get into her home even after all of the locks had been changed, and she was furious.

They chased their prowler all the way along the path, only pausing at the fork when they couldn't see him anymore.

They stood still, listening carefully. Maggie was grateful that the night was as warm as it was, otherwise she'd be shivering. She pointed to the short path to her left, wondering if she'd been correct before about the dock being a good escape point.

Sebastian shrugged as if to say they were already out running through the woods in the middle of the night in their pajamas, why not take one more chance?

Sure enough, as they reached the end of the path and cleared the woods, both of them fought to not skid down on the sloping ground.

He'd been here. The dock was still bouncing from the force of running feet. A smooth trail marked the water where a boat had been tied to the dock and very recently motored away.

Maggie held her hand up for Sebastian to be silent. Just barely—over the sound of her own heavy breathing—she could hear an engine. The trail in the water led to a small wake that led out the tiny alcove and off toward the left. Toward Lincoln.

"Son of a bitch!" Sebastian swore. Though he clenched his left fist, his right hand held the gun at his side and didn't move. He was right: he was well trained with that gun.

Maggie reached up, grabbed his fist, and unclenched it with her own fingers. Then slid her hand into his. Palm to palm, she felt her blood pressure drop just from touching him.

"We'll get him," she said, as though she and Sebastian were the only line of defense between an innocent world and a killer.

With a heavy sigh, he let go of her hand. For a moment, she paused, wondering if he didn't like the touch as much as she did. But then he reached up and threaded his fingers into her hair. Pulling her close, he kissed her with a force she hadn't expected.

When the torrent was over, once she understood that it wasn't that he didn't want to hold her hand, Sebastian rested his forehead against hers.

"I need you safe." He breathed the words out into the dark night air, then he added with a wry tone, "I want to continue what we started earlier."

Maggie kissed him back and whispered, "Me, too."

With another deep breath, Sebastian sighed to the sky and reached into his back pocket, producing his cell phone.

Maggie felt her eyebrows lift. She should have called 9-1-1. She'd been ready to but she'd … set her phone down back at the house? She didn't remember now, the shock of it all punching holes in her memory.

Sebastian began dialing.

CHAPTER FORTY-THREE

aggie stood in her backyard, still in her Bugs Bunny night shirt and her winter boots. But now she was also wearing a thin foil blanket that Marina Balero had brought her. The officer had given Sebastian one as well, and Maggie could admit it looked much better on him than her.

She clenched a cup of truly terrible coffee in her hands, also brought to her by the officer. Balero had made sure they were warm, but that wasn't the problem. The problem was that Maggie wasn't allowed inside her own home and it was lit up like a beacon as police officers combed the building, collecting evidence.

The neighbors had come out to watch despite the fact that it was now going on three am. But how could they not? The noise of police cars arriving, sirens blaring, in the middle of the night must have woken them. Then the officers racing through the yard and into the woods to meet the firefighter and the lawyer in their pajamas had to have been a show worth watching.

They'd had their statements taken right there in their foil blankets in the back yard for all to see. Sebastian had been smart enough to take a picture while the trail still showed on the water and he'd showed that to the police detective on the scene. Though anything the picture might have proven was slim at best.

They'd already been questioned by several other officers, both separately and together. But now another one—a young man that Maggie didn't recognize—approached them. "I'd like to ask you a few more questions."

Maggie nodded. She knew how this went. Different officers would have different priorities with the investigation—which was good, it got things covered—but it was a pain in the ass for witnesses. They also asked the same questions repeatedly, on purpose. It was a way to check for errors in the story, or things a witness might not remember clearly. Those things could change over time and with retellings.

Maggie took a sip of the coffee again and instantly regretted it. Now that it was getting cold, it was beyond terrible.

The officer went through the general information first. "What did the perpetrator look like?"

But neither of them could go beyond a general description of a person in shadow. Maggie couldn't even say for sure if it was a man or a woman. She was confident it was a man, and Sebastian believed that, too, but when she was asked why, she couldn't put her finger on anything.

Previously, they'd been asked about what they saw—about the things that could be used as eyewitness evidence in court. But this time, the officer took a different tack. "Do you have any idea why he might have come back?"

Maggie shrugged, but Sebastian offered, "The FBI was here just a handful of days ago. They obviously carted evidence out of the house, so I have no idea why anyone would have come back at all."

But Maggie thought maybe that was the issue. "Unless he didn't know that we found the jewelry at the back of the closet."

Looking up at Sebastian, she caught his understanding nod.

She wound up explaining to the officer who didn't seem to know about that particular find.

Interesting.

She would have thought the information of the closet stash would blaze through the station like wildfire. Maybe the FBI was trying to keep it secret, but she'd had an intruder in her home. If they couldn't keep her home safe, then she didn't care about their evidence.

She was going to give the police all of the information they asked for. "If they saw the FBI carting out documents and things, they might even think the jewelry was still under the floorboard. I don't know who has or hasn't heard about that ..." Maggie looked to Sebastian then to the officer.

Sebastian added, "Most of the firefighters at the station know about it. Maggie brought it to us before we realized what it was. And in fact, it was a group of us that figured out that we needed to hand it into the police."

The officer nodded, not offering information on whether this was news to him or not. His hands gripped the sides of his tablet and he focused on tapping out notes with his thumbs.

Maggie next explained about the stash at the back of the closet. "Both of these things were found in room five. The floorboard is still loose. The board in the back of the closet is still loose, but we closed all the doors before we went to bed ..." and there she'd done it. She'd just said "we went to bed." So that would be everywhere by morning. She tried to stay focused on the information. "If your people are in there now, and the door to five is open, and especially if that closet door is open, that would give you an idea what he was probably looking for."

They went on to explain again how they had changed the locks that evening. That they didn't know about the cellar access in the laundry room.

The officer raised an eyebrow.

"I inherited this home several months ago," Maggie told him, as if to defend herself. "I visited my aunt here during the summers as a child, and I cannot remember a time when that wasn't the laundry room, or when that old carpet wasn't there. If you look at the number of rooms this house has, you can understand why I would miss something like that."

Sebastian's arm came out around her shoulder and crinkled the foil as he pulled her close. No one liked being questioned. Maggie knew better than to get irritated. But she was.

"When will we be able to get back in the house?" Sebastian asked. And for the first time Maggie realized that if the officers looked upstairs, the bed she and Sebastian had been sharing would likely reveal what they'd been doing when they first heard the noise—and maybe why they hadn't caught on that someone was in the house sooner. She'd managed to skirt around it when questioned, but her clenched handprints were probably still pressed into the comforter.

Lovely.

"I don't know," the officer replied, tucking the tablet under his arm.

Sebastian was growing irritated now, too. "We're standing outside in our pajamas. We need to have access to our clothing. And we need to know when we'll be able to get back into the home."

He didn't demand that the officer produce the information, but he stated it in such a way that he brooked no opposition. Sure enough, the officer came back just a few minutes later and offered to lead them upstairs so they could change.

When the two of them met in the hallway again, the officer was still standing there. Probably to make sure they didn't mess with any evidence, either on purpose or by accident.

No privacy for a quick kiss, Maggie thought, but Sebastian had no such concerns. He reached out and took her hand and told the officer "You have my phone number. I'm taking Maggie out for breakfast."

The relief that flooded her was welcome. She hadn't even realized the amount of stress she was carrying, so she told the officer, "You all are welcome to check the house in any way you need while we're gone. Please collect any evidence that helps. If you remove anything from the property, I'll be needing an itemized list."

Damn if she hadn't had to say that more than once recently.

They were heading out the front door, discussing whether to take Maggie's car or Sebastian's bike. It wasn't as if every neighbor hadn't already been awakened but revving the bike down the street at an ungodly hour would not make her a beloved neighbor.

They were opening the doors to her car, when Marina came out the front door excitedly looking for them. Maggie waited while the officer came in close and spoke in a low tone. "I figured you would want to know. We already pulled prints from the back knob, scanned them and sent them in. This is not by any means a real confirmation, but the tech on duty tonight owes me a favor."

Maggie was confused. *They could find something that fast?*

Marina continued. "It's just a preliminary visual scan—not official—but AFIS already matched the prints to those found at the scene of several attacks of the La Vista Rapist."

CHAPTER FORTY-FOUR

M aggie was about to pass out into a serious carb coma by the time Sebastian opened the door to his apartment for her.

The sky was only just starting to lighten, but he'd taken her to a twenty-four hour diner and fed her pancakes and bacon and hash browns. It was exactly what she'd needed. And what she needed now was sleep.

Though her brain was wondering what the police were doing at her home—and whether or not the FBI had arrived—her eyes popped wide as she entered from the landing into the living room. "Holy shit. This is ..."

She could hear the grin in his voice. "It's what?"

"I don't know. Gorgeous?" It was masculine but really inviting and it ... "It looks so comfortable. I'll just curl up on the couch, okay?"

The couch looked fluffy and soft, like it would hug her if she just rolled right into it. There was a matching throw tossed over one end. It looked casual but there was no way the colors all coordinated like that without some effort.

He was laughing full-out now. "I told you, my mother is an interior designer. I told her I'd take care of it myself ..."

"You did all this?" Maggie was in awe. He'd been more than helpful and offered a great eye for her work, but this was ...

He laughed again. "No. I *told* her I'd do it, but she showed up and *helped*."

"Well, it's amazing." She'd not expected a man who spent his days in dull yellow gear and red trucks to have a home that felt so soothing and welcoming. Still, she was exhausted.

"Come on." He didn't touch her but led her down the hall and opened a door. "This is my room. You can have it for yourself or ..."

"Oh, I wouldn't kick you out of your own bed ..." but she wanted to share it with him.

Taking her hand, he pulled her into the room and flipped the covers back. "Crawl in."

Maggie kicked off her shoes and peeled her jeans and didn't have the energy for anything more. Sebastian disappeared into the attached bathroom for a moment and she was almost asleep when he turned up at the foot of the bed wearing another pair of plaid pajama pants. "Mind if I join you?"

She held out her hand to him and by the time she was settled in the crook of his arm, she was mostly asleep.

It must have been hours later that she drifted slowly awake. It was light outside, but the blackout curtains made the room feel like night should. No alarm. Warm bed. Sheets that smelled like ... Sebastian. And it wasn't just the bed that was warm, it was the man next to her.

Her hand was splayed wide on his bare chest and as she realized what she wanted, her fingers curled involuntarily. Sebastian's hand came up over hers ... he wasn't asleep anymore either. His mouth found her temple and he pressed soft kisses there, turning her on and stealing rational thought. He whispered into her ear, "I want to finish what we started."

She must have hesitated. Was she fully awake? She was, but she was certainly pulled under by the heat of him, by her own desire, and by the feeling that she didn't just want him, she needed him.

"I've locked and bolted all the doors. The sliding door to the balcony has a brace and I checked it. No one knows we're here."

He was reassuring her they wouldn't get interrupted this time. Thank God.

Maggie pushed up on one elbow, draped herself across him and kissed him with everything she was worth. Her fingertips traced the muscles of his chest and she felt his groan of satisfaction more than she heard it.

She didn't last as the aggressor for long. He peeled her hand from his chest, lacing their fingers together, and using that point of contact to roll her over. He had her pinned, settled between her legs, long hard body pressed against hers and she didn't protest.

How had she lived so long without this?

She was reaching for the ties on his pants again, sliding her fingers inside. She wanted to go slow, to savor every touch, relish in every slide of his tongue along her skin. But she didn't have the patience. She grappled with the fabric, sliding it down his legs only with his help.

When he was kneeling on the bed, fully naked, he looked at her and said, "You are wearing entirely too many clothes."

She wasn't wearing pants or shoes. "It's less than I usually wear."

"Still too much."

Maggie was laughing as he quickly stripped her naked. But the sound of his breath catching made hers catch, too. She didn't know why he wanted her as much as he did, but she wasn't going to waste it.

Her breath caught, waiting, until his hands were touching her everywhere, turning her on more … if that were possible.

She traced his jaw, the muscles in his arms and chest, wrapped her hand around the length of him, and stroked until he made her stop.

"Condom …" he practically gasped the word as he stretched out to reach into the nightstand drawer.

"I'm on the pill."

Instantly, he was back by her side. "Are you sure?"

"I offered." She was grinning at him, lifting up to kiss him, when she found herself suddenly flat on her back. His fingers stroked her until she gasped for more. Then as she begged for him, she felt the length of him at her entrance and the hot slide of him pushing home.

He was pulling back before she was ready. "More … please."

Those breathy sounds were hers, the groans of surrender his.

They moved together, straining to get closer until she was begging him to send her over the edge. Holding himself up on one arm, he reached the other hand down until his thumb found her slick and wanting. He stroked her while pushing into her and on the third time, she screamed his name.

CHAPTER FORTY-FIVE

Sebastian sat nestled into the corner of his couch with Maggie settled between his legs, leaning back against his chest.

He held his tablet in front of them, his arms looping around her as though the couch were its own private island and she was safe in whatever small shelter he'd made.

He'd packed the tablet at the bottom of his bag when he'd hastily left Maggie's house. An officer with the Redemption PD had searched the bag and either not found the tablet or not worried about it. Since their laptops had spent the night on the dining room table, they were getting dusted for prints and neither of them had been able to bring their computers.

This was their only way, aside from their phones, to search for information on Merrit Geller now. Their first problem was that they weren't sure who the man they'd seen last night was. But it was one of the best leads they had.

That and William Sanders, one of the other pictures that Marina Balero had produced as a suspect. When Maggie said she thought she remembered that name from Sabbie's records, that doubled down their suspicions.

Marina had produced three photos. That two of the men not only had ties to the boarding house, but had been renters there made Sebastian wonder if maybe they had the names of the Blue River Killer and the La Vista Rapist and the only thing left was to gather enough evidence for arrests.

Not that anyone had arrested anyone yet. Both men were still free.

Everything was shit right now.

He and Maggie were staying in his apartment because her house was being searched once again. It was the middle of the afternoon, and they'd slept late because they'd been up all night, dealing with break ins, *once again*. Maggie was losing work and time and possibly her reputation around town, *once again*.

He was losing work. But he wasn't going to leave her alone and, frankly, Sebastian had never felt better.

Having Maggie here, being with her, and knowing that she felt the same way he did more than made up for all the rest of it.

She leaned back into him, even as she reached up to tap buttons on the screen of his tablet. Sleeping with her in his arms last night had felt amazing, but while he'd been finally falling asleep, doubt had crept in at the edges.

Was she just tired or did she not want him anymore? Was she with him because she needed someone to keep her safe, and he could do that? Was she one of those women who couldn't stand to be single and flitted from boyfriend to boyfriend?

He'd reminded himself that none of that sounded like the Maggie he knew. It sounded like his own fears talking. He'd slept on it, but when she'd woken up, she'd cleared all of that up for him.

They were together.

Officially, she'd said. And the idea of Maggie telling people that she was with him was plausibly the best present he'd ever gotten. There was something very, very right about the feeling of her in his arms, whether that was naked and making love or curled up on the couch right now.

Though he had no idea if she felt it as deeply as he did, he was willing to wait to find out. And he was willing to do everything in his power to make sure that even if she didn't feel that way now, she would in the future.

"William Sanders has a horrible name," Maggie told him.

He couldn't help but laugh at her proclamation. "At least *Merrit Geller* is kind of unique. It helps to find him. That's why they three-name them, you know."

"Three-name?"

"Yeah. Like John Wayne Gacy and Lee Harvey Oswald and Mark David Chapman. If they have common enough names, the media three-names them so they don't get confused for other, innocent people who are unlucky enough to have the same name."

"Interesting," Maggie said as she pushed his hands out of the way. Breaking the loop of his hold, she hopped off the couch and headed across the room to her purse. Her ass looked good in those jeans. He wanted so much more than this, but it was way too fast and there was too much up in the air right now. So he kept his mouth shut and his eyes on the back pockets of her jeans.

Within moments she was on the phone. "Hey, Marina. Tell me you've got a middle name for Sanders?... Ah, perfect. Thank you! What? Oh? Okay, thanks." The exchange sounded more like she was calling for clarification on a cake recipe than information on a possible serial killer.

"Treat." Maggie smiled as she turned back to Sebastian and then spelled it. "He's William Treat Sanders and he's currently living in Lincoln."

"Marina gave you all that?"

Though Maggie nodded. Her voice said the opposite. "Noooo … No, of course not."

Sebastian laughed again. Good for Marina. He owed her one —or several—for sharing sensitive information because it would help keep Maggie safe.

"Also, the Redemption PD didn't find any fingerprints on our laptops that weren't ours. Mine all over mine, yours on your keyboard, apparently a few of mine on your keyboard?" She scrunched up her face as though that was the oddest thing about it.

Sebastian didn't care that she'd reached over and typed a few things rather than spelling it out and waiting while he typed far more methodically than she did.

She climbed carefully back onto the couch and settled in the circle of his arms. But just as she leaned back against him, her phone rang again. Popping up, she muttered something about how she should have kept it on her. And this time as she answered, she had a far more professional tone.

Sebastian sat up straight, as he listened to just the one side of the conversation again. Maggie stood rigid, the tension in her shoulders visibly tightening with each thing she heard. He was on his feet and standing behind her in seconds, though he wasn't sure what he could possibly do.

"Yes," she said. "Thank you. Okay. Yes. Yes."

What he heard told him nothing and he hated being in the dark, but at last she hit the off button and turned to look at him. Her eyes were covered in a thin sheen but she wasn't crying.

"They've finished and the house is open. I get to go in now and clean out all the black fingerprint dust and try to put everything to rights again." She sounded resigned.

"*We* will," he told her. She was probably the only woman he was willing to go clean a house that large for. But in a burst of brilliance, he realized he probably wasn't the only one willing to help Maggie out.

First though, he had to call the chief. He needed another shift off. And he couldn't just trade with someone—he couldn't pick up extra shifts until this was over. The problem wasn't the day, it was leaving Maggie alone for twenty-four hours. "I need to make a call or two. Are you good for a few minutes?"

She nodded but didn't move. Cleaning the house was daunting, but it shouldn't make her that tense or give her that thousand yard stare ... He definitely needed to get his shift subbed out.

He was just hanging up when Maggie's phone buzzed again. This time it was a text, then another and another.

She was flipping through them, her frown pulling tighter and tighter. At last, she turned around and showed him her phone and the picture that had come through. "Look what the FBI found."

It was just a picture of fabric with pen circles on it, large and small. The pictures showed it in blue light and red, each revealing some other hidden stain. It took a moment to see that it was a pillowcase. But the look on Maggie's face told him this was about much more than just a piece of bedding ...

CHAPTER FORTY-SIX

Maggie walked across the room in a daze and dropped down onto Sebastian's couch. It was a good thing the piece was large and cushy or she would have hurt herself.

This time, when he sat next to her, he wasn't wrapped around her comforting her, instead he was clearly waiting to hear what she said. "What is it?"

She took a deep breath. "Remember the itemized list that I made the FBI give me when they took things out of the house as evidence?"

He nodded.

"There were weird things on it, but I didn't think anything of it because there were so many weird things. It seemed like they were taking anything that could possibly be evidence of anything."

"But the pillowcase is important?" he asked.

"They found it at the back of the top shelf in the closet in room five. We must have missed it but, according to the list of what they took, that's where they found it."

"Why would a pillowcase be up there?"

"Apparently the FBI wondered the same thing and they tested it. It had Aunt Abbie's saliva on it."

"What?" Sebastian frowned suddenly, seeming to go through the same thought process she initially had. "I mean I guess if you drooled a little while you were asleep?"

"That would make sense," Maggie conceded, but that wasn't what Marina had explained. "The thing is, Abbie was a stickler for clean laundry, and she didn't sleep in room five. Ever." Maggie needed a deep breath to go on and was glad that Sebastian was willing to wait. "It had someone else's saliva on it too."

She watched Sebastian's face fall as he began to put the pieces together. "They were sharing a bed?"

"That would make sense, except that the evidence was found on *opposite* sides of the pillowcase," Maggie told him, repeating the information.

Sebastian frowned again, not following. Marina had needed to explain what it likely meant to Maggie, and now she had to tell him.

She needed a deep breath. "It looks like it's the pillow that one of them slept on, and that it was held over the face of the other."

"I'm sorry, *what?*"

Maggie didn't answer. She couldn't. When she found her voice, she barely managed to get the words out. "They told me Aunt Abbie died in her sleep, but now they think she was murdered. Something about the way the DNA and evidence is on one side—like he slept on the pillow more than one night. And on the other side the skin cells and traces of lotion are rubbed in, like maybe she struggled..."

"They think she was murdered?"

Maggie nodded and began to cry in earnest then. "That's what it looks like now."

"What did the autopsy say?"

She shook her head against his chest, getting her tears on his t-shirt. She hadn't cried or broken down despite having her home broken into or finding serial killer trophies in her home. She'd even suspected Abbie of falling for a serial killer. But this? It was the last straw. And Maggie felt like shit for thinking poorly of Aunt Abbie just because everyone else around her seemed to have no morals. "There was no autopsy. She was in her 70s and, at the time, it looked like a relatively peaceful death."

He held her close with one arm, and murmured, "I'm so sorry."

She watched as he ran one hand through his hair. He'd requested today off and at the time she'd pressed him to go to work, but she was glad now that he wasn't leaving. Though she didn't know if he could truly afford the time off anymore, she trusted him to make his own decisions.

Her heart twisted and she swallowed hard at the thought that Abbie had been murdered. It was worse than anything she'd imagined before. Previously, the victims had been people she didn't know. But this was too close to home—it was literally *in her own home*. It seemed now, the only reason it was her home was *because* Abbie had been murdered.

Sebastian's arms went around her and held her tight. Only then did she realize she was sobbing. Maggie took a few minutes to get herself together then realized she didn't know what she should do next. Looking to Sebastian, she said, "I don't quite know what to do now. I'm not an investigator. I don't work for the FBI. I can't solve this case. But I want to!"

He stayed silent for a moment and it all poured out. "I need to find her killer. I ... I told you I thought she might have been sleeping with the killer and I ... I feel *so awful* for thinking that."

"It was a reasonable assumption."

"No, it wasn't! I only thought it because—" She cut herself

off. This was what happened when she cried. She tended to tell people what she really thought.

Sebastian waited a beat, then whispered, "You can tell me."

"You'll realize that I'm stupid."

He shifted rapidly, looked at her like she was ... well, stupid. "How would I ever think that? I see you moving to a new town, starting your own business. You're a lawyer, and a damn good one from what I've heard. We all lock our keys in our cars sometimes, Maggie."

She wanted to laugh, and just wound up snorting a little. "Yeah, did you think you should marry someone then find him fucking your best friend in your bed?"

Silence.

Yeah. She was stupid. Stupid for trusting Ryan and Celeste. And stupid for telling Sebastian just how stupid she was now.

"They what?" He didn't seem to believe her.

"Yeah. About a week before the wedding. I mean, that's when I walked in on them." She paused, and sniffed. Better to tell the whole thing now. "He said he still wanted to marry me—"

"He thought you'd be *okay* with that?" Sebastian shook his head as if to rid an awful thought.

"They both did. Said it was the first time and it was a whim. But I'd found her earring in our room before, and Celeste said she must have dropped it when she came over." Maggie heaved a breath. Hopefully, Sebastian didn't think she was as dumb as she felt for not realizing all of it sooner. "And even if it was the first time? That wasn't forgivable. So I lost my fiancé and my best friend in the span of ten seconds."

"That sucks—"

But she was on a roll. "And my father the next day when I started announcing that the wedding was canceled."

"Your father? Why?"

"Because he thought I should forgive Ryan. He said the

wedding was too expensive to cancel and that all marriages had some adultery in them."

"What!"

Shit. If Sebastian didn't cut things off because she was stupid, he'd do it because she was so messed up. But it was a little too late to take it back now. "So, I guess my parents' marriage wasn't the good one I thought it was."

"Your mom passed a while ago, right?"

Maggie nodded, but said, "When I was thirteen."

The space between them descended into silence. What else could he say? He was too decent a guy to tell her to just go home. She waited him out while he took a deep breath and finally spoke.

"That's why you came to Redemption?"

She nodded. She'd only ever said that she "needed a change." It wasn't a lie, but it was nowhere near the truth.

"I'm glad you told me," Sebastian said, hugging her now and letting her sink into the relief that he wasn't pushing her away. "That makes more sense now why you feel you have to be involved in this."

"It *is* happening inside my house," she pointed out.

"True. Let's go back." He stood up as if the decision was made. "You're the best one to know what was there all along and what wasn't. You were even there as a kid when some of the boarders lived there, right?"

"Yes!" Maggie thought about it suddenly—she'd not put those pieces together before. *The boarders.*

Abbie hadn't let her interact with the boarders much. When she was little, they'd seemed more like part of the house, the same way other guests did at a hotel. But maybe she could remember something, maybe she'd met this criminal before.

"We'll put the place back together and maybe we'll find something new. We'll make sure the FBI and the police have all of it."

"And we'll lock that damned cellar door," Maggie added fiercely, wondering what other entries to her home might exist that she didn't know about.

"We'll check everything." He said it as if he heard her worries out loud.

She'd expected to move to Redemption, open her business, and spend her spare time painting the house. She'd thought she would meet the townspeople and make friends with other women her age. She'd thought her biggest concern would be drumming up enough business.

Instead, she'd met the firefighters and taken over Aunt Abbie's volunteer position at the station. Some of the older firefighters had remembered her from when she was a kid, and it seemed a natural fit. She dated Rex and then spent so much time watching Hannah for him. Now she was hunting a killer. None of what she was doing had been on her agenda.

But then again, neither had Sebastian.

"Okay," she agreed. "I'm ready to go."

He grinned. "Well, I need a shirt and shoes. And why don't you give me a few minutes to pack a bag?"

Sebastian suggested they take his car, just so hers wouldn't be obvious in the driveway. Then he drove them through Freddy's, the local burger joint.

They arrived at her house with hands full of hot burgers and cups of skinny cut fries. Opening the front door, Maggie headed for the dining room, but quickly realized there was nowhere to eat or even sit. Every surface was dotted with black fingerprint powder, in a few places it was bright green.

The chairs were pulled into the corners of the room, two of them still upside down, and the table was skewed in the room. The living room was entirely rearranged, and Maggie didn't think that if she even found a space, eating near all the black dust could be safe, so they settled on the front steps, watching the kids go by on their bikes as they ate the burgers.

They watched a young woman walking two large dogs. Just behind her was a man with a dual stroller. When they finished, Maggie wadded up her trash and took Sebastian's from him.

"I'm going to make a few calls," he pointed to his phone but didn't get up.

Nodding at him, she pushed the door open with her elbow and headed inside. She couldn't help but survey the damage, but in the middle of the living room she spotted black dust along the mantle and on the bricks that lined the chimney.

She almost dropped the trash she held. *Why hadn't she remembered before?*

CHAPTER FORTY-SEVEN

When Sebastian finally came inside, he expected to find Maggie pushing the furniture back into place or cleaning the smudges the FBI left behind. Instead, he found her kneeling in front of the fireplace, pushing at the bricks. Her fingers were dirty where she'd smeared the fingerprint dust.

"What are you doing?"

"I didn't remember," she said, out of breath and almost frantic.

He tried to stay calm because she wasn't. "Is the chimney another entry point?"

At least that made her sit back onto her heel and laugh. Then she stilled and her voice became wary. "At least not that I know of."

He wasn't going to go there. "Then what did you remember?"

"Old houses have secrets." She said it almost cryptically.

She was right, but it didn't actually mean anything. It didn't tell him why she was on her knees, pushing at bricks already covered in spots of black dust, the fingerprints standing out as stark reminders of her home being invaded again … "I don't understand."

"Aunt Abbie told me that when the house was built, there were soldiers in this area and they liked to leave secret messages. She said every hearth had a loose brick."

Interesting. Maggie was looking for a hidey hole.

"Did Sabbie show you which one?"

"Of course not. That would be too easy." She was still on her knees, still examining the bricks for something he didn't see and then pushing on each one.

She waved her now blackened fingers in an arc around the open fireplace. "Looking at the fingerprints here, I can tell you that she told *him.*"

Sebastian felt his eyes fly wide open. This time, he looked past Maggie. There were distinct patterns to the collections of fingerprints. There were a handful above the mantle, where Maggie had set pictures and a mirror—all of which had been moved in the FBI search, so he couldn't tell what those prints meant now. There were some at the side of the opening to the fireplace. And still others clustered on one or several bricks in a few different spots. But right next to them, whole swaths of brick were clean, with no dust or prints at all.

"Holy shit, you're right." Whether or not it was here, Sebastian didn't know. "Step back with me."

He put his hand on her shoulder and in a fluid motion, Maggie rose to her feet. Taking a few steps back, they examined the whole fireplace with a new plan.

Sebastian watched as she almost wiped her fingers on her pants, but then managed to lace them together and keep the fingerprint powder off her clothes.

"Do you see a pattern to it?" he asked.

"I don't know. My guess is that he was looking for a singular brick that comes out if jiggled the right way."

She took a breath and said, "The problem is that I can't tell which prints are me touching the wall to close the fireplace, or the FBI moving the pictures, or someone trying to find a loose brick."

"So, we start with the ones that have a lot of fingerprints."

"There's a few clusters on the lower left, and most of them are on the upper right. It looks like he didn't remember which brick, but he knew where to look."

The two of them now dove into it together. They pushed and pried and tried to budge individual bricks. The fireplace had been painted white at some point. The question was, was it before or after whoever-he-was had hidden information there?

"How did the crime scene techs even find all these prints? Who would look at a fireplace for clues?" Maggie eventually asked.

At least this was something he could answer. "They probably didn't. They look everywhere using special lights. Then they dust and collect every print they find."

"I thought the technique lifted the print ... so why are they all still here?"

"The tape they use lifts the top layer of dust. They don't need the actual print—the oils left behind—unless they're after DNA. And these days, sometimes they just photograph it."

They were still pushing on bricks when he had a thought. "Do you have Sabbie's prints on file somewhere? Does the city?"

"Why?"

"Do you think maybe her fingerprints are still in the house? Maybe some of these are hers." Nostalgia struck him. The techs might have revealed traces of Maggie's aunt still here.

"Her prints are on the documents, probably, but not on the walls or anything." She motioned to the windows where more black powder covered the edge as though tiny little dark snowfalls had simply deposited around her house. "I had a professional cleaning company come through. They cleaned every nook and cranny. It was so expensive."

"This place is so big and so full of nooks and crannies," Sebastian mused. It was no modern home, where the walls could just be wiped down. There was wainscoting in the dining room and a chair rail and crown molding in every room. He couldn't imagine being responsible for keeping it clean. "It's beautiful. And Sabbie loved this place."

"Then why didn't she take better care of it?" Maggie asked. "She didn't fix a lot of what needed it. The roof is old, and the floors have to be refinished. That wallpaper should have been replaced about three decades ago …"

He heard the sigh in her voice, but he also remembered Sabbie. "She just loved it exactly as it was, at least that's how I understood it. I don't know, maybe she didn't have enough money."

But he guessed Maggie knew that and he probably shouldn't have said it. Sebastian tried again. "Despite wearing those old jeans that had completely lost their color and those workman shirts, I always got the impression she chose that cabbage rose wallpaper and the fancy antique sofa."

"It is funny. So many things about Abbie were just about comfort. She was one of the first adult women I knew who fully understood that she was pretty, but that wasn't her value. Right down to that she never married and she ran this boarding house."

Maggie seemed caught in her memories for a moment, then she cried out, "Oh shit. I found it!"

CHAPTER FORTY-EIGHT

M aggie felt the brick wiggle under her fingers. But it wasn't enough to pull it out.

Turning to Sebastian, she told him, "We need a chisel and a phone to document it."

She pushed at the brick again. Jeez, she was such a lawyer. Over her shoulder, she called back, "Abbie's toolbox is on the shelf in the laundry!"

Then again, he might already know. He probably knew her aunt better than she did. Maggie pushed that thought away as she continued to work at the brick with her bare fingers. But nothing happened.

When Sebastian returned, they began diligently snapping pictures, chipping at the paint, and trying to break it loose.

Sure enough, when it came out, it wasn't just a loose brick. It was a *half* brick, leaving a space behind it. Sebastian was already reaching in for the folded paper they could see when Maggie gently pushed his hand aside.

"Can't touch. There may be fingerprints or other evidence. Let's photograph it like it is." She sighed. "And we have to call the fucking FBI again."

The last thing she needed was more fingerprint dust and more investigation. But that seemed exactly like what she was going to get. Though her fingers were dirty, she scrolled through her contacts looking for Watson or Decker.

"Let's call Marina," Sebastian suggested softly. "Marina's much more likely to share information. So if it goes to her first … I think it's perfectly reasonable for two average citizens—" they were not, not now, but Maggie didn't argue it. "To call 9-1-1 rather than the local Bureau of Investigation."

"Smart."

Five minutes later, a knock came at the door. Expecting to find Marina Balero, Maggie swung the door open and was saying, "Wow, that was fast." But instead, she looked directly into a broad chest. When she allowed her eyes to move upward, past the dark t shirt to the dark skin and broad smile, she found her friend.

"Kalan!" she exclaimed as she spotted Luke, Rex, Patrick Kelly, and his son Ronan standing behind him. Ronan was on A-shift, and the patriarch Patrick was an interim Captain. Two other Kelly sons were on units in Lincoln and Sacramento. Even in Nebraska there were Irish firefighter families. She loved them all.

"You found a sitter?" she asked Rex. It was a huge task for him to be here. Her eyes flitted from him to Sebastian, but there seemed to be no animosity.

"My first free day." He grinned at her.

And he was here? She saw Luke motion to a pile of supplies on the porch beside them. There was a janitorial mop and bucket, a box of various cleaning sprays, paper towels, shop cloths, and more.

"We're your cleaning crew." Patrick announced proudly.

Why? Her head whipped around to look at Sebastian.

"You volunteer for us," he said it as if it were no big deal. "So we volunteer for you."

She couldn't help it—happy tears rolled down her cheeks. The house was so big that even just the task of just putting the furniture back seemed daunting. She'd thought cleaning the fingerprint dust was going to take days ... except now it wouldn't.

She opened the door and five large men blew past her, carrying all their supplies with them.

"Holy crap," she whispered. These guys were no slouches either. The fire station and the engines shined. Their lives depended on the cleanliness and functionality of their trucks' instruments.

Though she was still in shock, Sebastian was not.

Apparently, he had called them. If she hadn't already been tumbling head over heels for him, she was now off the cliff for this guy. With no parachute. And she didn't care.

He'd taken charge, organizing them into pairs. Then he paused and asked Maggie what needed to be done first.

Before she answered, she caught his eye over the backs of their shoulders and mouthed the words, *Thank you.* His smile warmed her as much as if he was touching her.

"The kitchen needs to be first. We *need* the kitchen. If we can't cook and eat, we're in trouble. Next probably the dining room. The living room, then upstairs. Then my office," she said. There were so many rooms!

She was following them into the kitchen when another knock came at the front door. This time, when she opened it, she found detective Marina Balero.

It took a moment to organize everything that she and Sebastian had found. Then Maggie thought to tell the firefighters *not* to clean the living room yet. Not until further evidence was gathered.

The guys told her "no worries," and "just tell us where to work." Lord, she was buying them pizza and beer, or pasta dishes, or ... whatever they wanted.

After Marina took a preliminary look at the fireplace, she grabbed the comm on her shoulder and called in more officers. They set up another evidence gathering station, more pictures were taken. Maggie tried to both watch and clean. She couldn't just stand around and watch while the guys worked.

After pushing the couch and chairs back into their rightful spots, she headed to the dining room, where she could still see the fireplace. She moved the table back into place grateful that Abbie had been smart enough to put felt sliders on all the furniture.

Though Maggie kept one ear on the officers' conversation, her first priority was to flip the two upside down chairs. But as she bent over, she discovered there was not only writing but fingerprint dust on the undersides of the seats.

"Officer Balero?" she called out, curious now. "You took fingerprints from under the chair. Why is that important?"

"That's just it," Marina said as she headed over to see what Maggie was pointing at. "We don't know whose fingerprints they are when we find them. And we don't know what they'll mean, so we try to get everything we can."

"Were these useful?" Maggie pointed to the bottom of the chairs. Abbie had reupholstered these herself. Maggie had been a teenager at the time and Abbie had been so excited to show off the work. She'd found this fabric that she loved—which Maggie now realized didn't go with anything else in the house, but Abbie adored it.

Marina used a small flashlight to illuminate the pencil scratches. "It's dated."

Abbie was definitely a DIY kind of woman and, though she kept terrible records, she loved making scrapbooks and taking pictures. The year matched to Maggie's memory, but as she was getting ready to flip it back upright, she stopped.

"So are the fingerprints here from when it was reupholstered?" That would be ridiculous. *Wouldn't it?*

Marina flicked the light back and forth. The fingerprints became clear and easy to see, and even Maggie could see there were two sets of prints.

Marina tipped her head and continued scanning with the light. "Fingerprints can last forty or more years if they are undisturbed."

Maggie blinked, the smaller set of fingerprints was most liked Abbie's. Just like Sebastian suggested, something of her was still here. The other set looked larger, probably made by a man, though she knew better than to make that assumption.

"Have you ever reupholstered a chair?" Marina asked Maggie and Maggie shook her head.

"No, I just remember that I came back one year, and these were done. That year, actually." She pointed to the date.

"Well," Marina looked up at her, "Two people upholstered these chairs."

Once again, Maggie felt it like a blow and she realized something very important. Something that she wasn't yet ready to tell Marina Balero.

Instead, she nodded as though that was very interesting and went about setting the rooms to rights. She wondered what other surprises the fingerprints might reveal. But she was holding onto her secret for now.

CHAPTER FORTY-NINE

Sebastian probably groaned Maggie's name loud enough for the neighbors to hear. Just in case they hadn't missed the old bed creaking with every push and pull between them. Probably the FBI agents that were sitting out front casing the place now knew exactly what he and Maggie were doing.

He sighed with the release of being with her and realized he didn't care who knew.

He watched as Maggie's eyes rolled up, and her expression turned to pure ecstasy as he'd moved inside her. That was more than enough to make up for anything the neighbors might hear.

After a good handful of minutes of rough breathing to make up for the energy he'd spent, he curled his arms tighter around her and enjoyed the sensation of her curling into him too. There was no feeling quite like knowing Maggie wanted him.

He wondered if she was falling asleep when she said, "I have to tell you something."

His back stiffened. *That sounded more than a little bit ominous.*

He tried not to let his eyebrows pull together or his arms clench tighter around her. "What is it?"

"I asked Marina about the fingerprints on the bottom of the

chairs. There were clearly two different sets. She said it looked like two people had done the upholstering—which would mean the prints were old. She said they could last that long."

Sebastian appreciated that Maggie was more than willing to say this wasn't her field of expertise and willing to let Marina tell her how it had worked.

"So someone reupholstered the chairs years ago, and this is important?"

"I got on my phone and checked the contracts we photographed."

He didn't like the sound of that, but Maggie continued. Her body was tense in his arms, but there was nothing he could do but hold her.

"Merrit Geller was here when the chairs were reupholstered. And Marina told me that they weren't making an official call yet about the prints—that the lab wanted to do one more run—but it looked as if the La Vista Rapist's DNA was on that pillowcase."

Sebastian nodded along. The house was full of fingerprints and Marina had been feeding Maggie and him whatever information she could. So far, nothing had turned up from the Blue River Killer.

But the La Vista Rapist had left clean, fresh prints all over Maggie's house, and apparently older ones, too.

"Is it him?"

Maggie shrugged in his arms. "It's possible. But so far the two are not officially linked."

Sebastian understood. They had a name and a person who'd been here. Until they had something that could hold up in court to show that those prints belonged to Merrit Geller, they couldn't say the man was, in fact, the rapist.

"Surely, the FBI or the police in Lincoln are working on finding him. On getting a DNA or a fingerprint match?"

"That would be my guess," Maggie added. "Unfortunately, it

was Marina's guess as well. She's not part of the unit and they aren't sharing information."

"That sucks," Sebastian said, thinking that was the end of it. But it wasn't.

Maggie propped herself up on one elbow. "Here's the kicker: I remember when Aunt Abbie reupholstered the chairs. She told me how much she loved the fabric and she talked about when they had done it. She told me she had a friend who helped her ..." Maggie let the words hang in the air.

Sebastian put it together. "And those prints match the La Vista Rapist?"

"I don't know yet." She was clearly frustrated. "I mean, I looked around the house and it looks to me like the same prints. But what do I know?"

Sebastian wanted to squirm just as much as she was, but fought to stay calm. It seemed Maggie wasn't done dropping bombs.

"I didn't understand when I was a kid, but thinking back to the things she said, and what she talked about them doing together, and the way Aunt Abbie worked ... Sebastian, she was in love with him."

"Why do you say that?" He didn't remember Sabbie having a lover or even a boyfriend.

"She told me about her *friend*. I was just a kid. I didn't think anything of it, even as a young teenager. But looking back, thinking about the way she talked about this *friend*, he had to have been her lover."

The words were clearly not comfortable on her tongue.

Sebastian understood. His whole life, he believed Sabbie to be just an older woman. Only recently had he come to understand that just because people looked older than him didn't mean their lives were empty. But in his memories of Sabbie, she was only running the boardinghouse and handing out candy to the neighborhood kids.

"I'm afraid that, when they get this confirmed, they're going to discover that Abbie had a decades-long affair with him."

"That long?" He was surprised by Maggie's assessment.

"I don't know, but he kept coming back and he kept renting a room. She trusted him enough that she wrote him a contract on a napkin. And Abbie was in love with the boarder who helped to reupholster those chairs. I'm confident enough of my memory on that …"

She took a deep breath, "I'm getting more convinced that person was Merrit Geller and that he is also the La Vista Rapist."

This time her sigh was pained as she pulled out of his arms and flopped onto her back, exasperated. He wished they could make love again and at least release some of this awful stress.

She rolled only her head to face him. "We have to do something."

"Like what?" Concern bloomed in his chest. Maggie was the kind of woman who went after what she wanted. It was amazing and sexy but, right now, it was downright scary.

"I can't go on like this. This man has been in my house multiple times."

"The guys went around everywhere, and they didn't find any new entries." He protested but understood when Maggie raised an eyebrow.

"I appreciate their efforts and, in any other house, I'd feel safer. But I'm not confident that other entries don't exist." She paused. "Old houses have secrets."

Sebastian nodded. At least he was staying in the room here with her, rather than across the hall.

"He wants something that's still here." She said it with conviction.

But Sebastian didn't fully agree. "I don't know. He opened the closet, so he had to see that we found the second stash of jewelry."

"But he didn't get the brick," Maggie told him. "Who knows

what else he left hidden around this house? I've lived here four months. He was here off and on for decades."

He wanted to protest, but she beat him to it, switching topics like a racecar driver, and he didn't like it.

"I'm losing work, and so are you."

His lawyer was building a case, and he didn't think he would like her conclusion. She told him how she needed to get her life back together. And so did he.

Sebastian listened intently, trying to be open minded and ignore the dread that was closing around his chest, but it didn't work. Her next words made his blood run cold.

"He wants something here. I say we hold it out like bait."

CHAPTER FIFTY

Sebastian felt his heart go cold. He thought the topic had been dropped—after all, it had been three days. Maggie hadn't mentioned anything since the night she'd first brought it up.

Now he heard her talking to her clients and he realized he'd been wrong.

He was making lunch while Maggie finished up with a young couple who wanted to set up guardianship for their two young daughters should anything happen to them.

A-shift was on today, but once again he'd canceled. The chief was understanding about him not coming in, but Sebastian wasn't sure how much longer he could sustain that.

Maggie opened her office door and Sebastian waved to the couple as they passed through the living room and out the front door. When Maggie closed the door behind them, Sebastian couldn't help himself.

The words came out of his mouth in a flood of accusation. "You told them about the paper behind the brick!"

"Yes," she said, the word was delivered simply, with no argument.

"Why would you tell them that?"

"I've told several people," Maggie replied.

"Did you tell them it was a target list, too?" The very idea of what they'd found turned his stomach even though it would be important to the investigation.

When the police techs pulled the paper from where it was wedged they used tweezers to open it. Maggie had been allowed to take photos. Later, the two of them had put the list together on their own. Then Marina Balero had confirmed that they were correct: It was a list of targets.

Some of them were decades old. Many of the notes had been written in different pen, and appeared to be added at different times. Initially, Sebastian and Maggie had struggled by assuming that the list was all La Vista Rapist victims, but they hadn't all been. They weren't all names either, in fact, most weren't. Many entries were just dates, descriptions, addresses, or physical traits. But when they checked old news reports, they found each piece led to someone who'd been targeted.

However, some were La Vista Rapist victims and some were Blue River Killer victims. The list confirmed that the two had been working together, maybe finding each other victims. It was giving Sebastian nightmares.

"I didn't tell them what it was, just that we had found it."

"You told them that the police have it?"

"No," she shook her head at him. "Just that we found it."

"What happens when that information gets out?" What happened when her stalker—almost definitely a serial rapist— decided to come get his list?

Now, Maggie looked at him like he was being slow. "Exactly what I said will happen: he'll come back for it."

That was when Sebastian felt the floor drop out from under him. She'd *said* she wanted to bait her stalker. But when she hadn't said anything further, he'd assumed she dropped the idea. That had been his mistake.

"You're actually *trying* to get him back here?"

"*Yes*." Maggie said, putting emphasis on the word again, as though maybe he were being a little slow on the uptake ... and maybe he was.

"*Why?*"

"What other option do I have?"

That was when the argument really began.

"Lay low. Wait. Don't bring him here on purpose! You know what he does, Maggie!" He was practically yelling, the ramifications of what she was suggesting were possibly horrific.

"*Yes*." She said it again, with emphasis, as though he weren't catching on. "And by doing this on my time frame—at least as much as possible—I'm prepared."

"*Are* you?" He was so angry. So petrified. They'd finally found each other and ... this?

"As much as I can be. Besides, he's what fifty? Sixty years old?"

That didn't comfort Sebastian.

Maggie tried again, her tone soft even if her words weren't. "He's been at this for decades. He has to be older now."

"If he started young, he might only be in his forties," Sebastian argued back as though those facts might sway her.

"Okay," Maggie countered. "Let's say he's in his forties. That might make him strong and fit, but I'm ready for him."

"He struck again six months ago." Sebastian was breathing heavily, failing an argument that was too important to lose. He stopped there, thinking she would catch on. But then he decided it wasn't worth it to let her draw different conclusions. "Six months ago, he was strong enough to overpower someone. This time—" Maggie finally gave some ground, looking down and then to the side, but Sebastian didn't let up. "—you might be ready, you might have your baseball bat. But what if he has drugs? What if you don't see him coming?"

"I know what he looks like!"

"He knows ways into this house that we don't!"

She shrugged as though to say *what was she going to do?* and Sebastian thought what she should do is stop telling people about the page they'd found, stop spreading rumors that she had something he would want. Sebastian was opening his mouth to throw his next stone, but Maggie beat him to it.

"What *else* are we going to do?" She'd said it before as though it were rhetorical, but now she seemed to want an answer.

The good news was he had one. "We're going to lay low and we're going to let the police and the FBI find him."

"*We are?*" she demanded. "They haven't found him yet despite all the evidence we've given them. You and I are damn confident it's Merrit Geller, but he hasn't even been arrested yet. He's been active for over twenty years and *they haven't found him*. They're going to have to catch him in the act. Better me than someone else."

He wouldn't have thought he could get any more petrified, but that had done it. All he could think was *anybody but Maggie*. He was shaking his head 'no,' but she wasn't budging. "We just spent the last two weeks loading up the FBI and the police with *new* evidence, they're going to get him this time."

"It's been two weeks, Sebastian." She stood there in her suit and heels, looking professional and yet somehow angry. She'd pulled the clip from her hair, letting it fall down. Maggie was a sea siren now, one who would argue him to his death.

"Give them time." He was begging.

"How much time can we give them?" Her words were soft. She was actually asking him, but she had her own answer, too. "I'm losing clients. I've canceled them for FBI searches of my home. I haven't slept enough to figure out how to advertise. You aren't working at all." This time her hand waved at him. "How much longer can you sustain that, Sebastian?"

"I have savings," he told her.

"Good, but this isn't what they're for."

"Actually," he countered, finally having a point. "This is *exactly* what they're for."

Maggie nodded, conceding, but she played another card. "How many more shifts can you cancel before you don't have a job anymore?"

He didn't know the answer to that, but it wasn't many. He was a firefighter. Redemption was his hometown, A-shift was *his* shift. He would likely have to move to take a job somewhere else, because the chances of one opening up here were slim. It was part of what he liked about working here: No one was going anywhere.

"Sebastian," she told him, at least looking a little regretful now. "He's going to come back. He's already proven that we can't stop him. Our only hope is to control it."

But Sebastian was confident they couldn't.

CHAPTER FIFTY-ONE

Maggie was frustrated. Sebastian didn't like her plan and she didn't like her alternatives.

It had been three more days and nothing had happened, but there wasn't much she could do. She'd already told people about the paper behind the brick. Her hope was that word would get around town, somehow Merrit Geller would hear about it, and come back.

She wasn't sleeping well either. If she'd thought that every creak and moan of the old house disturbed her sleep when she first moved in, now it was ten times worse. Now, she *knew* someone had come into her home and that person was a serial predator of the worst kind.

She'd been messaging Marina daily, but aside from confirming that the fingerprints they'd found in her house all matched prints found at the scene of La Vista Rapist cases and none matched the Blue River Killer evidence, there was no new evidence.

Once again, she'd had only one client this morning. She needed to average almost three per day for a healthy schedule.

Sebastian's arguments didn't sway her. The La Vista Rapist

was going to come back to her home. She could either try to control the situation or let it surprise her. But she also understood that she couldn't just argue her way through a relationship, and she didn't want to lose Sebastian.

Last night over dinner, he'd asked her casually, "Can you sell the house?"

She'd thought of this already. *"Can* I? Like, can I get a real estate agent and list it? Yes, I already considered it. But who would buy it?"

"It would make a great BnB." He had that answer at the ready, she noticed. But that wasn't what she'd meant.

"Well, the town already has one. I don't think Redemption can support two. Once word gets out that there's a serial predator swinging by occasionally, no one's going to come."

He nodded.

She could sell the house, but she thought about it and she'd never be able to live with herself if anything happened. She wasn't sure how someone would list something like this anyway. Spacious interior, hardwood floors, serial rapist has a key.

And this was Abbie's legacy. Maggie hadn't felt it was truly hers until she had to defend it. But now? She had to defend Aunt Abbie's memory and her own sanity.

"Move in with me for a while."

That one she'd considered more carefully. He was already staying over, in her bed, each night, though he actually managed to get some sleep. He was used to waking up for an alarm and being ready to go, so he was practiced at catching his sleep where he could. She was not.

"This is my office," she said. "If we leave, we give him free range. He could come back, steal whatever he wants. If there's any more evidence here, he can get it, take it, and no one will ever know."

"I need you safe," he said as though finally arriving at the crux of the argument.

That part she understood. Reaching out, she laced her fingers through his. "I'm going to be as safe as I can. And I need you to be safe, too. I can't have anything happen to you, either. But I can't sit here and hide while he's out in the world. You're right, he struck almost six months ago. So, I would expect him to strike again anytime now, or maybe he already has. How can I hide when I may have the means to stop him? The upside is he's not a killer."

She'd watched as Sebastian's eyes bounced from the ceiling to the floor, to the other side of that comment as he desperately tried to process what she was proposing. He took a harsh breath. "He leaves his victims alive, yes, but he's destroyed their lives, Maggie. You don't want to be one of his victims. It's … awful."

"I know, and that's why I can't do nothing. I'm not better than any of those other women." She felt for them, for all his past victims and all his future ones. For Aunt Abbie. "They deserve safety too, and all the other women he's going to target? I can't sit here and let him do that."

Sebastian at least agreed with that, but he had his own contingencies. "I'm not leaving you alone until he's caught."

She nodded. "I can cut the cable bill, shave expenses here and there. If I can keep getting some clients, we can keep eating."

Here she was making plans into the extended future with a man that she hadn't quite agreed to live with.

"If I teach you how to shoot, can you do it?" There was only a dead serious gaze in his eyes. "Can you pull the trigger on a human?"

"I know how to shoot," Maggie said, and watched as he grinned almost as though he'd expected her to say that. "But the practice wouldn't hurt. It's been a while. And the answer is *yes,* I can kill him. The good news is, I know Merrit Geller's face, and I don't think I'll have any trouble pulling the trigger. You?"

He nodded. It felt good to finally have Sebastian on her side on this. But the good feeling was short lived.

Her phone rang. Seeing that it was Marina Balero finally reaching out to her for once, Maggie snatched it up. "Hello?"

There were no pleasantries, just the words, "I have bad news."

CHAPTER FIFTY-TWO

M aggie didn't sleep for the next three nights. Marina's news that the Blue River Killer had struck again was petrifying. Another woman was dead, maybe because Maggie and Sebastian hadn't been able to act fast enough.

Though she knew it wasn't truly her fault— the guilt was relentless.

She could still hear Marina's voice in her head. "She was blonde, like all the others. Late twenties." Maggie knew he struck younger or younger-appearing people—late twenties to even early forties. "She'd been out at one of the clubs."

The way Marina said it, with an air of resignation, told Maggie that whatever they'd been doing or however they had educated the public had not been enough. The Blue River Killer hadn't even had to change his MO.

She'd vented to Sebastian. "It's been a *week* since we found the paper behind the brick. It was a hit list with his fingerprints all over it! How hard is it to get Merrit Geller's fingerprints?"

Sebastian had sighed at her. "Not hard. But legally it can be a nightmare." He'd then raised an eyebrow at her as though she should have known that.

She did. She usually appreciated the order of the system, and she understood that it was just that, a system. But it was failing her now. And it had failed that young woman who's name Maggie hadn't yet learned.

"If her name's not released yet, that means they haven't told her family," she'd lamented to Sebastian before yet another sleepless night.

When she'd woken up—not rested—she'd rolled over to find Sebastian coming awake himself. She finally convinced him to go back to work. He'd protested. Hard.

"The La Vista Rapist isn't coming here. He doesn't care about the paper. Hasn't he proven that? Nothing has happened except you aren't getting paid and you are getting closer to losing your job.

She'd watched as his jaw clenched. She wasn't wrong, and she knew it. Still, he'd argued back. "You're more important than the job."

"I appreciate that, but what happens if you have to move to get a new position? This isn't tenable!"

"He's waiting for us to let our guard down." The deep sigh moved his bare chest, a sight she could appreciate even as he disagreed with her.

"Well then, it's time to look like we've let our guard down."

"What?"

"That doesn't mean *actually* letting our guard down."

They'd gone back and forth this way. Maggie wondered if the relationship could withstand the pressure of a serial predator bearing down on them. In the end, Sebastian told her he hated that she thought she could get away with it, but he backed down. He conceded that she was an adult, and he had to let her make her own decisions.

She'd raised her eyebrows at him. "I haven't heard that since I was a teenager and my dad thought I would learn my lesson."

"I'm sorry." He'd huffed the words out at her but didn't push more. "Please understand that I don't like the feeling in my gut about this."

She'd left it at that, hoping the residual anger would eventually fade, and Sebastian told the chief he'd show up for his next shift. She'd compromised on letting someone stay with her overnight when he was gone. It *was* a good idea, she wasn't stupid, and it made him feel better when he was clearly fighting trusting her decisions.

So he asked Jory Buckland from B, who readily agreed. Jory and Sebastian had gone to the academy together. The way he said this made Maggie think of her law school friends, though she was relatively certain the two trainings were very different.

That night Maggie had slept with Jory in Sebastian's old room across the hallway. She hadn't slept any more soundly than she did when Sebastian was here, but it was certainly better than if she'd been alone.

Three days later, Sebastian announced, "Jory can't make it tomorrow night. Now what?"

Maggie had made a bold move. "Did you meet the new neighbor? Two houses down." When she'd been with Rex, she'd fit right in with his friends. Now she had Sebastian's friends. She needed her own. So she'd made an effort to cultivate a friendship with the woman who had just moved in. "I liked her right away."

She didn't tell Sebastian that she'd been shitty about sticking to small talk and that she'd wound up talking about the Blue River Killer with her new friend. Instead, she figured she'd save Sebastian and the firehouse the trouble and said, "I'll see if I can line up my own bodyguard."

She'd headed over two doors and knocked on the front door of the pretty Victorian. Not as big as hers, it was certainly in better shape.

"Coming!" the voice had called out. Then Seline opened the door, wearing a lab coat and clear goggles around her neck. A triangular flask of equally clear liquid sloshed in one hand. "Maggie!"

"Oh! You're in the middle of something. I was going to see if you wanted to come to lunch. I have a question for you, so lunch is on me."

"I'm almost finished. Can it wait twenty minutes?" Her soft french accent tilted the letters even as she spoke them. Seline motioned Maggie into the house, and Maggie soaked up all the information she could. The layout was much like her own, only without the massive number of rooms. Seline's back room was larger than Maggie's, though. It had been recently converted to a lab, with a black top island that looked as if it had been built in. A sink was set into one end, and a raised bar featured an interesting array of outlets.

At the far end was a bunsen burner and Maggie watched as Seline set her goggles back into place and swirled the liquid. "You should stay on that side of the room. I don't think there are any fumes, but I don't have a hood in here yet."

Maggie looked up, and wondered how the woman would accomplish that. But the built-in chem lab was cute, even if Seline herself was very serious.

"I have to observe it for ten minutes." She swirled it again and made notes in her lab book.

Very scientific, Maggie thought, but stayed quiet.

"Where did you want to go for lunch?" Seline asked, though she didn't move her eyes. Apparently, she didn't need silence.

"I thought you might know?"

Seline laughed. "I'm sorry, I've only lived here for two weeks. I don't know the town very well at all."

Maggie had thought that Seline had come from somewhere else in Redemption. That must have been wrong. "Where did you move from?"

"Lincoln. I teach at the university. But I'm up for tenure and my schedule has changed so I only teach twice a week. The size

of the house here and the yard is worth commuting for classes."
She looked up and smiled. "It gave me the funds to convert this
room to a laboratory."

"The house is gorgeous." She'd be lying if she said she wasn't
a little jealous.

"Yours is bigger." Despite the accent, her grammar was close
to flawless.

So Maggie explained about Abbie and the boarding house
and then she suggested pizza for lunch.

"Oh! I love American Pizza, that sounds wonderful."

A few minutes later, Seline had peeled the lab coat to reveal
jeans and a short-sleeved blouse, and they headed out the door.
They sat at one of the sidewalk tables and ordered too much
food, and eventually Seline had worked her way around to,
"What was the question you wanted to ask me?"

"Oh, it doesn't matter. I thought you grew up in Redemption
and knew everyone."

"But you bought me lunch. So what was the question
anyway?"

As she bit into another gooey slice, Maggie told Seline more
about their serial predator. She mentioned the paper found
hidden in her fireplace and the need to find someone to stay
overnight with her. "I had hoped you might know someone that
I could ask."

Seline's eyes had gotten wider and wider as Maggie talked.
But, at the end, her expression snapped to serious. "I can stay
with you."

Surprised Maggie asked, "You're volunteering? I appreciate
it. But ..."

But the idea quickly took root. Having a second person on
scene would be smart and Seline was clearly intelligent and able
to think on her feet. And then the other woman surprised her.

"I am an excellent marksman. My father was in the COS—
French military, special forces. I have my own nine-millimeter

… pistol." She'd seemed to search for the last word, but she grabbed another slice of pizza as though this were an ordinary conversation and continued. "What do you think is the likelihood this man will show up tomorrow night?"

"Slim to none." Maggie sighed. "He hasn't shown up for weeks. We've changed all the locks and bolted the cellar door shut. He seems to have no interest in the last bit of evidence we found. But my boyfriend—" *damn, that sounded good,* "—is a firefighter. He works twenty-four hour shifts and won't go to work if I'm alone."

Seline smiled, a wide grin that reached her clear blue eyes. It seemed every emotion she felt played across her features. "I will bring a bag over tonight. Then tomorrow I can come through the back gate. No one will know I'm there!"

Seline was baiting the monster even more than Maggie had ever intended to. But damn if the fantasy of the two of them shooting him when he broke in wasn't tempting. Maggie knew that wasn't how it worked: Seline would be an extra set of ears and eyes for an incredibly boring evening.

"That sounds wonderful!" Maggie felt the relief slide through her whole system. Sebastian could go to work. "We can have a movie night."

Seline was still grinning as she reached for a third slice of pizza. She was smart, and apparently handy with a gun. Maggie thought it was great, but what would Sebastian say?

CHAPTER FIFTY-THREE

"Kane, Hernandez, fall back." The words were like music in his ear.

The struggle against the corn field fire had been epic and exhausting. It had started with the alarm hours ago and was nowhere near being contained.

Sebastian and Luke offered each other a subtle nod, acknowledging that they were getting relieved. They had, after all, been on the line the longest.

The Chief's voice came through the comm again. "Kelly, Smith, you're in."

Sebastian kept working, his second wind—or maybe third or fourth—giving out now that he knew his time was limited.

He and Luke had been digging trenches, hoping to stop the fire that ate dry cornstalks in a rage. The owner had passed, so the field wasn't planted. No one had watered it. The house had stood empty until a buyer had moved in just a few months ago. The buyer wasn't a farmer and didn't understand the fields still needed to be tended.

So, not surprisingly, it was now fully ablaze. The families at the neighboring farms were concerned. And the new owner was frantic.

Sebastian felt the tap on his shoulder and executed a carefully choreographed handoff. As he and Luke hightailed it away from the line, he lifted the mask from his face and breathed air that was cooler and less artificial tasting. It felt like heaven, though the sweat was still running down his spine.

He positioned himself not to bump Luke in their bulky gear as they rummaged through the cooler for a bottle of water, which he gulped in its entirety. Only when he'd drunk most of it, did he realize that the sun was coming up.

"Oh, that's beautiful," Luke commented as he crushed the plastic of his water bottle and screwed the lid back on.

The two stood there watching—grateful to not be digging—as the sun rose directly over the flames. The fire was nowhere near under control. "We are not walking off shift at eight a.m."

"I got nowhere I have to be," Luke commented and reached into a second cooler for an energy bar.

Sebastian polished off the water bottle and tucked the trash into the bag that had been set next to the cooler. "I wanted to meet the neighbor who was staying with Maggie last night."

"Don't trust her?"

On the one hand, Maggie was excited because she felt she'd made a friend, and Sebastian loved that. On the other hand … "I'm not sure about the two of them staying in the house alone. Not because they're women, but because I don't know Seline."

He had to trust Maggie's assessment of her and he *did*, his concern was mostly that Seline was blond, like the Blue River Killer's victims. "Two women in the house seems like way too much bait."

"He hasn't broken in again, has he?" All the guys knew what was going on, especially since Sebastian had returned to A-shift.

"No. Every noise and bump has turned out to be nothing." Nothing he could prove at least.

Of all the people Maggie could have picked, she'd chosen the best bait possible for both predators. It made him very nervous.

Seline's father being military and her claimed handiness with a gun was a plus. He felt better about Maggie as well after they'd been to the range several times. But he kept all of this to himself. Turning to the chief, he asked, "How much longer?"

The chief held up a finger, letting him know the man was calculating something. Sebastian reached for a second bottle of water. He'd drunk the first out of sheer thirst. The second he drank rotely, knowing that if he didn't stay hydrated, he didn't stay on the job.

His phone was back at the station, the digital world completely on hold every time they fought a fire. There was no room to be interrupted by messages and calls. The closest he could get now to messaging Maggie was to interrupt the woman from next door, who was filming the blaze on her cell phone.

But that was not allowed, for various solid reasons, and he was left trusting that Maggie was okay. He told himself that he would catch the marvelous Seline Marchand next time.

Maggie had clients this morning. And no one had broken in during the day. So, he repeated the mantra to himself, *she would be okay.*

He was still telling himself that at noon. When B-shift had arrived and the fire was blazing on … and his uneasy feeling about Maggie was growing stronger.

CHAPTER FIFTY-FOUR

M aggie had only seen one client that morning and she was already craving a nap. She and Seline had stayed up late the night before eating ice cream directly from the carton and watching Dirty Dancing. Seline had never seen it and Maggie had decided to correct that error.

It was possible she'd made a friend for life in the process, and it felt good to be in her thirties and making new friends of her own. Seline was smart, cultured, funny, and had the worst poker face ever.

Though Maggie hadn't slept any better than her usual, no one had disturbed the place. There weren't even the regular bumps and knocks she and Sebastian had grown used to investigating.

She had an hour between clients and was seriously contemplating the logistics of a power nap. Since many of her clients tended to show up early and she couldn't nap in a business suit anyway it didn't look like it would happen.

In lieu of her much-needed nap, Maggie headed into the kitchen and poured herself another cup of coffee. Maybe the caffeine would keep her awake.

Sebastian still wasn't home, but the local morning news told her the team was fighting a huge fire on one of the farms. So far, no one had been injured—which she expected, the guys were good at their jobs. But it was an all hands on deck situation. Another local team and a volunteer unit from Beatrice had been brought in to help.

Sitting down at the table, her shoulders slumped. She was still tired but tapped out another message to Sebastian, letting him know she'd added another client this afternoon and to let himself into the house.

Maggie had barely sat down when she realized the coffee wasn't going to cut it. Suddenly she felt even more tired. She was going to need actual food for fuel.

She shouldn't be this bad. Sure, she and Seline had stayed up late, but ...

Maybe she was just getting old. Maybe Aunt Abbie and her old woman ways were wearing off on Maggie. Then again, maybe she simply hadn't slept well in several weeks and her body decided that this was the last straw.

But the fun night of movies and hanging with Seline had been worth it.

Heading into the kitchen, she opened the pantry and stuck her head in. Potato chips? Given the junk food she and Seline had eaten last night, she knew she should find something better. She closed the pantry and heard a creak behind her.

Strange, she thought. The idea had barely registered before she had turned around and spotted the man standing in front of her fridge. He leaned back against the appliance, arms crossed, baseball cap pulled low.

Everything in her froze. She should have screamed bloody murder, but she was too startled.

She should have had her gun on her, but it was broad daylight and she was seeing clients.

She should fight, but he wasn't fighting her. Just looking up, kind face and clear blue eyes. Maybe this was just someone who wanted legal services? Was this Merrit Geller? Maggie couldn't tell.

So she stared at him.

He was grinning, but then he tipped his head as though to examine her and everything clicked. This was Merrit Geller.

For half a second she had the very odd reaction of wanting to pump her fist in the air and yell, *yes, we were right*. But it wouldn't be a victory if he got hold of her.

"Hello, Geller." She said it in her best unafraid voice, but the fact was she was petrified.

"Hello, Magdalyn," he replied.

Shit. Anyone guessing would have called her Margaret. He knew who she was. Though she hadn't voiced her thoughts about this to Sebastian, she'd known that Merrit Geller would kill her if he found her. He had to.

She could now definitely link him to everything in the house. His fingerprints would match everything else. Now that she'd seen him, she could ID him to the police. She didn't need anything more than she already had right now to confirm he was the La Vista Rapist.

But as her eyes darted downward, she saw that he was wearing thin, leather gloves.

Shit, she thought again. She blinked as he held up his hand and smiled, seeming to catch on to what she'd been thinking. *How had he read her so clearly?*

He was making no move to launch at her.

Maggie thought for a minute about what her next move should be. If he wasn't actively attacking her then she could think of an escape. She stayed still, not quite able to put her thoughts together. The fear was far more overwhelming than she'd expected it to be.

"Where's my list?" he asked.

The public didn't know that it was anything more than just a piece of paper, as far as Maggie knew. His words meant the list was, in fact, his.

"The police took it," she replied though, in her fear, her words ran together.

As she watched, his features contorted to rage, his fists clenched in the thin, evidence-concealing gloves. But he didn't move from where he leaned against her refrigerator.

Maggie hadn't moved from in front of the pantry. In fact, she realized she was leaning back on the door.

She would get out of this. He might know the house, but she did, too.

She'd been practicing what she would do if he got in. Here was her chance to make it pay off. She could run to the front door, but she'd have to be faster than him. She could run to the back door, but that would put her in the back yard, and further from help or anyone who could likely see her.

But running to the back of the house would mean she could get the gun she'd left on the shelf ... easy to grab, but hard to spot.

That plan would still leave her at the back of the house. The neighbors wouldn't see what was happening. They might not even hear if she screamed. She'd bolted the back door, since that was how he'd been coming and going at first. It would take too long to go out that door if she was being chased.

Maggie was on her own, so she made the decision to run through the back room, loop to the front door, and shoot if she had to. Now all she had to do was make a break for it without looking like she was getting ready to bolt. And she probably already did ... he'd read her clearly when she looked at his gloves. Maggie tried something else.

She looked Merrit Geller dead in the eyes and asked, "How did you get in?"

He laughed. "I walked right through the front door."

Her stomach rolled. She hadn't even locked it behind her

clients. He smiled again. He could probably read her stunned recognition of her own error on her face.

"But," she started to speak, the anger at herself leaking out around the word even though her mouth felt cottony.

Once again, he grinned. "Feeling a little sluggish, Magdalyn? That was some really good coffee ..."

Holy shit. He'd drugged her in her own home. She looked down to her hand, where she could barely form a fist. All the things she planned and practiced—punching him, grabbing her gun, running—none of it mattered.

Because she was moving through jello.

There was nothing she could do. Sebastian wasn't home and Merrit Geller was right in front of her and she couldn't fight.

CHAPTER FIFTY-FIVE

S ebastian was exhausted, but he found just enough energy to make a necessary run by his place first.

He was running out of clothes. He needed a second bottle of shampoo from his cabinet. He wanted the number of a florist so he could get flowers for Maggie. Her birthday was coming up.

All the things he needed were still at his place. He climbed the steps and fit the key into the lock. The apartment felt empty now. Aside from a few nights here with Maggie, he hadn't lived in his own home in a while.

So he gathered the things he needed and checked his phone.

Though Maggie had kept him up to date on her extra meeting and such, she hadn't replied to his previous message. But that was probably because she was still with her client.

Or maybe she was out to lunch with Seline. *No*, he thought, *scratch that*. His tired brain rolled over. Seline had left early to work in the city or something. That was why he wouldn't get to meet her today.

He headed back down to the garage, his bag now heavy in his hand. He aimed automatically for his bike before deciding on the car. Most days the bike was a great idea. But days like today, when he was completely exhausted, simply keeping it up right for the short ride was too much.

Waving to his neighbor as he pulled out, he waited on the gate that was so slow he might just fall asleep. Luckily, the drive to Maggie's was short and he parked next to her car in the driveway.

His heart loosened at the sight of the car, relieved that she was still here.

He headed through the side gate and walked the short stone path to the laundry room door. Sebastian entered the house trying to make as little noise as possible, something about the backyard bothered him, but he'd ask Maggie later. He just needed to see her.

Hoping not to disturb her with whatever clients she might be seeing, he didn't yell a ridiculous, *Hi, honey, I'm home.* But he felt like it. They almost felt like an old married couple to him, and he liked it. Knowing that he was in the right place and that she wanted to be with him as much as he wanted to be with her was freeing.

Once he saw her office door was ajar, he headed upstairs to drop his bag on the bed. But as he came back down the steps, he realized that he didn't hear her speaking to anyone. And there wasn't another car parked out front.

Sebastian began calling for her through the house.

But Maggie didn't answer.

He was a firefighter, he looked for kids who were hiding under beds while their house blazed around them. Though the image of the last child he'd found rushed back into his mind, he didn't panic.

He checked everything before he got worried.

But when his first sweep didn't reveal Maggie, he ran back through the house. He looked in every room and even knocked on the closed upstairs bathroom door and opened it when he got no answer.

"Maggie? Maggie, I'm home!"

Heading into Sabbie's office, he unbolted and opened the door to the balcony in case she'd decided to sit out in a chair and enjoy the sun. But Maggie wasn't there either. He ran back down the stairs and checked the front patio, still calling for her.

This time, there was no child under the bed to save. He was starting to get that sinking feeling he had as he handed Tyler Miller's limp body to his mother. The one that told him the child had been alive moments before … *and how had this happened?*

He dialed his friend. "Kalan, I can't find Maggie. Have you heard from her?" He almost hung up when the answer was no.

Sebastian regretted not making Maggie check in everywhere she went. It was daytime and all the break ins had come at night. He told himself she was safe. She was probably just running an errand and giving him a heart attack in the process.

He did have Seline's number. So he called her next. The sweet lilt of her French accent colored her words as she answered the phone. "Hello, Sebastian."

"Do you know where Maggie is?" He couldn't help the harsh tone in his voice.

"What? No. I left at seven-thirty. I'm in Lincoln, teaching. I had classes this morning."

Yes, he thought. That was exactly what he'd understood. School had recently started up again. He told himself that Seline was in the right place and everything was okay. Everything was fine. Maggie would be in the right place, too. But his racing heart didn't agree with the bullshit his head was pedaling. "Did she go somewhere for research? Her car is still here."

Many things were close by in Redemption. Had she walked?

"Maybe she hit the library, or the county clerk for records. She said one client was trying to divide some land …?" Seline offered and he felt his chest loosen from where it had tightened down to a pebble. That was a valid point. Chances were Maggie had simply gone somewhere. But she had to know she would petrify him if he didn't know where she was.

"Thank you, Seline. I'll check," he said, trying to keep his voice light and his worry from bleeding into someone else's life.

Sebastian bolted out the front door not sure which way to head as both directions lead back to the main street. He made a loop, trying not to look frantic, he ducked into storefronts, checked the library, and dialed her phone repeatedly.

When he'd completed his panicked search, he was back at her house, but hadn't found her. He went in through the front door again, checking rooms when he heard her phone beep.

Thank God, she was here. "Maggie!"

She didn't answer and he headed toward the sound. It beeped again, and this time he followed the noise to the kitchen. He turned the corner, concerned again when she wasn't there. When he saw her phone, unattended on the counter next to the pantry every cell in his body went rigid.

Why was her phone here if she wasn't? *"Maggie?"*

He practically screamed it as he ran around to the back of the house and out the back door. He knew, he *just knew*, she was gone.

He bolted across the yard almost missing the trail of footprints in the grass. The morning had been humid, which helped them fight the fire. It also made the grass more likely to leave tracks, and Sebastian didn't like what he was seeing.

It didn't quite look like footprints, but he moved fast and didn't analyze as quickly as he moved. When he reached the back gate, he saw it was unlatched.

He and Maggie had bolted everything. But now it had been opened and pulled almost shut, but it wasn't as they had left it. He tried to convince himself that Maggie had gone into the woods and hadn't told him ... and had left her phone behind?

No. She wouldn't do that.

Cold dread replaced the heat of rage again. If he looked back at the grass, and checked the marks from this angle, he could see now that someone had been dragged to the back gate.

Maggie was gone. And the La Vista Rapist had her.

CHAPTER FIFTY-SIX

"9-1-1, what's your emergency?"

Sebastian opened his mouth, but no words came out. His emergency was far too big to speak in a sentence or ten that had any clarity. He needed to run after Maggie, but he fought the urge because he knew protocol saved lives.

He could only hope that it would save Maggie's.

The voice repeated, "How may I help you?"

This time, he took what should have been a deep breath, but was merely a short chop of his lungs, and said, "My name is Sebastian Kane. My girlfriend, Maggie Willis has been kidnapped." He rattled off the house address. But he didn't stand still—he couldn't—so he bolted back into the house and looked around while he rattled off information.

The voice stayed too calm. And for the first time he understood why people got so frustrated with the dispatchers, even as he reminded himself it was her job to stay disturbingly calm. "And why do you believe your girlfriend was kidnapped?"

He wanted to yell but, instead, he snapped, "Damnit, Tracey. Talk to Officer Balero. She and the FBI have been working the Blue River Killer and La Vista Rapist cases. The rapist is Merrit

Geller—" he didn't care if he was wrong, he was naming the man, "—and he's been breaking in and leaving fingerprints all over my girlfriend's house for the last four weeks. They know this."

He took a breath as he heard Tracey tapping on the keys. At least he'd gotten someone he knew was competent, but as he dashed through the house, he didn't see anything new. "As of right now, Maggie's not here and there are drag marks out the gate in the back yard. I'm following them. Send Officer Balero and FBI Agents Watson and Decker. *Now.*"

He hung up then, realizing he would have been better suited to call Marina directly. So this time he did that.

"Officer Balero—"

He cut her off before she even finished her own name. "Maggie's gone." In a huff, he repeated what he had told Tracey at dispatch. He'd owe both of them an apology later, but he didn't care right now. He bolted out the back door. Even if it was protocol, he couldn't stand idly by.

"It looks like *what?*" Marina asked.

"Like someone was *dragged* through the grass and out the back gate, and you know that's how he's coming and going." He looked at the grass even as he ran past it toward the back gate.

"Holy shit." He heard her mutter the words and he could tell by the background noise that she was scooping her things off the desk—wallet? gun? badge?—and heading out the door.

What if he was running the wrong way? What if he should stay at the house?

He was practically yelling into the phone. "Come check out the house, Marina. We have to figure out where he took her. Get here ASAP."

Once again, he hung up the phone before the conversation was over.

The back gate swung behind him as he headed into the woods. He should call the FBI directly as well, but Watson and

Decker's numbers were in Maggie's phone. He'd have to trust Tracey and Marina to get them here.

What if Maggie hadn't been gone long? Had he wasted time checking the house and along main street? But if he'd barely missed her being taken, he might catch up ... he was in the woods and heading toward the dock before he even thought about it.

It felt as if he wasn't breathing, but he must be because he didn't pass out. His eyes darting back and forth, he searched frantically for signs that Maggie might have been taken this way. But he couldn't tell. He wasn't a tracker at all. So if a sign was there, he'd missed it.

He watched for other people using the trail today. They might have seen something. But the place was empty. Why was no one using the walking trail? He should have run into someone who'd seen a man carrying a grown woman through the woods.

But Sebastian was utterly alone. And before he'd realized how far he'd come, he was making the left hand turn to the short trail to the water.

He was running fast enough that he almost skidded to a stop, where the earth sloped down into the river, getting the tips of his toes wet. But the dock wasn't bouncing from someone who'd just walked across it. And the water was smooth as glass.

If Geller had brought her this way, it had been long enough ago that he hadn't left a sign.

CHAPTER FIFTY-SEVEN

Maggie sat in her little chair and seethed.

She heard voices coming from the room directly behind her. She was shut in her own small room but bound with tape and faced away from the door.

Not being able to see what was coming made her jumpy—which was probably the point.

She was livid. Mad with herself to the point where she was grinding her teeth. And Sebastian was going to kill her. He was right. She'd been wrong—*so wrong.*

She'd thought she was prepared to fight Geller, but she'd been ready for a scenario Geller had turned on its head. She'd thought he would come in at night, that daytime was perfectly safe. And she'd been so stupid that she'd drunk whatever drug he'd given her before she'd even known it was there.

She would have growled if she hadn't needed to keep quiet. Though she hadn't ever fully passed out, she'd definitely been unable to fight. Her thoughts had been sluggish and dream-like, escaping her grasp and changing to ridiculous even as she tried to hold onto them.

The worst part had come when she tried to hit or fight back.

It was like punching through water. Nothing landed. For all the force she put behind it, she would merely tap him. Geller had laughed at her attempts more than once, then just pushed her hand out of the way. He'd simply readjusted her over his shoulder or under his arm and hauled her along. There was nothing she could do about it except feel the terror of knowing he was stealing her away and she might never be found.

She had managed to kick one shoe loose along the path. But it had bounced a bit and landed to the side of the trail. It meant that Geller hadn't seen it, but it might mean no one else did either …

Her favorite business suit was now dirty and ripped in several places where she'd come into contact with branches and hadn't been able to even move herself out of the way. The suit was the least of her problems. But anger about her favorite clothing being destroyed helped keep her sane. Fear of what might come would immobilize her and that was the last thing she needed.

"I brought her to you," the first voice whined. Maggie now recognized that it belonged to Merrit Geller.

The cottony taste was leaving her mouth, but the plea from one psychopath to another made her bile rise. She fought it back down.

"I don't want her. It's no fun being handed playthings," the other voice had replied. Maggie didn't know this voice, but she could only assume it was the Blue River Killer. If it wasn't, then Merrit Geller had amassed a team of super-villains and she wasn't ready to deal with that possibility.

"I know she's not what you would have picked, but we need her gone." It was hard listening to two men discuss disposing of her body. But then it got worse. "She's Sabbie's granddaughter, so I wouldn't have picked her, but what's done is done. I play with her first, then you dispose of her."

Her stomach turned again. He had some allegiance to her

Aunt—not her *grandmother*, but now wasn't the time to quibble —that made him not want to hurt her? But he said he still would, and that made her more determined than ever to get out of here. Her hands and ankles were bound with tape—wider than standard duct tape and maybe a little sturdier. *Damn.*

The force of the binding on her forearms kept her elbows nearly touching in front of her chest. Another piece covered her mouth.

The second voice laughed. "I'm not your disposal system."

Now Geller's voice turned hard. "But we're in this together, your evidence was in that house, too. I've been hiding it for you for years and, if I go down, so do you."

"Please," the disdain was clear even from a room away. Merrit Geller wasn't even the scariest man in the room. The other voice went on. "Do your own wet work."

"It's not what I do." Geller bordered on whining now, and Maggie hoped she never saw the other man. He would kill her without a second thought and lose no sleep over it. "I'm sorry, is it not fun for you? I thought you liked it."

She was definitely listening to a conversation between the La Vista Rapist and the Blue River Killer. The comment about "hiding his evidence" was far too clear. She tried to remember what she could about the second voice, to think of descriptors for it. If she could get out of here, she would be full of evidence.

If...

Though Maggie had believed before that Geller would not let her live, this conversation was further proof of the things she suspected. But none of it mattered if she died. She could die full of all this evidence she had, but she'd still be dead. And they'd still be free.

The conversation moved further away and their voices garbled. While she could tell they remained at odds, she now had no idea what they were saying.

Swallowing hard, she took a deep breath and tried to think

through her options. Geller had drugged her, but she was coming around. If she was smart, and *lucky*, that would be his mistake.

She had no idea how the hell she was going to fight off two of them though.

Her eyes darted out the window, this time not just focusing on sunlight, but gathering intel. The glass had multiple panes with wood molding between them. She was probably in a small, cute, old cabin. And 'old' meant it was probably well constructed. It also probably meant the panes were real glass, which meant she could break them. But it looked as if she was going to have to open the window in order to fit out of it. Opening the window meant getting across the room and that meant getting her hands and feet undone.

This was going to take everything she had.

Maggie thought she remembered something about exercising toxins out of her body. That a person could get through something like, say, drunkenness, faster by exercising to increase their metabolism. She had no idea if that would work in this case, because she had no clue what Geller had given her. There was always the possibility that she was only alive because she was metabolizing whatever drug it was slowly. But dying from poison would be far superior to dying at either of these men's hands. She'd seen what Merrit Geller did to his victims. And he left his victims alive.

Those were not his plans for her though.

She had only one option for survival—for getting back to Sebastian—she was going to have to get the hell out of here herself. She looked around the room as far as she could see from her position in the chair and began to make a plan.

CHAPTER FIFTY-EIGHT

Sebastian bolted back to the house. The run to the dock had revealed nothing and had wasted his time.

Maggie either hadn't come here, or she'd been through long enough ago that there was no evidence. His phone buzzed in his pocket, and he pulled it out ready to answer … a social media notification.

He almost threw the phone, he was so angry. But he couldn't afford to turn off any alerts. His fists clenched, his jaw ratcheted down so tight that he thought he might crack a few molars. Maggie was gone and he couldn't even hit anything.

He thought about throwing his head back and screaming or growling into the air. He'd just found her. He'd argued with her so much that he hadn't fought her on Seline staying at the house overnight. He'd been so stupid to leave her alone, even for a few hours in the daytime.

He swallowed down the bitter rage and tried to move forward. The only thing that would save Maggie was moving forward. He could survive the Miller boy dying in his arms. But if he found Maggie and she didn't make it? If she was simply gone before he got there? He'd never survive that.

This was his fault.

His head fell forward and he squeezed his eyes shut, fighting the hot rush of pressure that wanted him to fall to his knees in the forest and give up.

When he reminded himself that he was trained to handle emergencies, he forced his mouth open, forced his lungs to suck in air, and forced his eyes open. Whatever he felt, he could suck it up. Maggie had it worse.

Through the sheen that blurred his vision, he caught a glimpse of pale blue to his right. He focused on it. Out of place in the forest, the color called to him, and finding out what the blue was seemed like a small task he could handle. As he pushed the shrub back, his heart clenched. A shoe.

A pale blue shoe that had to be Maggie's.

Snatching it from where it lay, he looked it over as if he could identify the shoes she wore on sight.

"Fuck!" he yelled at himself. He'd just destroyed evidence.

Too late to undo his own fingerprints. He yanked his phone out, fumbling until he almost dropped it, and then he took pictures of the shrub the shoe had been under.

Clutching the one clue he might have found, he bolted back toward the house. Not even five steps further, his phone rang and his heart kicked that it might be Maggie.

But it couldn't be Maggie. Maggie's phone was left behind. Maggie was gone. *Unless*, he thought for a moment, *everything he'd believed had happened was wrong.*

Looking at the screen, he saw an unknown number. Normally, he didn't answer those, but he'd never hit the button so fast in his life. "Hello?"

"This is Special Agent Watson."

"Yes?" Maybe there was good news.

"We're at the house. We've got techs dusting for fingerprints."

"Yes?" Sebastian breathed the word out again, still running

back toward home—a home that wasn't anything without Maggie in it.

"It appears that everything you said is correct. However, you've walked through the grass in the back yard and ruined some of the evidence."

"I know." He felt like shit. What if he'd destroyed even more evidence that could help them find Maggie? *Fuck.* But there was nothing he could do to reverse time.

His adrenaline spiked at the thought and his muscles threatened to shake. He was afraid there would be long, long years ahead of him to feel guilty about how he lost Maggie. He couldn't dwell on it now. "I think I found her shoe. What do I do?"

"Don't touch it."

He looked at it in his grasp. "Too late."

"We need you to come back to the house," Watson told him her voice turning sharp. "If we're going to find her, we need everybody in this together."

"I'm almost there." His words came in short, choppy phrases between breaths as he ran. "There was nothing I could see at the dock. So if he left with her from there, he's been gone for a while."

Sebastian stopped where he was. His eyes burning and his heart clenching as he made that declaration. He was thinking about saving Maggie, but if she'd been gone for a while, maybe it was too late. Maybe Geller had already hurt her. Maybe she was already dead.

But Watson was talking to him and he needed to pay attention because he had to grab any chance he could to save Maggie.

"—spoke with her clients from this morning. The first one, an elderly gentleman, Mr. Horace, believes he didn't leave until twelve ten." *Okay*, Sebastian thought, *Maggie had been alive and well until just after noon.*

"Her next appointment was at one-thirty," Watson was still giving him information and he did his best to absorb it as he ran the last distance. "That couple says they came by on time, but Maggie didn't answer the door. They called, left a voicemail, waited, and after a while they left. So we have a very clear window here."

Sebastian looked at his watch. It was almost three pm.

She'd been gone at least an hour and a half, long enough for the wake to leave the surface and long enough for Geller to take her plenty far away.

He'd stopped moving as his crazy thoughts had taken over. Now he was standing in the woods on the verge of breaking down, but he couldn't give in to the overwhelming urge. Standing here and crying about what might be wasn't his style. But his style was also taking care of other people's problems, not his own. He'd just gained a newfound respect for everyone who'd stood and watched their home and all their belongings burn right before their eyes. He was not handling this half as well as they did.

It wasn't time to get lost in self pity. It was time to move, and Sebastian started to run again. Watson kept him on the phone, explaining that they'd found no fingerprints from anyone other than him and Maggie.

The good news, he thought, was that between him, Maggie, Kalan, Luke, and the Kellys, they'd cleaned the house so thoroughly that any prints could be pinpointed to the last handful of days.

The bad news was they weren't finding any prints but Maggie's and his.

He spotted Watson as she held open the back gate and motioned for him to hop over the footprints at the entrance, and not further destroy any evidence. He handed over the shoe which she took without a word.

There were three officers in the yard between him and the

house. One was taking photographs, another seemingly looking for samples, and a third cruising the perimeter. Inside the house was crawling with people in white paper suits. At least the feds had all hands on deck.

For Maggie, he thought.

"Don't touch anything." Watson issued the stern reprimand as Sebastian walked through the back door. "Straight through and out the front."

He followed her, walking like a dead man, still not certain if he was breathing. As he watched, she handed the shoe to a tech and rattled off a few instructions. The one thing he'd found of hers was gone. But maybe it would still help them find her.

A small white tent was erected in the small front yard. The lawn sloped relatively sharply, and Sebastian's brain latched on to ridiculous details, like how someone had jammed the ends of the tent poles into the ground to help it stand even.

A table was set up in the center of the tent, officers and agents ringed it, even Marina Balero. But a handful of people he didn't know.

Watson walked him into the tent. "This is Sebastian Kane. He's our victim's boyfriend—" *victim, Jesus*. But Sebastian forced his focus. He had to keep his head in the game.

She introduced him to several officers, a few other FBI agents who specialized in missing adults, a third department was represented by a man in a forest green uniform.

His eyes were sharp, and he directed attention to a map, having barely looked up at Sebastian. That was good. This man was most focused on finding Maggie, and he could appreciate that. It took a moment for Sebastian to realize the man was a park ranger.

"This," Marina told him, "is Leo Evans."

The man shook Sebastian's hand with enough force to be reassuring in the most shitty time Sebastian had ever encountered. "It's nice to meet you. But why is there a park ranger here?"

CHAPTER FIFTY-NINE

The two voices were still arguing as Maggie struggled with the tape. Geller was trying to convince the other man —*William Sanders?*—to kill her.

"Just wait until I'm finished with her then dispose of her like one of your victims." He sounded so reasonable, as if they were discussing how to recycle cardboard. "If we mix up the M.O. it makes it harder for them to find us."

"I would agree," the other voice replied, just as chillingly cold in his tone. "But they've already found you."

The way this was going, the second man was fed up. Despite his reasonable sound, he was done with the conversation and was going to leave any moment now.

She could only hope he left without first killing her.

Maggie had been shaking her knees and rolling her shoulders and breathing as quickly as she could to get her metabolism up. It was exercise, and she didn't know whether it really did anything, but she did feel better when she flexed her fingers, she could see them respond quickly to each time she tried to move them.

The room had two windows, a closet hiding who knew

what, and a small table with a half-full glass of water. And her ... there was only what she had on her.

While she was clearly an idiot for not believing Sebastian, and for letting herself get drugged and kidnapped, she wasn't going to be an idiot anymore. Luckily, she hadn't been much of one in the days before this. She'd been watching forensics shows on TV and online videos about how to get out of being kidnapped. She now kept shoelaces in her pocket. Three of them, in fact. So she could hog tie anyone she could take down or use the laces to break the plastic if she was zip tied.

Unfortunately, she was not bound with zip ties. Fortunately, when they'd searched her, they'd patted her down for phones and keys, but they'd not taken her shoelaces. She also had one shoe left. If she could get to it, the near stiletto shaped heel would be a formidable weapon.

The escape artists online taught her how to get out of duct tape. This wasn't duct tape—Maggie was confident of that—but she hoped the same breakout technique would work.

Her fear tried to surface again, but she shoved it down deep. It wouldn't help her now.

Lifting her bound hands high over her head, she prayed. She hadn't told Sebastian, but she tried the technique she'd seen online once at home and it had not felt good, but it worked. If she slammed her hands down over her knees, using her hips and body as a wedge for her elbows, she could put enough force in the right place to tear the tape, and free her hands.

She took a deep breath and brought her arms down. The trick was doing it as quickly as she could. *Son of a bitch.* It was a good thing she had tape over her mouth, or they would have heard her yelp in pain.

It didn't work. This wasn't duct tape. It was something stronger, more cloth like and it was wide. A zip tie would have been thin and—she learned recently—could be sawed at with a shoelace. She thought about doing the same thing to the tape, but the tape was so wide that it would be much harder to get the shoelace strung through it.

She still had to do something. Maggie voted to try again.

She lifted her arms higher this time, hanging them hammer-style down behind her. For this to work it needed speed and commitment. She brought them down again. Again, the tape felt like it was trying to crack the bones in her wrists.

Geller had put several layers on to hold her tight. Maggie lifted her hands in front of her face to see if she'd accomplished anything other than hurting herself. She would have gasped if not for the tape over her mouth. She saw a small tear on the underside.

The trick did not work the way it did with duct tape. But she tried again and the tear became microscopically larger. *That was enough.*

Underneath the tape she muttered to herself, "I can do this all day."

So she lifted her arms again. And this time, furious, she slammed them down with all her might, and her hands split apart.

Her fists, tightened to help the tape split, fell to either side of her body.

Holy shit. Her hands throbbed. She flexed her fingers, only able to say that they were working and not broken. But her hands were apart, the tape split neatly down the center. She would have celebrated but this was just step one.

Reaching down, she worked at the tape on her ankles, unwrapping the sticky motherfucker was almost as difficult as splitting the one on her hands. She looked to the table and thought of using the glass to cut the tape but, with one shoe on, hopping around the room with her feet bound would be impossible. And it certainly wouldn't be quiet. Besides, maybe the water was poisoned. Geller had certainly seen fit to drug her once already.

Maybe the plan was to give it to her later.

Or just let her suffer and dehydrate while a glass of water sat waiting six feet away.

Continuing to pick at the tape, she broke one nail, then another. But at last she got her ankles free. It took another moment to wad the tape up to where it didn't want to cling to her fingers. She needed somewhere to put it that Geller and his partner wouldn't automatically see it. So she peeled her remaining shoe and padded softly over to the table, then stuck the wad underneath like a piece of chewed gum.

Now what? she thought.

She started to use her right hand to pick at the tape stuck firmly across her mouth. But her nails were broken, so she tried her left hand, but even that hurt. She was going to have a rectangular rash on her face, letting everyone know that she had been kidnapped.

She should be so lucky.

The real problem would be if no one saw her. If her body wasn't found. And no one ever knew that she'd had tape on her face. So once again, Maggie committed to fast and harsh and ripped the tape off.

Son of a bitch! She gasped as quietly as she could while the pain slowly ebbed.

But she was free.

What next? Go out the window? Look in the closet for weapons?

Her house creaked like nobody's business and this place looked even older. The trees outside the window made her think she was in a cabin. That made sense with what she remembered of the trip here.

No one knew where the Blue River Killer had been taking his victims, only where he'd abducted them from and where he'd been leaving them.

The La Vista Rapist tended to make do at the scene he was

already at. That would have been Maggie's home and Sebastian or her clients would have shown up. He'd planned this carefully ahead of time. And that alone made Maggie livid.

She held the shoe clenched tightly in her hand, her one weapon at the ready. But she'd prefer another. Then her eyes fell to the glass of water.

Leaving it here was truly a dumb move. They had to either believe she wouldn't get out of the bindings or it was drugged. She was thirsty, but the men were still arguing in the front room, and that spurred her on.

The tone of the conversation made her believe that Merrit Geller had something he was holding over the Blue River Killer. He definitely knew who the man was and Maggie wanted to know, too.

Could she peer through the lock and see his face?

No, she had to save herself first. She had to live to fight another day. If she saw his face and then died, it would all be wasted.

Peeling her jacket, she reached for the glass and carefully poured the water onto the floor, not willing to drink anything that had been left for her. Then she wrapped her jacket around the glass until only the silk lining could be seen. Putting it on the ground, she stepped down until she felt it crunch.

God bless high quality silk. She still cut her foot in the process. The jacket was already done for. Now it would have small pieces of glass clinging to the outside fabric. So be it.

She opened the jacket and carefully shook it out. It had muffled the sound of the glass breaking enough that the conversation in the other room hadn't lagged. She turned it right side out and carefully slipped back into it. If they came back in, she needed to look as tied up as possible.

Then she picked up four of the largest shards and slipped two into each pocket. Next, she carefully tiptoed to the window. She managed to flip the latch relatively quietly but getting it open would be another story. She probably couldn't break the window quite as softly as she'd broken the water glass.

She'd need to slide it up but, the moment she pushed on the sash, it made a noise. The two voices out front stopped.

Shit, she thought. As quietly and quickly as she could, she headed back to the chair and sat down facing away from the door.

Her jacket sleeves still had the tape on them, so that would look intact at first glance. She hid the shoe between her legs as best she could. She held her feet and hands together just as they had been positioned when she was bound. Lastly, she hung her head, so they wouldn't be able to notice the tape was off her face.

As soon as they got close, she would have to come up swinging.

"This is all new to me!" she heard from the outside.

"Do your own wet work! I didn't take her. This is on you."

She would have muttered an expletive but she had to sit still. The front door slammed but footsteps came up to the door behind her.

Once again, she wished she was facing the other way. But she needed to buy those extra seconds. She had to look like she was exactly where she'd been left.

Behind her, the knob turned.

CHAPTER SIXTY

S ebastian looked at the faces around the table.

It was Watson who told him, "We have enough evidence to arrest William Treat Sanders as the Blue River Killer."

"So, why haven't you arrested him?" Sebastian demanded.

"He's disappeared," was Watson's only answer, said as Decker replied. "He's in the wind."

That didn't help.

"But we've been tracking his movements."

Sebastian's eyes were bouncing back and forth like it was a tennis match.

"This," Ranger Leo Evans said as he pointed to a spot on the map in front of him. "—is a small section of the Rock Creek park that has cabins. Sanders' family owns one of them."

"It's close to water and we think this is where he takes his victims," Decker added.

Sebastian realized he was being given information that was still withheld from the public, probably in hopes that he could add something to it. He couldn't.

"We've been working on this for quite some time," Watson

told him, as if hoping he would understand why it had taken them so long. "Sometimes it takes months to pull this kind of evidence together."

Sebastian looked back and forth, "But it's not Sanders who has her. We think it's Geller, right?"

"Right. But Sanders usually attacks his victims where they are. He's clearly taken her somewhere else." Watson turned to Evans again, and he picked up the thread.

"The cabins were there before the land became a state park. So the owners are grandfathered in. The units don't see much use and they don't really have neighbors because they're reasonably far apart. The Sanders family has owned one of the cabins for three generations. The owners can come and go as they please, but the park rangers note activity in the area."

He looked to Decker then, and when he received a subtle nod in response, he plowed ahead. "The FBI contacted us and we pulled our information. We would have handed it off tomorrow or so, but your call bumped up the timeframe. The bottom line is that we can tie activity near this cabin to the time frames of at least six of the Blue River killings."

"Isn't that enough?" Sebastian asked frantic. But the Blue River Killer had murdered far more than that. *Only six?*

Watson looked to Decker, and then they both looked back at him. It was Decker who said, "It has to be enough, because it's all we have. So we're going to go perform a raid on these cabins. We're heading out in the next ten minutes, if you want to come with us."

"What if she's not there? What if he didn't go to Sanders' cabin?"

"Then he didn't go to Sanders place and she's not there." The answer was so simple and so stunningly awful that Sebastian's brain didn't want to process it.

"It's the only path we have," Watson offered solemnly.

Sebastian didn't know what to do. If he went, he had the

chance of being there when they found her. Or he had the chance that she was somewhere else, and he wasn't there to help. Sitting here meant doing nothing and waiting. He didn't have that in him. He was the kind of guy who naturally ran toward disaster—not a hero trait, just a hardwire in his system.

"Go."

He turned, having recognized the voice behind him. "Rex?"

Sebastian almost tripped over the stroller in front of his fellow firefighter. Rex had his toddler in tow, but he'd come anyway. Then Sebastian looked beyond him. Most of A-shift had shown up.

"We've got the house covered," Kalan told him. "If she shows up, we'll call you."

"My dad and Aidan are at dispatch monitoring all the calls." Though Watson raised an eyebrow at that borderline practice, Ronan Kelly didn't flinch. "We'll notify you if anything comes in that might be related."

"Go with them," Rex urged him. "Find Maggie and bring her back safe."

Sebastian nodded, glad that the decision was now made, glad that the guys were watching out for Maggie.

He bolted into the house and pulled his gun from the drawer by Maggie's bed. For good measure—and not to look like he'd just grabbed a gun—he also pulled his lightweight jacket off the hook. With one last glance at the bed they shared, he headed out the door.

They would head to Sanders' family cabin. It was a shot in the dark based on scant evidence. But their only options were that they were right or Maggie was dead.

CHAPTER SIXTY-ONE

The door opened behind her, the soft squeak of the knob an ominous sound.

Maggie knew it was Merrit Geller and she'd read the reports of his victims. She was not going to become the next.

He didn't say anything, just opened the door and presumably stood behind her. The room was too small for him to be more than a few feet away. She waited for his hand to touch her shoulder.

Maggie found it hard to keep her breathing slow and her head low, as though she were still drugged. But she forced herself to stay still.

She was sitting on her shoe and realized only now that was a mistake. She should have kept it in her hand, ready to make a move.

Making a small moan to cover her movement, she slipped her hand between her legs and grasped the shoe firmly.

Three.

Two.

One.

She popped up and turned to face him, screaming for all she was worth. Though whether that was because the noise simply came out of her with her fear or if she remembered from watching stupid online videos that noise was startling, she didn't know.

It was hard to tell if the scream accomplished anything other than him raising his hands in defense. Though he thwarted her blow a little, he didn't raise them up quite fast enough. She swung the heel for all it was worth, the sharp point aimed outward.

Even as she watched it arc through the air toward him, she realized the rubber tip on the end of the heel would reduce its effectiveness as a weapon. She should have pulled it off, made the heel sharper. Her stomach clenched as she both heard and felt the heel sink into the side of his neck.

Just as abruptly as she started screaming, she stopped. What if Sanders was still here? What if he was out front, and she had just alerted him?

Geller stumbled backward, the pale blue shoe sticking out of his neck where the heel was buried an inch, or maybe two, deep. Maggie let go and stepped back.

Once again, she saw her mistake too late. She should have pulled it out, let the blood flow from the wound. Instead, he screamed, "You bitch!"

And she watched his blood trickle down his hands as he reached up and felt the shoe stuck in his neck. Though he was occupied with undoing her damage, he was still watching her and still positioned between her and the door. The window was her only option.

But he wasn't disabled enough.

So she turned around, picked up the chair, and swung it at him from the other side. The old wood cracked against him, splintering into shards as the remains of the chair twisted in her hands.

It took only one step to reach the window, and she thought she might have made it before the chair clattered to the floor. Pushing upward on the window, her heart pounded and her mouth went dry when it didn't give.

But, in her fear and anger, adrenaline made her strong, and with a second massive shove, she managed to move it up far enough to climb out. As she slipped out and thought she was getting away, Maggie felt his hand wrap around her bare ankle.

Though she shook her foot violently, he didn't let go. Tumbling downward, she let her body weight pull them both forward, her head aimed toward the ground. Luckily, there were no sharp bushes beneath the window. She was merely falling to the forest floor, her hands out to break her fall, his hand on her ankle stopping her from hitting hard.

The window ledge cut into her leg, but he didn't let go.

Her hands were touching the dirt and she was halfway to the ground, but Merrit Geller was coming through the window too, his hand still tight on her foot.

Maggie braced her hands into the dirt, almost fully upside down, and shoved her foot backwards with all her might. When she succeeded in banging him into the edge of the window and making him groan, she did it again.

Only then did he let go enough for her to yank her foot away.

Tumbling into the dirt, Maggie scrambled upright and ran.

She had no idea where she was going. Her feet were bare, but she couldn't feel the forest floor other than to know that it pushed up against her, sending her bolting forward.

She had to look ridiculous in her once beautiful pale blue business suit racing through the woods in terror. But the only thing that mattered was getting away. Getting safe. Getting back to Sebastian.

She heard Geller bellowing as he rolled out the window after her. But then she heard another voice from the side of the house. "What did you do, Geller? Can't let her get away, can we?"

CHAPTER SIXTY-TWO

ear Lord, Maggie thought still tearing through the woods, he was still here.

It wasn't just Geller she had to run from.

Branches reached out and slapped at her. It was her fault—she had alerted Sanders—or whoever he was—when she yelled. Now, her only chance at safety was to keep going forward.

Behind her, Geller roared, seeming to ignore the other man. Maggie and Geller were in a battle for their lives. But whoever the other man was, he didn't seem to be chasing her, just chiding his partner for his failure.

Whatever made his adrenaline spike, this wasn't it. But she could hear him jogging along in the woods behind Geller. Maggie's fear was through the roof, her brain racing. She thought about things like getting her jacket caught on a branch and it slowing her down. She thought about how she was probably tearing up her feet, but she couldn't feel it.

None of that was important. She simply had to win.

If it was an endurance competition, she didn't know which of the three of them would be able to sustain the chase the longest —only that if she lost, she died. If it was about knowing the lay of the land, they had the advantage. If it was about strategy, there were two of them and only one of her. They could circle around and cut her off, flank her, trap her. If it was about hand-to-hand combat, she would probably lose that battle, too.

Her odds were worse than bad.

She remembered being in the boat. She remembered being pulled through the woods, but she truly had no idea where she was, only that it was the middle of nowhere. She would have to run as far and as fast as she could.

Even as that thought solidified in her brain, she tripped over a root and went down into the dirt face first. Her initial inclination was to push back up and keep running, but when she tried, she tumbled to the side and off the trail.

As she did, she grabbed frantically onto whatever she could to stop herself from rolling further. At last her hand clutched a large branch. It braced her, fresh and sturdy, stuck between two slim trees and broken on both ends. As she stood up, she realized she was still holding it and that she hadn't rolled more than a few feet off the trail.

Grabbing the branch with both hands, she tested it. For a moment it felt like the Louisville Slugger she kept at home. Yes, she could do this.

Maggie stood up slowly, trying not to make any noise as she tucked herself behind the trunk of a wide tree and waited for Geller to come close. Even as she pressed herself against the tree, she realized that he'd slowed down. He had to hear that she wasn't making noise, and thus not moving forward anymore.

Why couldn't a rabbit or a raccoon scuttle across the trail and make him think she was up ahead? She was no Snow White, clearly. The woodland creatures were avoiding her rather than helping.

She was breathing so heavily that all of Nebraska could likely hear her. But she stayed hidden behind the tree, waiting.

"Where are you, you little bitch?" The voice came out sing song at first, but sharpened to an edge by the time he got to the last word.

She didn't answer. His talking gave her a reference point for where he was, and he was slowly creeping closer to where she was hidden. Did he know she was there? And where was Sanders? Sanders could pop up behind her and slit her throat at any moment. But she couldn't afford to turn around. She had to focus on the threat she could identify.

There was noise in the distance, but Maggie couldn't place it. She took a chance and peeked around the trunk, hoping she could stay hidden. In a stroke of luck, she caught Geller looking over his shoulder—probably at the same noise she'd heard—and she took advantage.

Stepping out, her bare feet were now a saving grace, making little noise on the dirt trail. She swung the branch at his head as hard as she could and tried not to wince as it made a sickening crack as it contacted with the back of his skull.

The branch was less sturdy than she thought and split with the force of impact. A bellow emerged from his mouth and he swayed. For a moment, she thought she might have the upper hand. But behind her, a sickeningly calm voice said, "Hello Magdalyn."

There was no other option, she had to fight them both if she was going to survive. Maggie swung around, aiming what was left of her makeshift bat up toward the point where she'd heard the voice.

His hand came up to block the swing. His expression remained calm.

She'd seen this face before. This was William Sanders.

He didn't flinch with the hit, even though she had to have hurt his arm. It would leave a mark, but he wasn't even paying attention to her any longer. He tipped his head as though listening to something else, maybe the noises she had heard. Was it car doors closing? Could she be so lucky?

Maggie desperately wanted to turn and look, but she couldn't take her eyes off Sanders. His mesmerizing gaze was petrifying. His calm clarity in the midst of chaos chilling. When he grinned, it only froze her insides further. He would kill her right here and think nothing of it.

He said only, "I prefer blondes."

The noise behind her got louder, feet were tramping through the woods. She could hear the doors at the cabin slamming as someone rampaged through the place, at least she thought she did.

A loud bang startled her enough to turn away, but with her quick glance she couldn't see anything that told her what was going on. As fast as she was, Sanders was already down the trail ahead of her when she turned back to look.

Behind her, Merrit Geller's hand closed on her arm, yanking her around. She swung again with the stick, but this time it was ineffective. He'd pulled the shoe from his neck somewhere along the way. Blood was oozing down his collar, red and wet. She must have had the misfortune of puncturing muscle and not hitting anything valuable.

With a roar of rage that startled her spine straight, he pushed her backward until she stumbled and fell onto the ground. He was on her before she could react or fight back, his hands closing around her neck.

Though she fought and clawed, he squeezed until she couldn't breathe.

CHAPTER SIXTY-THREE

The cabin was empty.

Sebastian's heart raced as the FBI agents methodically slammed their way through the cabin yelling "clear" each time they found a room empty. The words ricocheted like bullets, the word hitting him each time that Maggie wasn't in there.

He could see into the back room, which held nothing but a splintered chair, lying in pieces on the floor next to a pale blue high-heeled shoe.

The shoe he had found *was* Maggie's!

But this one had blood on the heel, spatters on the side. He could only hope the blood wasn't Maggie's. Beyond the wreckage, the window was open.

She went out the window. Even as he had that thought, he heard the agents yelling to each other, "She's in the woods!"

Two cars were already parked at the cabin when they pulled up. Sebastian, a quasi-civilian relegated to the back seat, hadn't been able to see clearly on the ride up. Decker and Watson had talked the whole way, leaving him mostly out of the conversation, but it had been clear that they believed that both Geller and Sanders were here.

With Maggie.

His Maggie.

The agents were in the other rooms and far enough away that they couldn't stop him. Sebastian took advantage and slammed out the front door. They had protocol to follow, which he understood. He had protocol too, just not here. Here, his only job was saving Maggie, no matter what the cost.

He skidded his way around the corner and toward the back of the building. The clearing around the house was as small as the place itself and led into several trails, but one led directly away from the window. He bolted down it, deciding to take his chances there.

As he pounded his way along the trail, he saw broken branches and, ahead of him, he heard a struggle. *It had to be Maggie.* The sound gave him hope. If she was struggling, she was alive.

He braced himself for whatever he might find but told himself that keeping Maggie alive was his only goal.

He spotted a man from the back, presumably Geller, much further down the path. As the man moved and fought, Sebastian caught a glimpse of powder blue. Maggie!

She was on the ground and it looked as if Geller was trying to strangle her. But she was fighting back.

Sebastian ran like the hounds of hell were at his back. But they were in front of him. He pulled his gun even as his feet pounded down the trail and he prayed he would make it in time. Maggie was still so far away!

His brain was racing, letting him know to jump over roots and avoid low branches. He rolled his ankle but kept going.

He got as close as he dared before planting his feet and raising the gun. But he couldn't shoot. Any shot he took that would hit Geller might also hit Maggie.

"Geller!" he yelled, even as he heard the FBI agents racing up the trail behind him.

"Don't shoot!" Watson yelled, but he ignored her. He didn't give a flying fuck if Geller died.

Though Geller didn't loosen his hold on Maggie's neck, he turned his head and looked directly at Sebastian, assessing the new threat. Sebastian didn't look at him, but kept his eyes on Maggie. She was still struggling under Geller's grasp, on her back on the ground, and doing everything right from what Sebastian could see. But how much longer could she take it?

"Get your hands off her or I'll shoot!"

"Do it! You'll kill her, too!" Geller's eyes were as wild as his threats. He jerked, his hands clenching at Maggie's throat, the sound she made almost had Sebastian pulling the trigger.

The man almost looked high. But his next jerk made his hands slip and Sebastian could hear Maggie gasp for breath. The sound meant she'd gotten some air.

Thank God! But he had to disable Geller and fast.

Though Sebastian desperately wanted to rush the man and tackle him, Maggie was still underneath Geller, and Sebastian searched frantically for a way to fight Geller that didn't make things worse for Maggie. He wasn't close enough for a clean shot or even to tackle the man without giving him a chance to snap Maggie's neck before Sebastian even got there.

As he assessed what he could do, he saw that her movements weren't random. She'd been trying to get her knees up and leverage Geller's weight off of her. She clawed at his hands but then pulled them away toward her own torso.

Maggie's move was enough, and it sent Sebastian bolting forward. He could only hope he was fast enough, and he could kick the man off of her or tackle him—or who knew what? He didn't have a plan other than the pounding thought that looped through his brain, *Save Maggie.*

As he watched, she rammed her fists upward, taking advantage of Geller's distraction. But Maggie's hands burst apart from where she'd wedged them between Geller's arms, breaking his hold on her neck. Sebastian had been counting on that. It bought him the three seconds he needed to get to her.

She gasped for breath as Geller faltered, and Sebastian felt as though he were taking his own breath after being choked.

But he didn't get to revel in it. Something glinted in her fist, and with a furious jab, she aimed for Geller's neck. Though she hadn't breathed much at all in the last few minutes, the fury on her face told him she knew exactly what she was doing as she pulled her hand back and blood spurted from Geller's neck.

Even over her assailant's angry shout, Sebastian could hear Maggie breathing freely for the first time. He finally closed the distance as Geller's neck began spurting blood.

Maggie pushed him then, and he rolled easily this time. Her cut had him reaching for his neck. He could no longer try to kill her, his instinct to save himself would save Maggie. As he reached to staunch the gush, he collapsed and fell on top of her.

Even as she went to stab him again, Sebastian was finally close enough to do something. He grabbed Geller's shirt and yanked the man with all his force. He hoped the fabric strangled him and that it made the cut worse.

He hauled Geller backward, tossing him blindly aside like the trash he was as Sebastian dove for Maggie. Her hand was bloody and slipped away as Sebastian tried to hold onto her.

He'd seen the gash she'd somehow made in her attacker's throat. Good for her. Geller wouldn't likely survive it. But Maggie would.

"*Maggie!*' he shouted her name like a prayer and a relief even as he used his foot to push the gurgling man backward.

He took Maggie in his arms and listened to the heavenly sound of her labored breathing. She was breathing. She would be okay. But even as he told himself that his brain snapped back with a deep fear.

Next to him, Decker and Watson grabbed hold of Geller and yanked his arms behind him as they tried to help him to his feet.

They tried to staunch the flow of blood, even as they arrested him.

But Sebastian didn't care. His hands roamed her body, checking for broken bones, wounds, blood. There was so much of it. What if some of it was hers?

He grabbed her face, his own hand bloody now, but he had to see her eyes. He'd checked the Miller boy! Thought he was safe. The kid was breathing when Sebastian pulled him out. Until this moment, he'd thought getting here too late was his biggest fear.

"Are you hurt?" There were so many possible answers to that question, and he dreaded most of the answers. But he didn't let her answer. Turning to find other agents rushing toward the scene, he yelled at them. "Check her! Make sure she's okay! *Now!*"

"I'm fine, Sebastian!" Her voice was scratchy but the sound was beautiful. His head snapped back and he watched her eyes focus on him. "I'm okay."

She reached up to hold on to him, but Sebastian realized the blood on her hands was her own.

CHAPTER SIXTY-FOUR

Sebastian watched, helpless as the agents crowded around Maggie.

"I'm fine!" She insisted, but it wasn't good enough.

"Maggie!" He almost yelled it at her and watched as her head snapped back at the command. But he couldn't fix it, not yet. "Let them help you!"

"I'm fine."

"You're bleeding."

The agents were trying to check her over and he wasn't helping. But neither was she. And his heart wouldn't stop racing.

Logically, he told himself that she was talking. She was mad at him. And that meant she was healthy enough to do those things. He told himself she really was fine.

But illogically, he was petrified. People said they were fine when they weren't. The first thing they learned about medical cases was to look for shock. It could make people seem okay, then as the high of the fight-or-flight response wore off, their heart stopped.

Losing a child that way hadn't made him any more rational.

He dropped to his knees with a thud that would leave a bruise. He only hoped Maggie was around to tell him what an idiot he was. He grabbed her hand, still slick with fresh blood, and pled with her. "Please, I can't lose you! Let them be sure you're okay."

She sighed at him, clearly irritated, but as she agreed to his wishes, the agent pulled Maggie's hand from his.

"It's here. This is where the blood is coming from." He held up the wound for all to see.

CHAPTER SIXTY-FIVE

"It's time to go," Sebastian said to Maggie as he stood in the doorway to her office where she was hunched over her desk, typing frantically.

"What?" She looked up, confused.

He pointed to her hand wrapped in delicate white gauze. "Time to get your stitches out."

Her right hand now sported eighteen stitches where her glass shard knife had cut her as well as Geller. Though Decker and Watson had tried to save the man, he hadn't lived long enough to make it to the hospital. The shard of the drinking glass that Maggie had planted in his throat had done him in.

For himself, Sebastian was more than glad the man was actually dead. Maggie wouldn't have to testify against him or relive the experience. He couldn't get out in ten years for good behavior or some bullshit like that. As far as Sebastian could tell, Maggie felt no conscious guilt from killing Geller, though she did wake up at night sometimes in a cold sweat, jolting out of a deep dream. Sebastian made sure he was there to hold her and help her find some peace again.

She'd reached a point in the past few days where she mostly

rolled over, curled into him, and went back to sleep. Sebastian was convinced that Maggie was having more trouble dealing with the fact that her favorite aunt had an ongoing affair with the man for decades. She was still reconciling the adults she'd looked up to as a child with the realities that weren't all good or bad.

Her father had rushed in and told her she was an idiot for baiting a killer. Though Sebastian might have argued the same side and understood it came from fear, he'd told the man he could be nice to his heroic daughter who'd rid the area of a predator that had haunted them for decades or he could get the fuck out. Mr. Willis had not expected that. Maggie had tried to start rebuilding her relationship with the man.

The FBI was still combing all the data—bank accounts and letters Sabbie had kept and more—but the relationship had become clear. The bank statements showed she hadn't even charged Geller rent most months. The letters dripped with the gooey sentimentality of lovers and an old one with a pregnancy scare solidified that idea.

Though they hadn't spoken of it more than once, it appeared that Sabbie had finally found out who her lover really was … and he had killed her. That was what had Maggie grieving. And maybe justified killing Geller enough to not let it bother her.

Sebastian admired the crap out of her.

Now, she stood up and headed toward the front door, where she grabbed her purse and her phone.

Today was the first day she'd worn her new suit. She'd meticulously purchased a new favorite, this one the same pale blue as the one she'd lost. He'd been surprised by her choice, thinking the color might forever remind her of being kidnapped. Maybe it did. But maybe Maggie remembered it as the day she had triumphed.

She looked at her phone and frowned at him. "It's not time yet."

"Yeah it is," he told her, a grin on his face.

She raised one eyebrow at him as he reached out and took her left hand—the one that didn't have stitches in it. The one he had been holding for a week and a half now.

She was going to be fine. The bruises on her neck were mostly faded, the stitches were coming out today, and her feet had been fine for almost a week now.

He'd waited for this. "Follow me."

Sebastian watched while she set her purse back on the small table by the front door, then pulled her down the hallway. He tugged her past the boarding rooms, past room number five—now completely cleared out—and out the back door onto the back porch.

Two freshly painted Adirondack chairs sat to the left and Sebastian gestured to them. "What do you think?"

She gasped. "They're beautiful. What a great color. Are they mine?"

He smiled. He'd had to sneak them back here yesterday when she was out running errands.

Her surprise was thanks enough, but her joyful words and her arms around his neck were even better.

But that gift wasn't everything. So he pulled her past the chairs and sat her down on the back step, which still creaked every time someone made a move on it. He would have to replace it, maybe even the whole back porch. *If* she would let him. *If* she wanted this.

Taking her hand in his, he laced their fingers together, and put his other hand over hers. "Sanders is long gone," he started. "Decker called me today and said everything is cleared out from his house. No one's seen him, including the FBI who has run a massive series of stakeouts to find him."

Maggie nodded. "He made it very clear he didn't want me. He's some kind of freaking sociopath. But I don't think he was lying, and all his victims *have* been blonde."

Sebastian nodded. This was the most bizarre conversation he'd ever had—to acknowledge that a serial killer was out there, that his girlfriend had come face to face with the man, and that they still managed to feel that she was relatively safe from him.

"It's time to decide if you want me to stay here or not."

If she said *not*, he would put all kinds of security measures in place, still drive by the house in the middle of the night when he could. He wouldn't leave her unprotected, but it was time to make some decisions.

Maggie looked at him with one of those expressions that said, *You tell me what you want first.* She asked, "Do *you* want to stay?"

He'd thought about this. So he answered as he'd prepared himself. "I want to be with you." He squeezed her hand in his. "I've never met anyone like you. And ... um ..." the words choked in his throat.

But he finally found one that worked. "I'm *amazed* that you want to be with me."

Though Maggie opened her mouth to speak, he stopped her. "I want to stay with you. I see us as—" He paused again. He thought he'd had this all planned out, but it was harder to say than he'd expected. But once again he forced himself to say the words. "I see us as a long term thing."

He was rewarded with a heart-stopping smile. So he kept going. *All cards on the table, right?* "I want to do whatever makes that happen."

"Well then," she said, "You need to pack up and get out."

Her sweet grin didn't match the harsh words, but he still felt himself freeze. Sebastian reminded himself that if leaving now meant they would be together later, he could deal with it. He would do anything to make that happen. Even this.

"But," she said, leaning in, her words whispering along his jaw as she moved her mouth in small nibbles. "You come back tomorrow. Tonight, Seline is coming over and we're having

Girls Night. We're watching Love Actually, because she's never seen it! And maybe Austenland. And you're not invited."

She told him all this with sweetly whispered kisses. "But tomorrow, when you come back, I think maybe you should move in."

Hope bloomed in his chest. Sebastian reached up to hold her to him, taking her mouth with his, he reveled in the knowledge that Maggie Willis was his.

Forever.

CHAPTER SIXTY-SIX

Selene Marchand waited impatiently for the elevator to ding and the doors to open. She was already running late and the only ding she heard was her phone pinging.

With a sigh, she checked to see if it was her department head.

Luckily, not. But it was a text from her new friend Maggie.

— I'm still on for our sleepover tonight, but I wanted to warn you. Just got word that the Blue River Killer struck again.

What?

Maggie had said that guy was in the wind. The FBI said they were safe.

Another ding grabbed Seline's attention. Again, it was her phone and not the damn elevator arriving. She should have taken the stairs.

—Clearly, FBI was wrong. Seline, this victim was blond haired and blue eyed! Like you. Please, be careful.

That didn't sound good. But Seline was in Lincoln for the day, not Redemption. And she was going to be dead if she missed the *first* meeting she was supposed to attend this term.

She was up for tenure if this year went well. It had too; she was mortgaged to the hilt.

When the doors finally slid open, she ducked inside before they'd even reach their full width. Completely ignoring the man already in the unit, she quickly turned and jabbed at the 'door close' button, but nothing happened.

She did not have time for this.

Though she pushed and held the button, nothing happened.

It was easier to believe something was wrong with the elevator itself but, truly, it was just her own impatience.

The third time, the doors finally closed.

She looked up at digital floor number and watched like a hawk, but the number didn't change and she wasn't moving very fast. As she took a deep sigh, the floor dropped out from under her.

It had to be less than a split second—though it felt forever—before the brakes engaged and a horrifying squeal filled the small space. But the small box ground to a stop.

"*Ca suce des boules de singe!*" she cursed to herself. She could only hope the man next to her did not speak French.

At the same time, he muttered, "You have got to be shitting me," in English.

They were good and stuck now. According to the display they were now between floors and not moving at all. It was only then that she realized she hadn't even looked at the person she was now stuck in the elevator with.

He was large—both tall and broad shouldered—dark skinned and *very* good looking. On any other day, she would have appreciated the smile that came far too easily for the statement he'd just uttered. The smile was clearly trying to reassure her. It didn't work.

She felt her lips press flat. She tried to be a happy and cheerful person. But for all her forced positive thoughts, she was still stuck in an elevator with a stranger. And she was already running late to the most important meeting of the year!

She looked at the man again, suddenly wondering why he was already in the elevator when she was getting on at the top floor ... Then her stomach dropped as she saw the radio clipped to his waist ... and suspenders hanging down from thick pants.

She was stuck with a firefighter. Not that the elevator had caught on fire, but he was clearly here for a reason and the way her day was going it just might ...

He pulled the radio out and spoke into it as he pressed a button. "Guys. Come back. You're not going to believe this."

That was good, she thought. At least he had some communication. She'd gotten that ominous message from Maggie and then her cell had gone signal-dead when she entered the elevator shaft.

She heard another voice crackle back.

"Can they pry the doors open?" she tried the sweetest tone she could muster. If she was stuck, she might as well ask.

He put the radio back and only said, "They're coming."

"More firefighters?" she asked, hating that she sounded as irritated as she was. She needed an elevator repair person. Not a firefighter.

His head tilted at her accent. She'd been trying to minimize it since she'd first come to America as a teenager. It hadn't gone completely away. In times of stress, it leached even further into her words. It was almost too thick for her to be understood now.

"French?" he asked.

"*Oui,*" she replied, then asked again, "Who is coming?"

"Oh!" he said, as though he'd forgotten the original three-word question. "Lincoln FD and Redemption FD."

She felt herself blink at the admission. She was from Redemption ... what were her local firefighters doing here? And what was so wrong with this building that it required *two* teams of firefighters?

"We pulled someone out of one of the elevators about two hours ago," he volunteered on a heavy sigh. "We just completed our inspection."

Though she still faced the front of the elevators, she flicked her eyes sideways at him. "It did not work."

Thankfully, he laughed.

But right then, the elevator dropped out beneath them again. They hurled downward, and Seline grabbed on for dear life.

Thank you for reading! I love romances with real love and believable characters, and I hope you found all that in these pages. I want to fall in love right along with the characters, and I do, while I'm writing it.

About Savannah

I started writing when I was eight--I hand wrote an 80-page novella that I believed to be (adult) romantic suspense. I'm proud to say, I've gotten a lot better since then. I've grown up to be a nerd at heart! I love neuroscience and people watching, and if you look, you'll find some of that in each Savannah Kade book. Most days you'll find me in my office, looking out my window at a handful of the neighbor's cows, or watching my dogs or my cat roam the backyard.

Follow me, find me, ask me questions! I would love to hear from you.
www.SavannahKade.com
Savannah@SavannahKade.com

9 781948 059732